The Prospector

Riches and adventure lure a young man
west to the Rocky Mountains and
beyond.

James Oliver Virmala

Edition 1

Cover Photo By James Oliver Virmala

"The Tetons"

ISBN: 978-0-9972536-8-9

ACKNOWLEDGMENTS

I took a trip west this summer, in search of firsthand information of the places I have written about. I would like to thank all the people that took time to share with me about history of the area, or points of interest that I should see. The friendly greetings that I received in Elkader, Casper, Yellowstone, Mount Rushmore, The Badlands, Fort Laramie, Kaycee, Sheridan, Lander, South Pass City, and all the other places I visited, will provide me with material for my books and fond memories for the rest of my life.

CONTENTS

Acknowledgments   i

Chapter One   Pg 1

Chapter Two   Pg 9

Chapter Three   Pg 22

Chapter Four   Pg 39

Chapter Five   Pg 46

Chapter Six   Pg 58

Chapter Seven   Pg 72

Chapter Eight   Pg 93

Chapter Nine   Pg 104

Chapter Ten   Pg 135

Chapter Eleven   Pg 151

Chapter Twelve   Pg 164

Chapter Thirteen   Pg 181

Chapter Fourteen   Pg 207

Chapter Fifteen   Pg 229

Chapter Sixteen   Pg 248

Chapter Seventeen   Pg 268

BOOKS BY THE AUTHOR

Oli's Gold Book One
Search For Oli's Gold Book Two
Return To Oli's Gold Book Three
To Be A Mountain Man
Trouble On The Kansas Plains
Frontier Justice
Return Of The Mountain Man
The Tall Man
The Prospector
The Green Valley
Twilight Of The Mountain Man
The Mother Lode
Quest Of The Mountain Man
Journey's End
Rufus Pike
Rufus And The Pup
The Winding Trail Home
Rufus The Lost Years
The Kankakee Kid
Bogus Island
Tyler Tomas The Brothers' War
War of 1812 The Choice
Kyle Oliver The Next Horizon

CHAPTER ONE

The young man sat on the rough wooden porch, digging his toes into the dust. His unruly, sandy hair stuck out from the front of the worn felt hat, with its crowned top and slouching brim. His eyes were fixed on the news article he held in his dirt-stained hands. The headlines were about the gold discovered in California. It spoke of people finding a fortune in just a matter of months.

"Pup, put down that damn paper and get washed up!" his father barked. "I got supper ready here."

The young man carefully folded the paper and tucked it inside his loose wool shirt. He worked the pump at the side of the porch, filled the shallow basin and washed his hands and face. Pitching the water toward some chickens scratching for seeds, he chuckled and headed in to eat.

Pup, whose given name was Amos Mudd, was 18 years-old. He and his father lived in a scantily furnished, two-room cabin located in upstate Maine. His mother had died suddenly five years earlier and since then he and his father, Jacob, had lived a bachelor's existence on the 40-acre potato farm.

Amos seldom went into town to socialize because he was embarrassed by the condition of his worn and mended clothing. He and his father would work the farm planting, weeding, and then digging the potatoes. When time permitted they would work at clearing the last 10 acres to expand their fields.

On Sunday, Jacob would disappear to work on a boat he was building, or visit neighboring farms to talk about how the crops were doing. Amos was left to himself and would take his Leman .32 caliber squirrel rifle and hunt for small game. If the opportunity presented itself, he would try for a deer. Hours of hunting, along with a shortage of powder and lead, had turned him into an accurate shot. He didn't want to dine on potatoes only.

The boy had gotten the muzzle-loader from a hired man who had come to work at the farm when Amos was eight. He had been suffering from consumption and had died when the boy was 11. A note had been found leaving the Leman rifle to Amos, who had always admired it. While the stock was scarred from years of use, the firing mechanism was kept clean and oiled.

Amos sat at the wood plank table and scooped fried potatoes from the cast iron frying pan onto his tin plate. He picked up a slice of bread, ripped off a piece and mopped up some of the grease from the potatoes, then shoved it in his mouth.

"We got the last of the spuds in," Jacob said

around a mouthful of food. "Tomorrow I'll be bringing the first load to Houlton. You can work on the stumps with the mule. I'd like to plant a few more acres in the spring."

Amos sat at the table, his heart pounding under the dusty shirt. The meal suddenly lost its appeal. He had made a decision and had been looking for the right time to tell his father. He got up and scraped his plate into the slop pail and placed it on the washboard.

Without looking in his father's direction, he began, his voice barely audible. "Pa, I need to tell you something . . ."

"Maybe you can take some time to try and do a little hunting," Jacob said, shoving the last spoonful of the meal into his mouth. "Now that the spuds are in, it's time to put some meat on the table."

"Pa!" the lad said in frustration. "I . . . I won't be here when you get back."

"What the hell are you saying?"

"I am leaving tomorrow," the boy said, looking at his dirt covered feet.

"And just where is it you are going?" his father demanded.

Gathering up his courage, Amos looked his father in the eye. "I am going west. There is gold in California and I plan to go there and find some."

Snorting, the father tossed his plate toward the washboard. It missed and bounced across the floor. Both of them ignored it and continued with fixed stares at each other.

"Where in the hell are these ideas coming from?" Jacob asked his tone getting louder.

Unused to defying his father, Amos felt it important to explain. "I have been reading about the gold being found in California. Men are traveling to the west and become wealthy after a summer's work."

"You read about it!" Jacob scoffed.

"I promise that I will come back after I find the gold. We can buy another 40 you have always wanted and some new equipment," the young man said, trying to reason with his father.

The look of disbelief on his father's face was a look Amos had never seen before. "You are talking like a damn fool. If you walk out of here tomorrow, you can just keep on going . . ." His father's voice faltered.

Amos stood speechless as his father grabbed his hat and left the cabin. The young man went to the stove and picked up the kettle of hot water. As he washed the dishes, he struggled to come to grips with his father's reaction. He had not expected him to be in favor of having his son leave, but to be so vocal and to call it foolish was something else.

After he was done with dishes, Amos poured a mug of coffee and went to the porch to watch the sun go down. There was no sign of his father. From the porch he could see the sorting shed. The wagon filled with sacks of potatoes stood in front of the shed, ready for the trip to Houlton. The mule, Jenny, dozed in the corral. The team of horses was in the barn. He could hear them as they stomped and bumped against the sides of their stalls.

Amos slept in the loft above the second room in the house. At the foot of his bed were his bedroll, a coat, and a haversack filled with powder, lead balls, flint, a knife, fish hooks, food for a week, a change of clothes, and other things he thought he might need on the trip.

He had started putting it together almost a year ago, when he'd first read about the gold strike. Amos had also put aside the money he had earned from trapping. It was not much, but it would help him get a few things as he ran out.

He had gotten a map from the school master and had traced a route from Maine to California. He had read whatever he could get his hands on about the frontier. He knew he'd have to find some work on the trip. The long hours working in the fields and handling bags of potatoes had left him in excellent shape.

After the sun had set, the lad fed the horses and mule. Normally, his father would do this while Amos cleaned up after their evening meal. Tonight he had no idea where his father might be. The crestfallen boy stood in the corral and brushed the mule in the darkness. He did it mostly for companionship. He didn't want to lay in the loft with the silence and his thoughts.

It was late when Amos finally climbed up to his bed. He had hoped that his father would have come back so he could try and explain why it was important for him to leave. Since his mother had died, life on the potato farm had become more of an existence rather than a home. He and his father worked, ate, and slept.

He missed listening to his mother talking quietly with his father while Amos lay in the loft. They would talk about the future. She would laugh at something funny that his father had said. After she was gone the boy would go to sleep early and dream of his mother.

After a sleepless night, Amos got up. It just beginning to get light in the east. The boy had laid listening for his father to return. He crept down the ladder from the loft carrying the haversack, coat, and bedroll. Amos looked into his father's room. The bed had not been slept in.

After returning from the outhouse, Amos made some coffee and sliced some bread. He poured honey onto the bread and sat at the table, alone, eating his last breakfast in his father's house. For a moment he realized that being alone would be his father's future. Maybe that was why he was against Amos leaving.

The young man decided that there was no reason to delay any longer. He looked down at his bare feet. He hadn't gotten his boots for winter yet. Last years had split at the soles and were less than useful. He would need to get some if he was going to walk all the way to California. He hoped that the money he had would be enough to purchase a pair in one of the towns he would be passing.

Looking around the cabin one more time, he blew out the lamp. Tying the coat and bedroll to the haversack, he slung it over his shoulder. He picked up his squirrel rifle and stepped out of the cabin. Looking up, he stopped short. His father was standing in front of the barn.

Amos debated if he should just walk away or if he should say goodbye to his father. Knowing it would be a long time before they spoke again, the lad walked over to the barn. His father turned away from him and went into the barn.

Standing with his mouth open, Amos stifled the torrent of angry words he felt build up inside. About to turn away, he stopped when his father emerged leading the mule. Jacob's face was drawn and his eyes were red. The last time the boy had seen the look on his father's face had been after his mother had passed.

"You'll need the mule to make the trip," his father said, his voice lacking strength. "You should lead the animal some of the time to give it a rest. I ain't got a saddle, but maybe you can pick one up somewhere."

"Pa, I can't take the . . ." His father held his hand up, stopping his son from talking.

"You'll need shoes," his father continued. "Hanson's Mercantile just got some in. Take this so you can buy a pair." Jacob held out $4 for Amos.

With a shaking hand, Amos took the money. His father had never given him money before. When Amos needed something, his father would bring it back with him from a monthly trip to Ashland.

Taking the lead rope from his father, Amos promised, "I will bring the mule back to you when I come back from California."

"I built this farm for your future," Jacob said. "Together we worked hard to grow it and make it pay. It is not there yet, but it could be some day."

Before Amos could respond, his father turned away. "Be safe, Pup."

The young man fought back the tears as he left leading the mule. This was not the way he wanted his leaving to go. He vowed as he walked that he would return with gold and make his father proud of him.

CHAPTER TWO

The low-cut boots cost $3 leaving an extra dollar. With that Amos purchased two pairs of woolen socks. Old man Hanson kidded the boy, "New boots and socks. You plan on doing a lot of walking?"

"I'm heading for the gold fields of California," the boy proudly stated. It felt good saying it.

His mood had improved during the two-hour walk to town. He thought about things he might buy with the first gold he found.

"California! The hell you say," the surprised merchant said. "That's a damn long way. Does your father know about this?"

"He told me to have a safe trip," Amos retorted.

"You sure you ain't running away and stealing that mule outside?" Mr. Hanson asked with skepticism on his face.

"He give me Jenny and the money for shoes," Amos said, feeling his ears turn red.

"Well, heck kid. You ain't even got a razor yet," the sarcastic owner laughed.

Rubbing the fuzz on his chin, the boy answered, "Pa said my whiskers are slow to come in. He told me when the time came, I could use his."

Reaching under the counter, the merchant brought out a small wooden box. With a kinder manner he handed it to Amos. "Let me give you a going away gift. I took this shaving kit in on trade after old man Kinney died. His wife traded it for a new bonnet. Take care of it and it will last you until your wife can trade it in."

Now Amos was in a full blush. He hadn't had much experience with women and the thought made him uncomfortable. "Thank you Mr. Hanson. I promise to take good care of it."

Before leaving town, the young man put on his new boots and socks. Standing for a minute, he decided that they felt just fine. Taking the lead rope, he and the mule headed west. Less than a mile later his new boots came off and he hung them over the neck of the mule.

* * *

It was September 1850 when Amos headed out on his great adventure. He had traced out a route that would take him directly west across Canada and then he would enter back into the United States in Michigan. From there he would travel south and west to St. Louis, then join a wagon train to California.

Looking at the route on his small map, it

seemed very achievable. He figured that in about 4 months he would be sitting beside the stream in California, panning gold. All he had to do was get to St. Louis in time to catch a wagon train. If he traveled fast, snow in the mountains shouldn't be a problem. If it did delay the trip, then he would be there first thing in the spring and have the whole summer to pan gold.

As he traveled the first day, Amos alternated between walking to break in the boots and then riding the mule to give his sore feet a rest. He stopped by a small stream for the night. By the time he had the mule settled and a fire going, the sun was going down. The young man was not new to camping out. Often, while hunting, he would spend several nights in the hills.

He had taken a small pot and a frying pan for cooking. Tonight he made coffee to drink and ate the bread he had packed from breakfast. He put some cheese between two slices and then warmed them over his fire. The meal was satisfying and the coffee was strong.

He thought about things he needed to help him on the trip. First, he had to get a saddle for his mule, Jenny. He could use it when riding, or to secure his belongings. Clinging to the bare back when riding over the hills and ridges of Maine had left his legs cramping.

With the meal done, Amos spread out his bedroll and crawled under the blankets. The sounds of coyotes and night birds was comforting. Using his coat as a pillow, he was soon asleep. The rain didn't start until well after midnight. At first he was confused when the light drizzle began to pellet his face.

Shortly he awoke to a steady downpour. Grabbing his blankets and his coat, he dragged them under a pine tree. While the tree helped some, the damp gear and night chill left him shivering. He had hung his haversack on a pine branch not far from the tree he was crouching under. With luck the rest of his things would stay dry.

Just before daylight the rain stopped and the wind picked up. Amos sat on his ground cloth against the tree, wrapped in his soggy blankets and coat, his face buried in them, taking advantage of his own warm breath. The young man dozed fitfully until the first sign of light showed in the east.

He scoured around beneath the pines, collecting dry cones and other tinder. His teeth were chattering by the time he had the fire going. Amos turned from side to side, warming himself. The first rays of sunlight revealed steam rising from the mule. He went to relieve himself and then checked on his haversack. Everything had come through the rain okay.

Amos planned to let his coat dry while wearing it, but spread his blankets over some bushes. He put water on to heat, to make oatmeal for breakfast. He had to forgo his morning coffee. With only one pot, he had to choose between the drink or porridge. Eating the hot oatmeal warmed him. He scooped a cup full of water from the stream and drank it down.

It was almost noon when his blankets were dry and he was ready to travel. The young man frustrated to lose most of a day on the road so soon. Leading the mule, he said, "We got to do better than this, Jenny. In the next town, we got to pick up a fly tarp and check on a saddle."

The narrow, rutted road wound through the

timber-covered hillsides. Amos traveled with the .32 caliber loaded, in case he spotted some game. As he walked, he would whistle songs his mother used to sing to him. A cool breeze was blowing in from the northwest, with the promise of colder weather. It was fall, and the leaves would soon be changing.

Fall was the young man's favorite time of the year. The heavy field work was finished and he could spend more time hunting and fishing. He and his father would butcher a hog once the November snows had come. They would smoke the hams and side meat.

Some would be made into sausage, head cheese, or canned as pickled pig's feet. The rest was hung in the sorting shed and remained frozen for use during the winter. His father was handy when it came to cooking, and during the slow season he would put together some grand meals for the two of them.

Amos had quit school after his mother had died. His father needed the help on the farm and figured that his son had all the book learning he needed. The young man had always enjoyed school and read, wrote, and ciphered well. The school master had continued to loan Amos books to read.

Movement on the road ahead caught Amos' attention. A partridge was moving under a tag alder bush. Astride the mule, the boy stopped the animal, took aim with the Leman .32 and squeezed the trigger.

Immediately following the impact of the rifle against his shoulder, Amos fell backwards off the startled mule and landed flat on his back. The barrel of the rifle came down and struck him on the cheek bone. With the wind knocked out of him and dazed from the blow to his cheek, Amos struggled to get up, fighting for air and wrestling to get out of his haversack strap.

Sitting in the middle of the road, he finally got his breath back. The mule stood looking back at him about a hundred feet up the road. The partridge flapped its last, under the tag alder bush. The anger he felt at the mule quickly ebbed when Amos realized that the animal had had no warning that he was about to fire the rifle within inches of its head.

Getting up, feeling a little sheepish, Amos called to the mule, "Jenny, you just stay there while I get the packs and my supper."

With some pride, he saw that his shot had taken the head clean off the bird. No meat would be wasted. He slowly approached the mule, talking softly to it. Once he had the lead rope, they were on their way. Amos had hunted before with the mule, and shot with it near him. In those instances, it had been aware that the gun was about to go off.

If Amos had been able to travel straight as a crow flies, he would have cut several miles from the trip, but it was said that the animals had followed the streams and the Indians had followed the animals. Once the white man came, he built the roads following the trails made by the Indians. They wound back and forth along the lowlands.

Late in the fourth day of the trip, he saw smoke from a small cabin. A burly, dark-haired man sat on the front porch, smoking a pipe. Amos waved and called out, "You wouldn't have a place for a traveling man to sleep out of the weather, would you?"

"That depends," the man replied. "You willin' to split enough wood for our supper?"

"I sure will!" Amos said enthusiastically, "and I got a couple rabbits to add to the meal."

The burly man's name was Hardy. He would spend his summers hunting and fishing and basically loafing around. Come winter he would go to a logging camp and earn what money he needed to get by. While Hardy cleaned the two rabbits, Amos took the two-bit ax and split enough wood to last his host for a week or more.

Amos felt good after swinging the ax. He hung it on the wall next to the stack of wood. Taking an armload, he headed into the cabin. He was greeted by the smell of rabbit frying on the man's nine-plate stove. Some slightly dark sourdough biscuits sat cooling on the sideboard.

"Supper will be ready in about 20 minutes. Grab the kettle and you can wash and shave in the pan just outside the door," Hardy told him. "Got a fine mirror to admire yourself in."

Thanking him, Amos walked outside with the hot water. Rubbing the soft whiskers on his cheek, he felt almost grown-up. Mr. Hardy just assumed he had been shaving all along.

Filling the enamel basin, he reached into his haversack for the razor box. Sliding open the cover, there was a cup, soap, a brush, and the straight-edged razor. The cover had a mirror on the inside so a man could shave while traveling.

Amos had seen his father shave many a time. He would strop the razor on his leather belt. Then he would add a little water to the soap in the cup and use the brush to make suds. The young man was about to remove his belt when he noticed a leather strop hanging near the mirror. Opening the razor carefully, he held one end of the strop and ran the razor up and down.

Amos had no idea how long he should do this, but after a few swipes he figured that the razor was ready. Then, pouring a bit of water into the cup, he swirled the brush and dabbed the suds on his beard. Taking the razor, he tried with both hands to hold the instrument. Finally, he was comfortable with the razor in his right hand.

Starting like his father, at the middle of his ear, he began to shave. At first, no whiskers came off. After adjusting the angle of the blade, he had success. He also had some blood. With half his face shaved, resulting in several nicks and cuts, he had no choice but to keep going.

With the razor pulling and scraping his face, Amos finally finished his first shave. The water in the basin was red with his blood. Hardy had a towel hanging near the basin for drying your hands or face, but with all the cuts the young man didn't want to make a mess of the towel. Digging into his haversack, he pulled out his extra shirt and dried his face as he attempted to stop the cuts from bleeding.

"Supper's ready," Hardy called. "Get it while it's hot."

Quickly, he put the razor kit back into his bag and went into the cabin. Hardy looked up smiling. He then burst out laughing. "What the hell happened? Were you in a fight out there, or was you to a dentist for a bleeding?"

Deciding to face up to his inexperience, Amos laughed along with his host. "To tell the truth, it was the first time I fought the razor and I believe it won the fight."

After a good laugh by both men, they sat down to a meal of biscuits and rabbit. Hardy had dusted the rabbit with flour, salt, and pepper. He had jam to put on the biscuits. Amos chewed his first bite with his eyes closed, enjoying the tender meat. They had hot tea to wash the meal down with.

After the meal was over Hardy offered to give Amos some tips on using the straight razor. The young man shook his head. "No thank you. I think I will be swearing off the bloody thing."

Again, they laughed until their sides hurt. After cleaning up from the meal, Amos went outside to take care of his mule. The cold air felt unusually cool against his whiskerless face. Hardy had a team of horses in a small barn next to his cabin. He would take them to the logging camp and haul wood out with them. He told Amos that he could give the mule some grain and hay.

The cabin had only a single bunk. The young man made his bed up next to the stove. Hardy brought out a bottle of brandy and poured some into two tin cups. "This will help us sleep and keep the night chill off."

Taking a gulp, Amos fought to breathe as the burning liquid went down his throat. "Take it easy, my friend," Hardy cautioned him. "Brandy is meant to be sipped and enjoyed."

Amos had had a beer or two in the past and had assumed that the brandy would be similar. His father had never allowed hard liquor in the house. Jacob's father, back in England, had been an abusive drunk. When Jacob had come to America, he had vowed that he would not follow in his father's footsteps.

The young man liked the warming effect that the brandy had on his body, but declined the offer of a second drink. "I have to be up and going early in the morning. I got a long way to go before I get to the gold fields of California."

"I heard they had struck it out there," Hardy acknowledged. "I understand a fellow discovered a nugget in a stream out there."

"What I was reading," Amos said, "a man can get rich quick."

"Or poor," Hardy warned him. "I run to Georgia 20 years back and thought I could get rich. I rushed to the banks of the Yahoola Creek with a sore-footed horse and what I thought would be enough money to set myself up. I found a few thousand dreamers had gotten there before me. Hell, I didn't even have enough money to buy a meal at the prices they was selling them at, much less a pan and such."

"After spending a month working on another man's claim for food and a place to sleep, I headed back for the logging camps in the north. I won't say it wasn't exciting. For those that found a bit of gold, there was wild times with rot gut whiskey and willing women. If you didn't die from the bad drink or get shot by someone wanting to get your claim, you just might have gotten out with enough money to run to the next strike you heard about."

Hardy painted a pretty gloomy picture of life in the gold fields, but Amos was sure that it wasn't like that in California. There was plenty of room for everyone and he would just stay shy of the whiskey and women. One thing he would heed from the logger's warning was he'd best arrive at the fields with enough money to set himself up. While traveling, Amos would find work when he could and not waste the money he earned.

Amos was up early, and went out to relieve himself and check on the mule. On the way back into the house he grabbed another armload of wood. Stopping a moment at the mirror, he inspected his handiwork with the razor. There were a whole lot of whiskers he had missed, and where he'd shaved clean, there was a cut or two.

Smiling, he mumbled, "I wonder if a man can trade a razor for a saddle."

Hardy had traveled to Montreal and Bytown, in the past and gave Amos advice on the best routes to travel and places he could stay. He recommended traveling up the Ottawa River from Montreal until he arrived at the fork of the Mattawa River. That would take him into Petite Rivière, or Small River, and then to Lake Nipissing. It was a canoe route that had been used over a hundred years, and the way furs and timber were brought to Montreal and Quebec City.

Amos was busy making notes on the back of his map as Hardy spoke. The logger had recommended selling the mule in Montreal and then purchase another animal once he reached Michigan. The young man couldn't even consider it. He had promised to bring the animal back to his father.

The logger watched as Amos got the mule ready to leave. "How are you holding your stuff on the animal?"

"I carry the haversack and stuff," Amos explained. "When I get tired, I climb on Jenny here and rest while I ride."

"Well, damn it, man, you are still carrying the stuff even when you're on the mule."

"Oh, you're right about that," the young man admitted, "but, as soon as I can, I plan to get a saddle so I can ride and then hang this stuff on it when leading Jenny."

Hardy kicked a chunk of wood toward the pile Amos had chopped. "You split a hell of a lot of wood for me. Follow me a minute."

From one wall of the barn he took down a dust-covered sawbuck pack saddle. "I ain't got a blanket for you, but I want you to take this and let the mule carry your gear. If you load it light, it shouldn't rub the back too much. First place you can, you should get a blanket."

"It weren't that much wood," the surprised young man said.

"Take it and get it on that mule before I change my mind," Hardy insisted.

Amos walked away from the cabin leading the mule with his newly acquired sawbuck pack saddle. He still cradled the squirrel rifle under his arm. Hardy stood and watched the young man leave. "He's a good man. I hope the hell he gets over the dream of California," the logger said.

The second day after Amos left Hardy's cabin, he stopped at a small livery stable and swapped the shaving kit for a blanket to use under the pack saddle.

CHAPTER THREE

The young man and his mule sat on a rise above the St. Lawrence River, looking at Montreal. He had been told by a local merchant that the river was being dredged, to deepen the waterway past the city and allow larger vessels to navigate further along the St. Lawrence.

Amos could see the church spirals of Notre Dame and others rising above the bustling city. When he closed his eyes, he could hear the bells, trolleys and the rhythm of industry that was the life blood of Montreal. Looking around, Amos wondered what it must be like to live with neighbors' houses sharing walls with your house.

In about an hour the ferry that would carry him across the river would be pulling up to the short pier below him. This would be the mule's first ride on the water. He hoped that it wouldn't give him trouble. A mule kicking at everything could be a problem on the ferry.

It would also be Amos' first ride on a ferry. He watched teams pulling wagons, lining up to board the boat. Two men with loaded push carts waited patiently, sharing tobacco. The ferry would cost him $1, which would take a big bite out of his funds. He had been on the road for 10 days. His food, other than a little bit of cheese, was gone.

He tried to see beyond the city through the morning haze. Somewhere to the west the Ottawa River flowed. He planned to travel on its south side as he headed west. October was only a couple days away. Snow could start at any time. The route he was taking stayed busy as long as the water was open. As soon as it froze over he would be traveling with little outside contact. Amos was depending on being able to gain information from other travelers about the route ahead.

Amos took up the lead rope of the mule as he watched the sidewheel steamboat approach the pier. As it came to a stop, a ramp on the front was lowered and the onboard passengers began to exit the boat. A man was having some trouble with a skittish horse. Amos looked at Jenny. "See that unruly horse? I don't want to see you doing anything like that."

The young man's fears were unfounded. Jenny walked on to the ferry and stood quietly like an old pro. Amos believed that he was more nervous about the transit than the mule. The smell of coal and wood fires drifted past the ferry as it slowly moved across the river. The ferry's stacks spewed black smoke from its boilers. Icy rain began to spatter down from the sky.

The ferry would be docking at the widening of the Ottawa River delta, which was part of the Lac des

Deux Montagnes or Lake of Two Mountains. Amos would be west of Montreal and would be happy to be back in the less populated areas. He was brushing the mule to keep it calm when the ferry bumped against the far side pier.

Amos was one of the last ones off the ferry, followed only by the two men with push carts. He spotted a small market not far from the pier. He stopped and purchased a loaf of bread and some of the local sausage for 25 cents. Walking a short distance from the market, he sat on a tree stump and ate part of the bread and sausage. If he was careful, he could make two more meals from them.

Using the stump, Amos got onto the mule and headed it upstream toward Bytown. He was told it was a four-day ride between Montreal and Bytown. The rain had stopped, but a frigid wind was blowing from the north. Amos wrapped his blanket over his coat for more warmth. He urged the mule along the rutted road while he sat behind the sawbuck pack saddle.

He noticed that the softer hardwoods had started to change color, displaying their brilliant reds. Within three weeks, most of the leaves would change and the tree branches would be bare. Looking over the river, he saw a raft of rough-cut square timbers lashed together as it floated past him. Two men sitting next to a crude shelter erected in the center of the raft waved to Amos.

By midday the sun broke through the clouds. Amos sat on the bank of the river, with the sun warming his back as he ate some more of the bread and sausage. The mule pulled at the sparse grass a short distance away. The sound of horses approaching caught his attention. Glancing over his shoulder, he saw two men riding towards him.

"You wouldn't have a little extra food to share?" the stockier rider inquired. Amos looked beyond the stocky man and saw a slim stoop-shouldered man holding back a bit. Both men stared at the sausage and bread on his lap.

"Much as I would like to share," Amos apologized, "I am wondering where my next meal is coming from."

"I'm Hal, and this is my partner, Rod. Mind if we set for a minute?" the stocky man asked, swinging down from his horse.

"Plenty of room, help yourself," the young man offered. Amos set down the wrappers holding the rest of his food and laid the rifle across his lap, aiming toward the river.

Noticing the movement, Hal sat a bit further away and asked, "You any good with that rifle?"

Before answering, Amos waited for Rod to settle down next to Hal. "I usually hit what I aim at."

"Good to hear," the stocky man said, smiling. "It appears we are headed in the same direction. Maybe we could travel together and you can help us hunt for some meat." He patted the revolver in his waistband. "I can't hit the side of a barn with this thing."

"I'm headed for Michigan right now," Amos replied. "You're welcome to ride along."

"It's a bit farther than we are going, but your company is appreciated," Hal said. "You know what. I could go for some coffee. The morning was nippy and it would warm the insides. We got enough for a pot. Could you go for some?"

Feeling awkward that these men were being so generous and he hadn't offered them any of his food, he answered, "That would be good. After it's done, I got a little bread and sausage to contribute."

"That ain't necessary unless you can spare it," Hal said. Poking Rod with his elbow, he said "Get us some wood and put together a fire and get the pot and coffee.

"You offer the coffee and make me do it," Rod grumbled as he went to find some wood.

Chuckling, the stocky man said, "He ain't too ambitious, but he's a good man to ride with."

Hal was making small talk about the Canadian winters. Amos heard Rod coming back with the wood and turned his head toward the sound. There was a flash of light and he felt himself falling forward. Then his head was under water.

Struggling to push himself back out of the river, there was another blow across his back. Momentarily stunned, he lay struggling for breath. Hal was yelling something at Rod and Amos heard the sounds of their horses. They were galloping away.

Struggling up the bank, spitting mud and leaves, Amos saw that the men's plan had been to steal his mule with his gear. When he had fallen forward the Leman rifle had been under him, and in their haste to get away, they had left it.

Grabbing the butt of the rifle, he pulled it up. With no time to check the weapon, he lay on the bank and put the rifle to his shoulder. Praying that the barrel was clear, he took aim and squeezed the trigger. The .32 caliber ball struck the stoop-shouldered man, causing him to jerk and drop the mule's lead rope. Slumping forward over his horse's neck, he clung on as he and Hal disappeared into the forest.

Lying on the bank with the empty weapon, Amos was thankful that they kept going. Trying to stand up caused pain to shoot through his head. Putting his hand to the side of his head, he realized that his hat was gone. After the worst of the pain had subsided, he reached for a sapling to try and stand. He saw that his hand was covered with blood.

Finally getting to his feet, he saw the mule standing, looking back at him. He whistled and called to the animal, "Jenny, for God's sake, come here!"

Hesitantly, the mule walked toward the disheveled Amos. Stopping 40 feet away, Jenny stood with her head up and nose high, prepared to flee at any moment.

Attempting to straighten up, a spasm shot through Amos' back. Clinging to the sapling, he let out an audible gasp. He stood waiting for the spasms to subside. "If those son-of-a-bitches come back, I am in trouble."

Finally, his back relaxed, leaving only the throbbing in his head. Using the rifle to support himself, he walked toward the mule, speaking softly to calm it. As he approached it, Jenny reached her head out to greet him. Clutching the lead rope, he pulled the mule next to him and used it for support.

He knew that the first thing he needed to do was reload the rifle, in case the riders circled back. The vision of the smiling Hal patting his revolver was still in his mind. Wiping mud off the rifle butt, he looked over the rest of the gun. It needed cleaning from falling under him on the bank, but that would have to wait.

While he loaded the muzzle-loader, he winced as he used the ramrod. He hoped that his back was only bruised. Amos decided that he had to carry some reloads on his person, in case he and his gear became separated again. Leading the mule back to the river bank, he saw his hat floating well away from the shore, on its way to Montreal.

His package of food had been kicked during the attack. Both the bread and sausage lay in the dirt. Wrapping them back in the stained paper, he put them into his haversack. He started to feel nauseous, no doubt from the blow on the head. Fighting down the urge to vomit, he took the lead rope and started walking west.

As he walked, his back seemed to loosen up. Rather than throbbing, his head now had a dull ache. When he touched the impact area he felt the dried blood on his hair and right ear. The cut scalp stung when his fingers brushed by it.

After an hour of walking, he took advantage of a windfall and climbed onto the mule. The late afternoon wind was cold on his hatless head. He thought about the men who had tried to rob him. He didn't understand people who preyed on the unsuspecting. The realization that he had shot a man sent chills through him. He had never fired at a man before and wondered if he had killed him.

He didn't recall aiming and firing, but the sight of the man grabbing the horse's neck kept flashing through his mind. The elation he felt when he knew that he'd hit the man was the same feeling he'd had when bagging wild game. Amos knew that the trip west would have its share of danger, but killing men had not entered into his thinking. Most of all, one shouldn't feel good about it.

The young man began to have trouble focusing and hanging onto the back of the mule. He guided Jenny up a small stream, away from the road along the river. Stopping at a flat, grassy area, he clung to the sawbuck pack saddle as he slid off the mule. Amos gripped the side of the animal, unable to straighten up.

Amos' back had stiffened up and the exertion of dismounting had caused his head to start throbbing again. "I am in trouble, Jenny," he moaned.

The warmth of the mule against his cheek felt good. Riding against the cold wind all afternoon had left his face stiff and numb. Slowly, the young man straightened himself and began to search for tinder and wood. With great effort, he had a small fire going. Amos removed his gear from the mule and picketed the animal.

Dipping his pot into the stream, he filled it and put the water on to heat. Opening the haversack, he rummaged through it for something to clean his head wound. He hadn't thought to pack any towels or rags. He looked at his shirt, that was last used after he'd shaved. He pulled it from the bag and set it next to him.

His food was mostly depleted: A little cheese, the sausage and dirt-covered bread. Amos had been sure that there would be plenty of game and had planned to supplement his diet with it. He didn't factor in that hunting took time out of traveling. If game only used the roads, he would have been all set.

He had plenty of salt to season his meals. "I wonder how long I could live on salt-water soup," he said, hefting the bag.

While the water heated, Amos cut a tag alder and rigged up a fishing pole. A quick search under some rocks and rotting logs produced a few worms. They wiggled in the bottom of his tin cup. Amos warned them, "If you don't catch fish, you go into the salt soup."

Smiling at his own humor, the young man tossed his line into the stream. In short order his attempt was rewarded when the piece of stick used as a bobber went under water. He pulled up an eight-inch shiner. After using up his bait, he had a half-dozen shiners. They would make a moderate meal for the hungry traveler.

The water was steaming when Amos got back to his fire. He poured some into his frying pan and picked up the spare shirt. Using the sleeve on one side, he wet it in the pan and began to wipe the dried blood off the side of his head. Tenderly, he cleaned a large lump caused by the blow to his head.

After an attempt to clean up, he rinsed the shirt sleeve in the stream and washed his frying pan. Hanging the wet shirt near the fire, he looked at the fish. Too tired to clean them, Amos stuck them into the pan with some fat to fry. He added coffee to the remaining water in the pot.

While the meal was small, the fresh fish was a pleasant change. He made the coffee weak, to conserve his supply. With the warm food inside him,

Amos felt much better. Glancing at the darkened sky, he saw that the stars were obscured by cloud cover. Amos cut and layered some balsam branches. He then lay his blankets over the branches and his ground tarp over the blankets. He would have to sleep on the damp ground, but at least his blankets wouldn't be soaked in case of rain.

The injured, exhausted young man slept soundly. The sun was full up before he awoke. He sat up. His back was sore, but not as stiff, and while his head was tender the ache was gone. Amos poked through the ashes of his cook fire and found a few coals. Once he had the fire going, he warmed up last night's coffee.

He ate the last of the bread and sausage. The dirt on the bread ground between his teeth. He finished the meal with a cup of stale coffee. Getting his mule and gear ready to go, he grumbled to Jenny, "Last night's meal was a hell of a lot better than this morning."

For the rest of the way to Bytown, Amos lived on a rabbit and several small fish. When the lights from the town came into view, he was truly relieved. He had had no human contact since his run-in with Hal and Rod.

In the distance he spotted a large barn next to a small, clapboard-sided house. The wide double-doors of the barn were open and a shaft of light was cast across the barnyard. As he rode closer he could hear excited voices coming from the barn.

Stopping next to the corral attached to the north wall, Amos looped the mule's lead rope around the middle rail. After running his finger through his unruly hair and rubbing his hands across his heavily stubbled cheeks, the young man walked into the barn.

A lantern was hung on the front inside wall, next to what appeared to be a small office. Another lantern hung over a stall in the back of the barn, where the voices were coming from. Amos walked past other stalls, with curious horses looking toward the sounds.

A large red mare lay in the stall, giving birth to a foal. A young boy struggled to hold the head of the mare down while a small, wiry man with a tobacco stained-beard crouched behind the animal with his arm inside the animal up to his armpit.

"Hold the damn head down, junior!" he snapped. "If she stands back up, I'll never git the head turned around. The horse may end up dying!"

Without thinking, the strapping Amos entered the stall and helped the boy hold the animal down. He spoke softly to the frightened horse, trying to calm it. As he and the boy fought to keep the mare from getting up, the old man worked to straighten the unborn foal.

All of a sudden, there was a shout of success. "I did it! Now, push Nola!"

In the next few minutes the slippery newborn emerged from the exhausted mare and lay on the bloody straw. The old man grabbed a burlap sack and started to rub the foal down. Pointing at Amos, he said, "Give the mare that warm water, if she'll drink it. Junior, git the blanket for the mare."

Realizing that the old man wanted him to give the water, he picked up the bucket sitting in the corner of the stall and offered it to the mare. After taking only a quick drink, the horse lunged forward, standing up.

Amos had to duck out of the way to stop from being knocked over.

Looking to find its foal, the horse turned around, afterbirth still hanging under its tail. It pushed the newborn with its nose, encouraging it to stand. Amos helped the old man put the warming blanket on the mare and then followed him out of the stall.

"Damn glad you come in when you did," the old man said as he reached a hand out toward the young man. "They call me Tuck."

Taking the hand, Amos replied, "The name is Amos Mudd. I hail from Maine."

With a nod of his head to follow, Tuck headed for his office. The young man followed, wiping the sticky birth fluids from his hand.

The old man produced a jug from the side of a scarred deck. Taking a couple of tin mugs off hooks on the wall, he blew them out and then poured a measure of amber liquid into each. Handing one to Amos, he invited him to have a seat.

Taking a sip, Amos smiled. "Damn good hard cider." The fermented brew warmed his empty stomach.

"I got two trees in the back. The apples ain't worth a damn, but they sure make a good cider," Tuck said proudly.

The young boy came back into the barn with another bucket of water. He brought it to the stall, and then came to sit near the men. "This here is Junior," the old man said, nodding to the lad. "He's my son's oldest boy. He spends time with me to help out with the horses."

The lanky, freckle-faced boy had a thick crop of red hair. He appeared to be about 12 years-old. "My pa works at the narrows block house on the Rideau Canal."

"Rideau Canal?" Amos asked.

The old man poured another measure of cider into each cup and then tore a piece of tobacco off the plug in his shirt pocket. Before putting it away he offered a chew to Amos, who declined.

"The Rideau was built to prevent you Yankees from cutting off supplies to Montreal after the war between us," Tuck explained. "It took over 40 locks to lower the level from the Ottawa River to Kingston. The canal connects a couple rivers and several lakes as part of the route. The boy's pa is in the army and is stationed in one of the blockhouses. They was built to defend the canal."

"We aren't fighting with Canada," Amos said, confused.

"Not now, but back in 1812 things were pretty hot between us. It was in the '30s before the canal was finished, and we were friendly with you folks by that time. It still works for bringing supplies up. It is easier than dragging the goods overland past the rapids. That will end once they deepen the St. Lawrence."

By this time the two men were on their third measure of hard cider, and Amos was feeling a little light-headed. Junior sat, fascinated, listening to his grandfather. The old man would spit into the straw and then take a drink of his cider while catching his breath between stories.

"Things are changing though," he said, shaking his head. "Word is that the army will be giving up the canal. Come winter, there is a section that is cleared for skating, probably the longest rink in the world, but not too wide. There are those that even want to change the name of Bytown to Ottawa. Colonel John By put his life's blood into building the canal. I guess Ottawa sounds better than Bytown."

Amos' eyes were getting heavy, and he was having trouble paying attention to Tuck's stories. Suddenly, the old man said, "Hell, we got a pot of venison stew on the stove. Come in and join us for some supper."

Wide awake at the thought of food, Amos stood up and stretched, steadying himself against the wall. "I have a mule I should do something with at the corral."

"Put it in an empty stall and fork some hay," Tuck instructed. "Junior and I will go git the chow on."

While he was light-headed from the cider, Amos' stomach burned with hunger. He watered the mule before leading it into the stall. Jenny anxiously went after the hay as it was tossed into the stall.

The old man had hung his hat on a peg near the door, revealing his bald head. Amos placed the haversack on the floor next to the door and leaned his .32 Leman beside it. There was a pail of water and an enamel basin on the side board. The men washed their hands and faces before going to the table.

The stew was excellent. They ate in a small kitchen, warmed by a 10-plate stove. It was a neat room, with pans and pots hanging on the wall behind the stove. A sideboard with shelves built above it was on the back wall. Two doors led into what Amos guessed were bedrooms. It was a warm and cozy kitchen, with a homey feeling, much different than the house Amos had grown up in.

Tuck continued to talk on and on about the canal, fishing on Big Rideau Lake, and changes in Bytown. Amos barely heard any of it as he helped himself to seconds and thirds of tasty stew that was served with a dark bread and buttermilk.

Once they finished the meal, the young boy began to clean up and do the dishes. Tuck poured coffee from a pot on the back of the stove and put a bit of rye into each cup. Handing one to Amos, the two of them went and sat on the front porch.

The porch faced east, to get the early morning sun and then shade in the afternoon. A lean-to full of split wood protected the porch from the wind on the north side. Tuck was suddenly quiet as he looked out over the fields. The two men sipped their coffee royals and enjoyed the stillness of the evening.

Amos broke the silence. "If you don't m, I would like to sleep in your barn tonight. I am headed west, eventually to California. I have run into a few unexpected things on the trip so far."

"The boy has two bunks in his room. You are welcome to sleep in the house," Tuck offered. "I figured you might be a bit down on your luck. The side of your head is a mess and I didn't see any hat. Your clothes look like you've been living in them for a while."

Amos felt his face turn red. He was thankful that they were sitting on the darkened porch. "I had a couple of lowlifes try and steal my mule and gear a few days ago." He couldn't tell the man that his clothes, although a little soiled, were as good as he had.

"I board horses for folks in Uptown. They come over the Rideau on Sappers Bridge and take rides south along the canal," Tuck told the young man. "Often they will bring some food and stop near one of the locks and watch the men work the gates as boats go through."

The old man paused for a moment. "You know, Amos, I am some behind on my work due to a bout with the crud. If you would be willing and had the time, I could sure use a hand around here for a week or two. I saw you work with the mare keeping it down."

"The boy is a lot of help, but with school and spending time with his pa, he can only do so much. It would be heavy work, cleaning stalls, spreading manure, brushing stock, and a shed I've been trying to get built behind the barn."

Amos thought about the offer. What he heard was three meals a day and a warm bed. Winter was fast approaching, and he needed to get westward. "I can spend a few days helping you, Tuck. But I got a lot of miles to cover before hard winter sets in."

"Good. Very good. Any days you can give me will be a great help," the old man said. "I got pretty dirty climbing into the south end of that mare. I asked Junior to heat some water to wash up. There will be plenty enough for you, too."

Then he added, "The work will be tough on the clothes. I got some old pants and shirts my boy use to wear. He was about your size. I'll dig them out so you won't ruin your stuff. Oh, and I got a hat you can wear to keep your head warm."

Amos heard the old man spit and then shift his weight on the chair next to him. The young man's pride was hurt a little. Was Tuck making all these offers because of the condition he'd arrived in? Again, he was thankful that it was dark. Fighting to make his voice light, Amos said, "You are being too generous. I will work hard for you."

"I need to go check on the mare and foal," the old man said.

"I'll go with you and check on the mule."

CHAPTER FOUR

There were two clean sets of clothing waiting on the bunk when Amos came in from the barn. Huck was in the other room cleaning up. While the clothes showed signs of wear, they had no damage or patches. After digging his spare long johns from the haversack, Amos went back into the kitchen to take his turn washing.

He cringed when he saw his reflection in the mirror behind the bucket of hot water. He still had crusted spots of blood on the side of his head. The scrawny whiskers that had grown out barely covered the nicks and cuts on his face, and he was badly in need of a haircut.

Stripped to the waist, he scrubbed himself clean. Tuck came out of his bedroom, put some wood into the stove and turned down the dampers. Noticing Amos' back, he said, "That's one hell of a bruise you got there."

"Yes, it felt pretty painful," Amos agreed.

"The fellow that hit me is carrying a .32 ball in his back as he tried to get away with my mule. I figured his is worse than mine."

As the old man headed back toward his room, he called over his shoulder, "Served the bastard right."

Amos was up before daylight. Dressing quickly, he clamped his new hat on and walked toward the barn. A quick search provided him with the tools that were needed to clean the stalls. Tossing the manure into a wheelbarrow, he then gripped the handles, pushed it up a short plank in the back of the barn and dumped it onto the pile.

He then pitched clean straw into the stall. After an hour's work he finished the last stall, which held the mare and its foal. The little colt was contentedly suckling the mare. The afterbirth that had fallen out the night before was gone. Most likely the cats that ran around the barn had taken it.

The young man had just finished pitching fresh straw into the stall when he heard a shout from the porch, "Breakfast is ready!"

Amos carefully brushed any of the straw from his borrowed clothing. He then hurried to the house, where he was greeted with the smell of pancakes. A generous stack sat on his plate, with a pitcher of maple syrup and bowl of butter next to it. A steaming pot of coffee sat on the stove.

After the meal was finished, Junior headed for school. Tuck and Amos went out to spread the manure. A team of horses pulling a wagon was led to the manure pile. The two men used forks to load the wagon. Then, while Tuck drove the team through the field, Amos spread the load, pitching it out the back with a fork. Taking only a short break at noon, the two men made a significant dent in the pile by late afternoon.

Amos put the team up and brushed them, while the old man went into the house to clean up and start supper. The next two weeks flew by as task after task around the farm was finished. One evening, after an all-over bath, the two men sat on the porch.

"It is time for me to continue west," Amos told his friend.

"I could use your help through the winter, if you would be willing to stay," Tuck offered.

"When I rode into your place I was at the end," Amos admitted. "I don't think I could have ridden another mile. You recognized it even before I did. I will never be able to repay what you did to help me get back on my feet. But now I have to go. Maybe I'll come back this way sometime and hear some more stories about the Rideau."

Tuck paid him £5 in Canadian money for the work and insisted that he take the clothes and hat. The old man also gave him a canvas bag packed with coffee, side meat, flour, beans, and cornmeal. Amos hung his haversack on one side of the sawbuck and the canvas bag on the opposite side. One other thing he had was a plug of chewing tobacco in his pocket, a new habit he had picked up.

With his mule packed, Amos waved to Tuck and Junior. He walked north along the canal in search of the first bridge across. The sun was bright and the leaves were in full color. With his mood matching the weather, he strode briskly, humming a tune his mother used to sing.

Amos stopped at a mercantile on the west side of Bytown. Tuck had trimmed Amos' hair and let him use the scissors to trim his beard. He had decided that he didn't want to go through the world looking like a wild man, so he purchased scissors and a small mirror to add to his gear. He also picked up a fly tarp, some hard bread, and several pieces of jerky.

The first evening he stopped a short distance from the river. Clouds had come in and there was the smell of rain. Rigging his new tarp, he put his gear underneath and then put together a small fire. By the time he finished his meal of coffee, fried side meat and bread, the wind had picked up. The colorful leaves cascaded down around his camp.

"We got a storm brewing!" he shouted to the mule. Pulling the picket, he led it to water and then picketed it closer to camp. Jenny licked at his coat and shoved him with her nose. "Missing the warm stall and hay, are you?"

He dug into his haversack and took out a piece of the hard bread. Breaking it into pieces, he fed it to the mule. "This is the best I can do, old girl."

The wind was pulling up one end of the fly tarp. Using a hatchet, he reset the stake. Laying it back on the haversack, he poured another cup of coffee and sat with his back to the wind, collar turned up, sipping the hot brew.

With the meal done, he dumped the remaining grease from the frying pan and rubbed it with leaves. Tossing it under the tarp, he checked the pot. Deciding that there was enough left for morning, he set it next to the fire.

Large drops of rain began to fall. Amos

grabbed up some kindling for the morning and ducked under the tarp. Barely had he set the wood at the foot when the rain came down in earnest. The darkening cloud, blocked the last of the waning sunlight. He checked to make sure that the rain wasn't getting to his rifle.

The young man usually enjoyed the sound of rain, but having it only inches away on the tarp made him feel vulnerable. The fact that he was staying dry made Amos smile. The fly tarp was well placed for the storm. He lay under his blanket, warm and comfortable. Sleep came quickly.

Braying from the mule brought Amos wide awake. The rain had stopped, but the cold wind was still blowing. Pulling his boots on, he came out from the fly tarp in his long johns, the .32 Leman ready for action. Jenny had pulled the picket rope loose and was standing a distance from the camp, continuing to raise a ruckus.

The wind brought him the appalling smell of skunk. Walking up to the mule, his worst fears were realized. Jenny had investigated a passing polecat and had been sprayed. Picking up the lead rope, he struggled to get the fearful animal back to camp. Tying the mule to a pine branch, he crawled back under the tarp and sat in the center of his blankets.

His hands had become coated with the skunk spray from the lead rope. "Damn, that stinks," Amos muttered. Then he called out to the mule, "I guess I may as well get used to it. We'll be living with the smell for some time."

The first hint of light began to show in the east. Thankful that morning had arrived, the young man finished getting dressed. Putting the kindling on top of the wet ashes, he struck the flint, sending sparks into some tinder. After he got the fire going, he set last night's coffee next to it to warm up.

It was finally light enough to check on the mule. He was thankful that most of the spray had missed the animal and had not gotten into its eyes. The lead rope and the mule's front right leg had caught the stream. He kept clear of the area that the skunk had sprayed to prevent picking up any more of the smell.

Hurriedly drinking the lukewarm coffee and chewing on some jerky, Amos broke down camp and packed the mule for travel. The smell of the skunk was giving him a headache. He had left the lead rope soaking in the clear water of the stream while he got things ready. Taking it out, he swung it around the trunk of a pine to get the water out and, with luck, some of the spray.

The day remained cold. The heavy cloud cover cast a gloom over the land. Just the day before, the sun had made the fall leaves look brilliant. One night of wind and the heavy rain had all but stripped the foliage from the trees. He wore his dark blue pea coat, which fell just below the waist. It protected him from the chilling north wind. Amos also had a pair of choppers with a buckskin outer shell and a wool inner liner to keep his hands warm.

His father had gotten him the pea coat the year before on one of the trips to sell potatoes. He had met a former sailor who had been down on his luck and was looking for some drinking money. The choppers were useful when working on the farm during the bitter Maine winters. One other item he had was a tuque, or stocking cap, that Tuck had given him while working on the farm.

Today he had all the cold weather gear on. His new crowned, flat-brim felt hat was rolled up and tied to his haversack. The only thing he wished he had was a pair of high cuts. They were a laced boot that came halfway up the calf, to be worn once the snow got deeper.

Late in the afternoon he spotted three men sitting around a fire near the river bank. With his Leman rifle cradled in his arm, ready for quick action, he slowly approached the fire. "Hello the fire!" he called. "Can I come in?"

One of the men stood up, looking toward Amos. He had unbuttoned his coat and carried a Colt Paterson in his waistband. "If you're friendly, you are welcome," was the response.

"I am friendly," Amos replied, "but my mule came face-to-face with a polecat last night. We might smell a mite."

He heard the men laugh. The man standing waved him over. "No man is refused the hospitality of our fire, but we would appreciate if you took the seat downwind." Another course of laughter erupted.

CHAPTER FIVE

When traveling, most men one met are good and willing to share with a fellow traveler. Hal and Rod were an exception. Their type are few, but a man always had to be careful. Tying the mule next to the men's horses, Amos sat just back from the fire, still carrying the .32 Leman. A pot of beans was boiling on the fire and a pot of coffee sat next to the coals.

"Grab your cup. The coffee is hot and the beans will be ready soon," a round-faced man with red cheeks said.

Retrieving his cup from the packs, Amos held it out so the man could fill it. The coffee was good. "My name is Amos Mudd. I've traveled from Maine," the young man said, introducing himself.

The man who welcomed him in had a ruddy complexion, broad, strong shoulders and large, calloused hands. He pointed to the round-faced man. "This here is Leroy Armand." Then, at the short, barrel-chested man with one good eye, "That's his brother Henri. I'm Jacques Larue, they call me Jake.

We are headed for the logging camp just above the Mattawa fork."

"I'll be taking the Mattawa to Lake Nipissing," Amos told the men.

"You're welcome to travel with us," Jake offered. "There is safety in numbers and you have a good-looking rifle there. Are you good with it?"

"I generally hit what I aim at," Amos replied slowly.

"That's good. You can be the hunter of our little group. If you shoot it, Leroy here can make a fine meal for us," Jake assured their new member.

The conversation gave him chills. It was like the one with Hal and Rod.

The men had their shelter up already. Amos excused himself and went to rig his fly tarp. While he worked, he kept the rifle within reach and an eye on the three men. The three men continued to talk and kid each other while they waited for the beans to get done.

With the tarp up and his gear stowed, the young man went to check on the mule. Getting a better look at the animals, he saw that the two horses were over 16 hands high, were muscular and had powerful hind quarters. They were draft horses. The other animal wasn't a horse, but rather another mule, much the same size as his mule. The animals were intended to skid logs, or pull sledges loaded with logs.

When he got back to the fire, the three men were sitting with tin plates filled with beans. Amos ladled some of the bubbling beans onto his plate and sat down to eat, keeping the three in front of him.

"That's a damn fine team of draft horses you have there."

Henri looked up from his meal and smiled. "They can out pull most of the scrawny animals you find at the logging camp."

"We won plenty of money out pulling those that thought their horses were better," Leroy bragged.

"The mule you got there is the same size as my Jenny," Amos said. "Is it yours, Jake?"

"That it is," the man replied. "Makes me an extra few pounds at the camp each month and they supply the feed."

Pouring another cup of coffee, Amos inquired, "How long will it take us to make the fork of the Mattawa?"

"Seven, maybe eight days to the fork," Jake replied. "The camp is about another day beyond the fork along the Ottawa. We cross the river two days before reaching the fork. The trail on the north side isn't as good, but it's the best place to cross."

Henri and Leroy got up from the fire and started collecting the dishes. "We best get these cleaned up and get some sleep," Henri said.

Amos pitched in, helping secure the camp for the evening. For the first time around these men, he left his Leman .32 out of reach. He volunteered to take the animals to water. While the stock drank, the young man looked back at the camp. He was confident that he had joined good men to travel the road with.

The men had pitched a good-sized tarp to sleep under. They offered to let Amos sleep under it, but he had already set up the smaller fly tarp. It was decided that in the future only one tarp would be set up. The snoring of the men was the only sound that night as the frigid cold settled into the river valley.

A heavy frost coated the woodlands when the men awoke. The naked tree branches extended toward the sky. The frozen grass crunched under the men's boots as they readied to leave. Leroy had made a pot of coffee while the others put packs onto the animals. They made a meal of coffee and hard bread. Amos provided the hard bread.

"We call this stuff hardtack or sea biscuits," Henri said as he dunked it into his coffee.

"Or tooth dullers," Leroy laughed.

Jake came to the fire. "Tonight we will be eating rubaboo."

"And what is rubaboo?" Amos asked.

"We got some pemmican from the Metis in Montreal," Jake explained. "Leroy here mixes it with flour and water and makes a tasty soup. Some folks hereabouts call the soup rubaboo."

Tuck had told Amos about the Metis, who were a mix of early European men and women with the Algonquin, Cree, or other tribes. They were known in the area for drying strips of meat, pounding it almost to a powder and then mixing it with fat. Sometimes dried berries, choke cherries, or cranberries were pounded and included in the mixture. The result was called pemmican and was carried by trappers and other frontier men to provide a quick, high energy meal. Generally, it was made into a soup, or fried. If necessary, it could be eaten raw.

With the packs on the animals, the men headed

upriver, their frozen breath hanging in clouds behind them. Leroy and Henri led their horses while Jake led the two mules. Amos was free to go ahead and hunt for fresh meat.

He rejoined the men for a midday break. He was able to add three partridges and two rabbits to their larder. After a meal of venison jerky, the group continued on. Amos hadn't gone far when there was a crashing in the brush ahead of him. He caught sight of the white flash of a deer's tail.

The rest of the afternoon, Amos trailed the deer. It remained just out of the range of a killing shot. The sun was low when he heard the hammering of tarp stakes being driven in. Following the sound, he found the men camped at a small inlet to the river. There was a wide area covered with brown grass. The stock was busy eating their fill while Jake watched them.

Leroy had just finished cleaning the birds and rabbit. He looked up at the young man approaching. "Tonight we eat like the queen herself. The soup can wait for another day."

"No luck hunting this afternoon?" Henri asked.

"I chased the legs off a nice whitetail but never got close enough for a shot," Amos replied.

Henri fixed his one eye on the Leman. "You got a fine rifle there for smaller game, and maybe something bigger at close range. What you need is something like my converted Brown Bess."

He went over to the packs and came back with the .70 caliber smooth-bore that had been converted to percussion caps. Handing it to Amos to look over, he continued, "If you get within 100 yards, the musket will bring it down."

The gun was heavier than the .32, but would give Amos an advantage. "I'll use it tomorrow," he said, thanking Henri.

Using the Dutch oven that Leroy had, Amos mixed up some sourdough biscuits. They were golden brown and ready at the same time that the game was finished roasting. Spirits were high that night as the men ate the hardy meal. Jake brought out a bottle of cognac and poured some into each man's coffee.

The plummeting temperatures continued. The next morning there was ice along some parts of the river and the inlet was solid ice. Amos left carrying the Brown Bess, hoping to startle another deer. Jake had given him the Colt in case he ran across some small game.

"If you shot a rabbit with the Bess, all will be left is ears and tail," he'd said, laughing at his own joke.

Amos liked the feel of the Colt Paterson. It was a five-shot .28 caliber. He carried it under his coat, in his waist band, loaded with four shots. Jake had warned him that if all five were loaded he could accidently lose his manhood if he tripped.

He shot at two rabbits with the Colt, missing both. His shine for the handgun was beginning to dull. He had just assumed that if he was good with the long gun, the same would apply to the other. Just before noon, he spotted a partridge sitting on a balsam branch.

Setting the musket down, Amos took his time, leveling the Colt, putting the bird into the front site, then squeezing the trigger. The partridge fell to the ground, flapping its last. The young man rushed over and picked up his prize. Disappointed, he saw that the shot had gone through the breast. He had been aiming for the head.

Muttering he said, "It's a small ball. Shouldn't be too much meat wasted." Sticking the bird into the game bag slung over his shoulder, he picked up the musket and continued.

He had ranged too far ahead to join the others for the midday break. There had been a couple of buck scrapes and Amos had heard the sound of antlers clashing together in a dispute of territory. The sun was starting to get low in the afternoon sky when he spotted two whitetail deer.

An eight-point buck had its head down, following the scent of a doe. A younger spike horn stood a way off, watching the elder animal. Standing, hardly breathing, Amos waited, concealed by some low spruce trees. The larger buck was out of range and moving away from him.

With his eyes fixed on the spike horn, Amos waited. If it continued to shadow the eight-pointer, it should pass less than 60 yards in front of him. The shadows were getting thicker in the woods and the two deer were taking their time.

All of a sudden, the large buck's head came up and it looked back at the spike horn. It snorted loudly at the small buck. The next thing that Amos expected was to see the eight-point deer turn and chase the spike horn. He readied himself to take the shot at the larger buck as it passed him.

The scent of the does in front of him must have been too strong, because after a head shake the eight-pointer headed out, following the females. After a moment, the young spike horn started ahead, his eyes fixed on where the other buck had disappeared.

The large musket felt clumsy in Amos' hands. He brought it to his shoulder and waited, feeling the pounding of his heart. After all the years of hunting, he was still filled with excitement at the prospect of bagging a large prey.

Unexpectedly, the young buck stopped and looked in his direction. *Close enough,* Amos thought, and with the sights lined up on the buck, he squeezed the trigger. The muzzle-loader belched smoke and fire sending the .69 caliber ball flying at the deer.

Whether it was seeing the flash of powder or the impact of the ball, Amos couldn't be sure, but the spike horn jumped to the side before tripping and rolling to the ground. It struggled to stand up before collapsing. Pushing through the evergreen branches, the young man ran across the open ground to the deer. He poked it with the barrel to make sure it was finished.

With shaking hands, Amos reloaded the musket. He didn't want to be found without a loaded gun in the wilds of Canada. Leaning the musket within reach against a poplar tree, he pulled his knife and began to gut the deer. He kept the liver and heart, stuffing them inside the game bag.

With the front legs lashed between the small horns, he took the loose end of the rope in one hand and picked up the musket with the other. He had no more than a half-hour of daylight left and had no idea how far he might be from the other men.

Grasping the rope tight, he started walking north toward the river. Head down, leaning against the rope, he walked. While the deer had only been a spike horn, it was still a good-sized buck. Dragging a deer over snow would have been much easier than over the frozen ground.

Amos stopped to rest. His breath was coming hard and he was beginning to sweat. That could be the death of a man in frigid temperatures. He unbuttoned his coat to try and cool off. Amos knew that he had to slow down. Darkness was rapidly approaching, but he had stars to follow. Once to the river, he would follow it to the camp.

The howl of the wolves somewhere behind him broke his plan to pace himself. Soon he was all but running, with the deer flopping over deadfalls and the uneven ground behind him. At any moment he expected to feel something leap onto his back and drag him down. He switched hands, pulling the deer to relieve the pain of the rope tightening under the weight.

At last he saw a lighter area ahead. "Let it be the river and not a clearing!" he shouted to the darkness around him. Coming to the river bank, he felt some sense of relief. He was wet with sweat. Looking up and down the river, he couldn't be sure whether the rest of his party was downstream or upstream of him.

Pulling the Colt, he raised it in the air and fired a shot. He stood still, gasping to catch his breath. His eyes were closed as he listened for an answering shot. Nothing. His best guess was that they were still downstream of him. Taking hold of the rope with his aching hand, he started walking. If he guessed wrong, he would have to abandon the deer and walk back. He was too wet with sweat to spend a night. He would be dead from the cold by morning.

Less than a mile downstream, he caught the flicker of a fire. Relief flooded over him. In a hoarse voice he shouted, "Hello the camp!" He heard shouts in return and soon there were running footsteps and shadowy figures coming at him out of the dark.

Jake reached him first. "We was just about to come looking for you!"

"I have been dragging this deer all over hell's half-acre," Amos said, handing the rope to Jake.

Leroy gave Amos a bowl of pemmican soup as the exhausted man sat next to the fire. There was also a biscuit left over from the night before. The soup was hot and tasty. Dunking the biscuit into the thick broth, Amos wolfed it down. Despite the hot soup and fire, he began to shiver. The cold night air and the sweat on his skin was making him chilled.

While Henri built up the fire, Amos retrieved a change of clothing from his haversack. He stripped down in front of the roaring fire and put on the dry clothes. Leroy had the buck hanging on a pine branch and started to skin the animal. Slowly, the shivering subsided and Amos was able to tell his fellow travelers about his day. Just as he finished howls from the hunting wolves reached their ears.

"They are following the scent of the deer you dragged," Henri surmised.

"You got the liver?" Leroy called, interrupting.

"It's in the game bag," Amos said, picking it up from next to his sweaty clothing.

Taking the bag, Leroy reached in. Dumping

the contents onto the ground he grunted, "Damn mess of feathers and blood."

Jake poured some cognac into a cup for Amos. "This will warm your innards."

The men were excited about the prospect of venison steaks, making Amos proud that he was able to provide the deer. He had given the Colt back to Jake, who loaded it in case it was needed.

Care was taken to make the camp wolf-proof that night. The stock was brought in closer, the deer meat was hung out of reach in the pines, and the rest of their food was stored under the tarp. Henri kept the loaded musket within reach.

Sometime during the night, Amos was woken by the snorting of the horses and braying of the mules. He felt snowflakes hitting his face, carried in by the cold breeze. Pulling the blanket over his head, he drifted back to sleep.

An inch of snow had fallen by daylight. The flakes clinging to the tree branches made the area a winter wonderland. Pulling his boots on, Amos walked away from the camp to relieve himself. He found tracks of the wolves as they had circled, looking for a way to get to the venison.

Leroy had the fire going and was slicing the liver into the frying pan when Amos returned. "Ain't nothing like liver in the morning. Only wish I had some onions to throw in."

The young man noticed that the liver was lightly floured and Leroy had included the partridge and the deer heart in the pan. Jake came walking in from upriver. "Good thing you dragged the hide and head a good way from camp. The damn wolves ate everything, including the hair."

Henri was watering the stock. Leading the animals back, he said, "Poor critters spent the night watching the wolves circle."

The smell of the meat frying had everyone anticipating breakfast, as they sipped their coffee and watched Leroy at work. As soon as the tender liver was devoured, the men set about breaking camp. With wolves in the area, they decided that Amos should walk with the group rather than hunt.

CHAPTER SIX

As the men trudged on leading the animals, thick clouds were building to the west. Henri sniffed the air and declared, "We'll have snow by tomorrow and it will be a good 'un."

"We got snow now," Jake said, pointing at the fluff on the ground.

Henri snorted, "You'll not call this stuff snow come morning."

Amos walked enjoying listening to the two men banter back and forth about the coming weather. He was in agreement with Henri about snow coming. He just hoped it wasn't too big of a storm. He had miles to go before winter set in.

Looking back, Amos caught sight of something following them. Staying a way back, the wolves were still hopeful of getting at the deer meat. Leroy saw him looking back. "They will follow us until we reach the camp. Then the smell of man will be too strong for them."

Amos wondered if the smell of four men didn't discourage them, then what would happen when it was only one? The wind was picking up as the dark clouds moved in. By the time they made camp, a damp snow that stuck to everything was falling.

They staked the animals on a grass-covered area. Amos watched over the animals, carrying the Leman .32. He half-hoped that the wolves would come close enough to get a shot at one. He had heard that wolf skin made a warm winter coat.

The sun had already set when Leroy called out that supper was ready. Amos pulled the stakes and brought the animals into camp. A picket rope had been stretched between too poplar trees for tying the stock. Covered with the sticky snow, he headed for the fire to get the venison steaks.

Extra wood had been put onto the fire before the men crawled under the tarp to eat. Extra supports had been put in to hold the snow load. The meat of the young buck was tender. They cut strips with their knives and speared them to bring the juicy meat to their mouths.

Amos soaked some hard bread into the juice left in his plate from the venison. The coffee pot sat just inside the tarp. Gripping the handle, he poured more into his mug and offered some to the others. Leroy made a strong coffee, and that's the way Amos liked it.

With the meal finished the men rubbed snow on the plates to clean them. It left them coated with fat from the deer, which would go fine with their next meal. After stowing the plates and mugs, they got out their bedrolls. In the dim light of the cook fire, there wasn't much they could do other than go to sleep.

Amos put his coat and hat on and went out to check on the horses and mules. The snow-covered animals were standing, contented and dozing. He stood under a pine that protected him from the falling snow. Taking the plug of tobacco out of his shirt, Amos ripped a chew off.

Rolling it in his mouth, he thought about California. Snow wouldn't be a problem there. He imagined sloshing gravel from the bottom of a creek and seeing a gold nugget appearing. He had been told that everything at a gold strike was expensive, but heck, with all that gold he would be able to afford it.

Amos had stopped talking to everyone about heading for the gold fields. Most of those he talked to thought it was a fool's errand. They didn't know what he knew. He had read and studied and understood what was out there. From now on, he just told them he was going west.

It was peaceful chewing the tobacco and watching the fire beyond reflect off the snow. The flakes looked like diamonds. His thoughts were interrupted by the lonely howl of a wolf. Shortly, several others answered. They sounded far off and shouldn't be a problem for them.

Spitting out the plug, he headed back to the tarp. Ducking under the edge, he crawled into his blankets. The others were already sleeping. The tarp gave them just enough clearance to sit up, and both ends were held down with wooden stakes. A rope went through the middle and was tied to trees. He lay next to one of extra posts holding the tarp against the heavy snow.

Sleep came quickly to the young man. He had only a couple more days traveling in the safety of these men, so he'd best rest well while he could. A loud crack brought Amos awake. He attempted to sit up and was smashed down on his back. The weight of the tarp had him pinned.

He heard the shouts of the other men and felt them kicking and fighting to get free of the snow-covered tarp. Someone was shouting his name. "I'm . . . I'm over here! I can't move, hard to breathe."

There was movement above the tarp near him, and then a knee was planted in his groin. "Ah!" he shouted, "You're on top of me!"

Quickly, the snow was removed from the tarp and he was free to sit up. Sitting exposed to the weather, Amos searched for his boots. Pushing his feet into them, he gathered up his coat and blankets, then shouted to the others, "Let's get under the pines!"

Shortly, four disheveled men huddled under the snow-laden branches of a large white pine. Their fire had been long smothered by the heavy snowfall. The wind was calm, allowing the snow to build up on whatever it landed on. The cracking sounds of branches and trees giving way around them was constant.

Everyone but Henri had managed to grab some of their blankets or coats as they'd ran from the collapsed tarp. Their one-eyed friend had but one boot, and no blankets or coat. Amos had his coat on, so he let Henri share his blankets to keep from freezing.

The crack of a branch and then the thud of the branch and snow falling directly behind them startled the men. "I hope the hell the branches above us hold up," Jake growled.

Sitting crowded together underneath the pine, they shared the blankets to keep the snow off. The men dozed off and on through the night. At first light they looked in disbelief. There was at least two feet of snow on the ground.

"You said it would snow, Henri," Amos recalled.

"By Jesus, I didn't expect this," he said in awe.

The men pushed the snow back from their blankets and then sat back. It continued falling steadily as they watched the white world around them get brighter as the sun rose behind the cloud cover.

Henri leaned toward his brother. "Leroy, can I borrow one of your boots? I got to go take a piss."

Wrapped in a blanket, Henri waded through the deep snow. "See if the horses are okay," Jake called.

One at a time the men waded away in the snow, just far enough to clear the tree, to relieve themselves. Jake came back muttering, "Had to dig a hole so me bum cheeks didn't freeze."

The levity helped to raise the spirits of the stranded group. Leroy turned to his brother. "Give me that boot back. The snow just tumbled off the pine next to us. I can get a fire going and at least make some coffee for us."

Amos had the most winter wear with him, so he volunteered to burrow under the tarp and find what was needed for the morning meal. Trudging through knee deep snow, he made his way back to the mounds that defined the tarp.

Kicking snow with his boots and scooping it with his hands, he was able to clear an area near the edge. He continued to kick the snow clear while fresh snow fell, trying to cover his effort. With a space cleared, he pulled up the end of the tarp and started crawling under it, pushing up the tarp and snow as he went. Soon, he was engulfed in darkness. When he felt a blanket or some clothing, he would pull it toward him to take on the way out.

Just before reaching the supplies, his hand came down on Henri's boot. He stuffed it inside his coat. Once at the packs he was weak from pushing up on the snow-covered tarp. He didn't dare lay down, because he feared that he wouldn't be able to push the snow up again.

Feeling around, he found the pack with the coffee pot. Leroy kept the ground coffee and beans in the same bag. Gripping it, he pulled. The pack didn't move. "Come on you bugger," he shouted and heaved on the pack. After several attempts the bag started to move.

As he grunted and pulled on the pack, Amos attempted to pull the blankets and clothes he had come across with him. His burden was becoming too large to drag when he felt the tarp come up behind him. It was Jake coming to help. "Couldn't stand watching you anymore," he said. "I had to come and help."

"Much appreciated," Amos gasped.

They left the pack just under the edge of the tarp and dug out the things Leroy would need. Jake grabbed the blankets and clothes and brought them to the tree. He heard Henri call out, "Did you find my boot?"

"Got it under my coat, keeping it warm for you!" Amos yelled back.

Gathering the things that Leroy would need, Amos waded through the snow to the pine. There was a small fire going. Filling the pot with snow, Leroy put it onto the fire. "Did you find any mugs?" the round-faced man asked.

"Damn, you're right," Amos sighed. "Next trip in I'll look for some."

Once back with the other men, Amos pulled the boot out from his coat for Henri. Then, sitting against the tree, he opened his coat to cool off. Snow had gotten between his low-cut boots and his ankles. They were numb from the cold.

The men spent the day digging out the tarp and their gear and moving it to the pine tree. They tied and wrapped the tarp around the tree, wigwam style. The snow continued to fall steadily. By early afternoon the wind started to pick up, blowing the loose snow, causing whiteout conditions.

The men sat together, clumps of snow buffeting the outside of the tarp as they fell from the pine branches. The wind howled and tore at the tarp. In their cramped space, the men fought to keep the swirling snow out of the shelter.

Leroy had melted enough snow to fill all the canteens. The men kept them inside their coats. With the blowing snow, it would be impossible to light another fire and cook, so they ate chunks of pemmican broken from the frozen block, and jerky.

Unable to lay down inside the cramped,

makeshift shelter, they sat, huddled together for warmth and slept. Every once in a while, someone would stomp their feet to make sure their toes weren't freezing. They couldn't go out and check on the animals. If they did, there was nothing they could do for them anyway.

The second morning after the storm began, the wind died down. Slowly, the stiff and cold men climbed out from under their shelter. The sky was clear and the sun was bright, making it difficult to open their eyes. Walking on feet that felt more like stumps, Amos made his way to the animals.

The horses and mules snorted and stomped, welcoming the company. "I ain't got anything to feed you," he said as he untied the animals, letting them roam to find any tender branches to chew on.

As he walked, feeling came back to his feet. The sensation of pins and needles made stepping difficult. He kept moving to get things circulating. Jenny came over and pushed at him with her nose. "I got nothing for you, mule. Try the small poplar or the cedar." He patted her on the forehead and moved away.

The wind had blown the snow into large drifts, leaving some of the ground almost bare. The river was over half-covered with ice. It was the end of October and early for such a snow. Moving out today was not even considered. They would need all of a day to get things back in order for travel.

Jake was kicking through the snow, looking for items that might have been left after the tarp had been removed. Henri joined him in the search. Amos watched the horses and mules paw under the snow for brown winter grass, while he made sure that the animals didn't wander too far. Leroy worked at making a hot breakfast.

They hung the tarp between two pine trees, putting the center higher to keep the sides steeper. The windward end of the tarp was closed off and Leroy had built the fire at the open end. By the time the coffee, beans, and fried venison were ready, the camp was most livable.

With the meal finished, they strung another line to dry the items that had gotten wet during the storm. Breaking the ice near the bank of the river, an opening was made for the animals to drink. Amos spent an hour chopping firewood. The exercise helped get the cramps out of his muscles.

Jake scouted around the area for any wolf tracks. Coming back, he stated, "The snow is even too much for the damn wolves. They have moved out."

After spending their time readying for travel the next day, all the men were glad to turn in as soon as it became dark. They all slept soundly after two nights of less than restful sleep. While the stars marched across the sky, a hungry fox wandered around the camp, picking up discarded scraps of food.

Shortly after daylight the group was back on the trail. Winter had come early to the North Country and the loggers were anxious to get to camp. Amos walked quietly, knowing that by tomorrow the men he had joined would go one way and he another.

Some of the snow drifts were waist-deep as they pushed their way north. To make travel easier, they strung out single-file, with the man leading breaking trail. By taking turns, travel was less tiring on everyone. They rested midday under a stand of tall white pine. Leroy made a pot of coffee for the men to dunk their hard bread into.

Jake sat next to Amos. "You have been quiet today."

"I suppose I have," the young man replied. "You and the brothers have been good company. Tomorrow you cross the river, and me and the mule will be on our own."

"How far west are you headed?" Jake asked.

Looking at his newfound friend, Amos hesitated and then told him, "All the way. I will stop at the Pacific Ocean."

There was a look of surprise on Jake face, "You're not going hunting gold, are you?"

The young man wiped his nose with the back of his gloved hand. "I am going to hunt for gold. They say along the American River men are getting rich."

Expecting Jake to ridicule him, Amos sat with his jaw set. Jake looked him straight in the eye. "I wish I had your courage. Each year I spend the winters felling trees and dragging them on the ice of the river. Come spring, I ride the damn things down to Quebec and then work in sawmills. It keeps me in vittles and cognac. But there is no adventure."

"I had expected to be in Michigan before winter set in, and if the snow wasn't too deep, I planned to continue to St. Louis," Amos admitted.

"I doubt this snow will stay," Jake said. "A couple of sunny days will melt much of it. But anything that falls after November 1st will last until spring. You can expect the nights to be cold, building ice on the river."

"Drink up the rest of this coffee before I dump the grounds," Leroy called out, bringing an end to the conversation.

Amos was in better spirits through the afternoon, joining in with the kidding and joking. It was like a burden had been lifted talking with Jake. Much of the excitement of going to California was having someone to discuss it with.

That night they camped at the crossing. Leroy separated all of Amos's gear that had gotten mixed with theirs. He gave any extra food, including a leather bag of pemmican, to the young man. Amos made more of the sourdough biscuits in the Dutch oven, while Leroy made beans with molasses and fried side meat.

"We will eat well tonight," Leroy declared. "We celebrate the departure of our friend from Maine."

Henri said, "And I'll not forget you went and got me boot under the tarp."

Laughing, the men set down to eat. By the end of the meal, the mood became more somber. Jake got his cognac out and poured some into each man's coffee. "We can't be sitting here moping. Our friend Amos is heading out on an adventure!"

In the quiet of the evening, the young man worked at arranging his packs. "Leroy, I might have to give some of this back. My packs are full up and I still have some to go."

The cook came over with another canvas bag, "This should help you." Then his face became sad and Leroy turned away. "You have a safe trip, Amos

Mudd."

With his gear ready for morning, Amos walked over to the windfall, where Jake was sitting while smoking a short thick stub of a cigar. Sitting next to him, Amos took out the plug and tore a chew off it. For several minutes the two men sat in silence, enjoying their tobacco.

Jake blew a smoke ring and watched it disappear. "Amos, how much money you got for your trip?"

"I got a couple American dollars and almost £3 Canadian," the young man replied.

"Not much money for such a long trip," the broad shouldered friend said.

"I'll find work along the way," Amos said confidently.

"Work takes time," Jake stated. "Despite what you might think, the gold won't wait. Soon, the bigger companies will come and squeeze the men like you and me out."

"I plan to keep going until the winter forces me to stop. My plan is to join a wagon train in the spring, and by mid-summer I will be panning for gold on the American River."

"Come winter, you will be hunting for a place to stay warm, Amos," Jake warned him. "You won't find winter work where you're going. Come spring, you will be broke and starving, a poor candidate to join the wagon train."

"Damn it, Jake!" the angry young man growled. "You agreed that California was a good idea. Now you talk like it's dumb."

"Easy, my friend," the broad shouldered logger said. "I don't think you realize there ain't no way to get across to Michigan until spring. All trade and travel has stopped on the Nipissing, and when you finally get to Georgian Bay where you should board a boat to Michigan, you will find none going. Not to mention you won't have the money to pay fare anyway."

"What if I go north and cross at the top of Michigan?" Amos said stubbornly.

"Well, my friend, you will arrive at the St. Mary's River, starving, half-froze and broke. You will be alone. Your mule will have starved long before you get there and you will be eating its meat to stay alive."

The young man looked at his friend in disbelief. Just the day before he had said going west would be an adventure. Now he spoke as though it would be a death sentence. "Jake, you leave me speechless the way you are talking."

"Amos, it is not as dark as you think," Jake assured him.

"Not as dark, for Christ . . ."

"Amos! Keep the lord's name out of this!" his broad-shouldered friend warned. A bit more gently he continued. "There is a way if you want to listen."

The young man was flushed from being reprimanded. His first impulse was to grab his gear and leave this very night. The trouble was, what Jake was saying made sense. Amos had read about the Donner party eating human flesh to survive in the mountains.

"What would you suggest, Jake?" Amos asked, ready do dispute anything his friend said.

"I think you should come to the logging camp and work the winter with me," Jake said, seeing his friend stiffen. "Come spring, with money in our pockets, we can travel together to California."

Amos almost missed the last part of what his friend had said because the first part of the statement had his hackles up. After a moment, the young man blurted out, "You! You want to go to California with me?"

"It sure as hell beats working in the mill next summer. I'll go, but only if we start in the spring."

CHAPTER SEVEN

Amos' first view of Jasper's logging camp was a row of low, log buildings that the men slept in, two large log barns to house the stock, an open lean-to with a forge for the blacksmith, a row of outhouses made from hand-sawn planks, and a long, log building which served as the mess hall.

The roofs were either shingle or birch bark. All the buildings had a window on each end and plank doors. The ground was covered with patches of snow, and muddy roads ran past the buildings. There were large log sledges sitting around the camp, to be used once enough snow fell.

To the west, next to the river, were sets of stringers lined with logs. A dozen men were hewing the logs into square beams with axes. Men with horses or mules would pull the logs onto the stringers and then remove the hewn logs. The sounds of chopping and men shouting commands to their stock or other men was a constant din.

A large log cabin sat just above the stringer area and was used for managers to eat and sleep in. Next to it was the camp office used for the records, medical, and payroll. The men led their animals to the office and tied them to the rail in front. The first thing they needed to do was to check in and get their work and bunk assignments.

The office was hot and smoky. A short, stocky, bald man was in front of the open potbelly stove and stabbing at the wood with a poker. "Damn thing cooks me or freezes my ass!" he complained.

"Charlie, you are still fighting the old stove," Jake said, laughing at the office manager.

Slamming the door, he looked over his spectacles at the arrivals. "Jacques Larue, I was wondering when you would get here. I hope you still have that mule. Ah, Leroy and Henri, good to see you boys. I imagine you have your team with you?"

"We do, Charlie, and they are ready to work," Henri replied.

Looking at the young man, he asked, "And who is this with you?"

"This is Amos Mudd, a logger from Maine, and he also has a fine mule," Jake said, introducing his friend.

"Excellent, excellent. You men will be in cabin three. Stow your gear and bring any extra food to Pelletier. If it is acceptable you will get a credit for it. Put your animals in the barn, I think the north one has room. If you haven't eaten, Chef will give you something. Then see the log boss for your assignments," Charlie said, then went right to shuffling papers on his desk.

Jake reached inside his coat and set a bottle of cognac onto the desk. "Make sure you file this, Charlie."

Beaming from ear-to-ear, the office manager put the bottle underneath his desk. "Thank you, Jake. I'll drink it to your good health."

Standing outside, Henri was laughing, "We got three, hot damn!"

"What's so good about cabin three?" Amos asked Jake.

"We are closest to the mess hall and furthest from the outhouses."

The low, log building had rows of double bunks facing toward the center isle on each side. There was a stove in the middle of the isle. Gear was stored in wooden trunks underneath the bottom bunk. Pegs on the end of the bunks were used for hanging coats. The men would line their boots up around the stove to dry them at night. Near the door there were plank tables and stools made from split logs, with legs for the men to use playing cards or putting sealer on their boots.

The four men quickly chose a bunk, tossing their gear onto it, then took their animals to the barn. They spotted a bearded man with a bent nose. He spat a stream of tobacco juice onto the fork full of manure he was loading onto a wheel barrow.

Seeing the men leading their animals into the barn, he dropped the fork and gave them a broad smile, exposing the few blackened nubs he had for teeth. "About damn time, Jake!" he shouted. "Half the season is over and you finally drag your lazy tail in here."

"How the hell are you doing, Pap?" the broad shouldered man asked, shaking the old man's hand. "My friends and I need some first-class stalls for our stock."

"Why hell, Jake. All my stalls are right up there," Pap said, pretending to be insulted.

"You remember Leroy and Henri, here," Jake said. "I got a new man here. He is very important and comes all the way from Maine. Meet Amos Mudd."

Pap looked the young man up and down. "Don't know too much about men from Maine. I'll just have to take your word."

Suddenly, both men were laughing and slapping each other on the back. "Follow me, I got you some good stalls a short haul from the manure pile."

The light in the barn was dim, and the sweet smell of hay mixed with the pungent odor of manure reminded Amos of the barn back home. After stripping the remaining gear off the animals and stowing it in the stall, they gave the mules and horses some hay. With the animals taken care of, the men went to find the log boss. Jake paused at the door and reached into his coat, then brought out a bottle of cognac for the hostler.

While walking to find the boss, Jake told Amos that each owner could take care of his own animal, cleaning the stalls, brushing, and feeding. Or if they wanted to, Pap had a couple of young boys working for him, and if you gave the old man 10 shillings a month he would have the boys do it. Jake never said if that money ever got to the boys or not.

The young man was also told that the log boss

liked to be called, Boss. They found him coming out of the mess, chewing on a thick slice of fresh bread folded over a slice of cheese. "Glad to see you boys," Boss said. "Things are gearing up here and we been shorthanded. You got your team, Leroy?"

"I got them and they are ready to work," the round-faced man said.

"We got trees cut on the north track. You can take the team and start skidding them to be hewn," he ordered. "Henri can work with you."

Boss looked at Jake. "I suppose you got your mule with you."

"You know I do, Pike," Jake replied.

"Take it over the hewers and pull logs on the stringers." It was obvious that Boss didn't like being called by his name, Pike.

Looking over at the young man, he wrinkled his nose. "Who might you be?"

"The name's Amos Mudd. I come from Maine . . ."

Interrupting, Boss snapped, "I don't much care where the hell you come from. Can you handle an axe?"

"Both right and left, Boss," Amos replied.

"Go relieve Gus on the stringers," Boss ordered. "He clipped his foot this morning and has been slower than molasses since. Stop in the office first and let Charlie know what I put you doing."

"He's got a mule," Jake pointed out.

The log boss scowled at the broad-shouldered man, then he said to Amos, "Work the week with the broad axe and I'll have Pap look over your animal."

The young man's first impulse was to let Boss know that his Jenny was fit and ready to work, but Pike turned and walked away, his thoughts elsewhere.

"You go see Charlie while I fit some harnesses on my mule," Jake said. "Then I'll take you to the shaping stringers."

It was just past midday, and the men had missed the chance to have something to eat. Amos wished that they had gone to see the cook before finding the log boss.

Walking through the ankle-deep muck on the path, the young man stepped onto the porch and attempted to stomp some of the mud off his boots. Charlie was working in a ledger at the stained makeshift desk. He looked up and asked, "Did Boss assign you?"

"I'll be squaring logs," Amos replied. "He said maybe in a week he'll have me work with my mule."

Snorting, Charlie said, "They overwork the damn animals to death and he has yours sitting in the barn. Well, starting pay for an axe man is £9. If they have you work with the mule it will be £10 for you and an extra £2 for the mule."

Amos turned to leave, when Charlie stopped him. "Before you go, grab a pair of high-cuts. There's no place for low boots in the camp. They are £2. We'll take it out of your first pay. You best grab a tin of the sealer, too. Anything else you need, just let me know."

The young man saw the shelf stacked with boots. He went over and picked up a pair that looked like they would fit. Seeing this, Charlie objected. "Don't just grab them. Try the boots on and make sure you leave room for double woolen socks. If you want, I'll get rid of the old ones for you."

While Amos tried on a couple pairs, he figured socks were something that Charlie also sold. After finding a pair that fit to his satisfaction, the young man headed for the barn, carrying his muddy boots. He was sure there was a rule that low-cut boots had to be worn in the summer and Charlie would sell them, new or used.

Jake had the mule harnessed when Amos arrived at the barn. He told the young man that Pap would have a harness ready for his mule when Boss put it to work. Seeing his friend, the broad-shouldered man smiled. "I see Charlie sold you some boots, hey."

"Yes, he did. Charlie mentioned they work the animals to death. Is that true?" Amos asked his friend.

"Company stock can be treated pretty rough. Some of the drivers are on piece work and push their teams to their limit," Jake told the concerned young man.

The smell of fresh-cut pine was strong at the hewing stringers. Gus was happy to see his relief and limped toward the mess. Amos hefted the broad axe. He then ran his thumb across its edge. It was okay, but could use a stone or file. A man with stooped shoulders and a thick moustache sneered as he watched Amos. "You gonna admire that axe or swing it?"

Amos guessed that being introduced as a logger from Maine wasn't enough to gain the respect for the old timers. He knew he would have to prove it, especially since he had grown potatoes in Maine.

It was the stoop-shouldered man that he was working with and they were following the roughers that had scored and removed the majority of the wood from the side of the log. Amos and his partner went down each side of the log, finished it to size with right and left handed broad axes. Starting toward the lower edge of the side, they would work their way up, removing a thin layer of wood, smoothing and sizing the side to the chalk line the group leader had laid down. The stoop shouldered man started down the left side of the log and Amos worked on the right.

The long-time logger swung in a rhythm with the broad axe, quickly removing the rough, unfinished wood, leaving it sized and flat. Amos followed him on the right side of the log. He was not nearly as efficient. It was taking many more swings to achieve the desired result. The young man swung faster to try and make up for the extra swings.

When his hewing partner reached the end, he pulled a whetstone from his back pocket and expertly touched up the edge of his axe. Amos reached the end, breathing hard. Motioning the young man to get out of the way, the old logger took the cant hook and turned the log. Without a word, he moved to the next roughed log that had only the two sides left to finish and started working back along the chalk line, squaring his side. The young man followed his lead, working the other side.

Well behind the experienced man, Amos struggled, swinging the axe as fast as he could. Reaching the end, he stood leaning on the axe and gasping for breath. His partner called out, "Take her!" and a man with a horse secured a chain to the end of the squared log and pulled it from the stringers.

"You listen to me, boy," the old logger said.

"You best sharpen that damn axe before you cut yourself. Ain't nothing as dangerous as a dull axe!" With that he kicked the box at the side of the stringers, rattling the whetstones.

While they waited for the roughers to score and trim their next log, Amos used the stone and sharpened the broad axe. With the sharper edge, Amos was soon following the rhythm of his partner and they finished the sides without any waiting.

Four logs were being squared on the knee-high stringers at one time. The men worked in two pairs, cutting from opposite ends, leaving men on both sides to use the cant hooks to roll the log for the next cut. As each log was finished, a man with mules or horses pulled it to an area where they would eventually be put into the river and then lashed together, making a raft to be floated downstream in the spring. Two young boys ducked between the stringers, grabbing the slabs of wood and throwing them onto a short sledge. It would be pulled to the river and the waste wood would be piled along the shore, to be washed away with the spring floods.

As much as 30% of the log was disposed of during the squaring process, but trees were plentiful and it was required to ship the logs. The squared logs were floated to Quebec City, where they would be loaded onto ships. Amos was glad that when the rafts were floating downstream come spring, he and Jake would be heading for California.

By the end of the evening, Amos was working with just his long john top on. His arms ached from the constant chopping. The brief rests when the roughers hadn't finished the next log was welcomed.

Once all four logs were removed, the men rolled the next four logs on, using the cant hooks.

There was the sound of a metal triangle being struck. The men stopped work and grabbed up their shirts and coats. The man who Amos was working with was named Shane. He told the young man to keep his axe and sharpen it on the hand-cranking stone after supper.

Chef Pelletier put on a fine spread for supper. Amos and his friends hadn't eaten since morning. The long table had plates of bread, bowls of bear meat stew, and plenty of coffee. The men ate at a long wooden table with split log benches on each side. One end of the mess had a large cast iron stove for heat and cooking. Shelves of supplies and counters for preparing the food ran along the back wall. Below the floor was a root cellar where squash, potatoes, and other various root vegetables were kept, as well as hams, bacon and pemmican.

The loggers weren't bashful, grabbing their shares of the meal, or more. At the end of the meal one slice of apple pie was served to each man. Amos sat drinking his coffee and enjoying his pie. Jake produced a small metal flask from his pocket and poured a little cognac into the coffee.

Henri and Leroy sat at the table, having difficulty keeping their eyes open. "If I am this tired every evening, I am going to pay Pap to take care of the horses," Henri complained.

"Me too," Leroy agreed. "I don't need to clean stalls after working behind the horses all day."

With the meal done, they walked outside and took a seat under the long porch that ran the length of the mess building. A few of the men were throwing knives, axes, or hatchets at the end of a four-foot diameter log. A young man named Jamie was making bets and cleaning up against all comers.

Jake smoked a cigar while Amos chewed tobacco. Henri and Leroy excused themselves and headed for their bunks to put their gear away. Leroy had brought some pemmican and side meat to Chef and had been given a credit that could be spent at Charlie's store.

"Is it cold in California?" Jake asked.

"In the mountains it is," Amos replied, "but where we will settle won't be too bad."

"How about logging?" Jake probed.

"I read that there are trees so big, ten men hand-to-hand can't reach around it."

The broad-shouldered man scoffed, "I doubt that."

Spitting his chaw onto the ground Amos stood up and stretched his sore muscles. "Maybe so, but I would sure like to see a tree that big. I got to take care of Jenny and then get the broad axe sharpened. I'll see you later in the bunkhouse."

Jake remained on the porch, enjoying the cigar and sipping on the flask of cognac. Amos lit a lamp and carried it to the back of the barn. Jenny's head was over the side of the stall, welcoming her master. Amos hung the lamp on the rafter next to the stall and got the fork to clean the stall. After finishing his chores, he watered and gave the mule some hay before beginning to brush the heavy winter coat.

With the animal taken care of, he headed for

the bunkhouse. The men had a hand-cranked grinder for sharpening the axes. He brought his over and put a good edge on it. Jake and the brothers were already asleep. Amos put his gear under the bunk and rolled out his bedroll. Within minutes after lying down, he too was sleeping.

There wasn't much variation to the days in camp. After a breakfast of porridge or pancakes the men began work. Lunches wrapped in paper and string were piled on a table near the door. They would contain bread with meat or cheese to be eaten midday. The men would grab one on the way out from breakfast under the watchful eye of Chef.

Just before sundown the triangle would clang, signaling the end of the day's work. Amos was told that baths would be offered on Saturday night, with Sunday being off to take care of personal stuff such as laundry, mending, or repairing harnesses. Payday was the last Friday of the month.

After three days working with the broad axe, his mule was needed for skidding. Amos and Jake's mules were put together as a team to skid down logs off a ridge. The trees were felled with axes. Two men worked each tree, chopping the notch first, to determine which direction they wanted the tree to fall in, and then finishing the cut with two-bit axes from the other side.

They would then limb the useable part of the tree and then chop through, topping it. Clear logs brought the highest price, so much of the log at the top was left to rot. Felling the tall white and red pine had its dangers. Dead branches high in the tree could fall, striking the choppers. The men called them widow makers. Also, trees leaning put the wood under stress and could split and hit one of the men if they weren't fast enough to get clear. When a tree did this, it was called jackknifing.

After the mules brought the logs down from the ridge, an old-timer they called the bucker would measure the logs and mark them for cutting to length with a bucksaw. Once bucked into shorter lengths, they were piled to be hauled by the sledges. The bucker probably had the most important job. If a tree was wrongly measured, it could render a valuable log to useless wood.

The muddy roads had frozen, making travel easier. They had several days of snow, and the sledges were put to use. New men came in every day, leaving their farms behind and looking for winter work. Jake and Amos would wave when they passed Henri and Leroy with their team. Boss pretty much left them alone. He had all he could do harassing the new men.

The one bright spot in the camp routine was Saturday night. There was a building, half log and half canvas, called The Shanty, three miles from the camp. It had cheap whisky and working girls. The crew had Sundays off, so after hitting the wash house on Saturday night they would crowd onto a sledge or two and head over for some entertainment.

Jake had told Amos that after payday the camp was almost deserted. By the third Saturday after payday, most of the men were broke and just hung around camp. Amos looked forward to his first Saturday night.

He had heard a lot of talk about The Shanty from men who had worked the camp the year before.

While Grady, the owner, might water down the rye, he never put anything in it that would hurt the men. The women used the rooms in the canvas-covered section to entertain their clients.

Amos entered the wash room for his weekly bath. A large caldron was used to heat the water. It hung above an open fire pit in the center of the room. A raised plank floor was built around the pit, and log walls supported the louvered roof, which let the smoke and steam out.

The young man stood naked next to the caldron and ladled water into his bucket. Moving to the wall with the hot water, he set it on a bench and scrubbed himself from head to toe. Charlie sat near the door with towels. If a man used one, a small deduction was taken from his next pay. Using the mirror and scissors, Amos trimmed his hair and beard. Dressed in clean clothes, he put on the pea coat and stepped outside.

The men were already climbing on the first sledge. Running to the bunkhouse, Amos stowed his dirty clothing and got some money out of his haversack. Hurrying back to the sledge, he saw his friends already seated. "Over here, Amos," Jake called.

A layer of logs had been left on the sledge for the men to sit or stand on. The young man had barely sat down when Boss walked up. "You men can have your fun tonight, but if any of you are unable to do a day's work come Monday, you will be sent packing," he warned.

The man driving the team slapped the reins on the backs of the horses and the sledge jerked forward. In his haste to get to The Shanty, the driver kept the horses at a trot. The sledge bounced over windfalls, stumps, and rocks beneath the snow. The men hung on, knowing that if they fell off, they would be walking the rest of the way.

At last the lights of the low log building came into view. A whoop went up from the men. Before the sledge came to a stop, some of the men jumped off and ran, stumbling towards the door. Two soot-covered lanterns burned near the front, to light up the yard. The sound of women's laughter reached the men as the sledge came to a stop.

There were other sledges and teams standing in the yard, with some saddle horses tied to the rail toward the back of the yard. The hard-packed snow in front of The Shanty was stained with vomit and urine from the merrymakers inside.

The din from the loggers already inside was almost overwhelming as Amos walked into the place. Several lanterns hung from the low rafters, providing dim light in the smoke-filled room. The smell of spilt beer and rye mingled with the sweat of the patrons was strong.

A heavyset man with a stained apron and bushy moustache was the owner, Grady. He made his own beer, which was drawn from barrels behind a long plank bar and served in tin mugs. The rye bottles lined the back bar, and most men bought a bottle and were given a glass to drink it with. The floor was thick with sawdust, to soak up the spills and whatever else needed soaking up.

Two potbelly stoves warmed the place, one near the back where the girls worked and the other near the front. Split wood was piled near each stove. Three bartenders worked behind the bar, serving the throngs of men that leaned against the bar or sat at the tables playing cards.

There was a makeshift stage at the back of the building, and some of the girls would put on a show singing and dancing to try and raise the interest of the loggers. A man with a concertina would accompany them. When the show was on, an attempt was made to keep the noise down so the singers could be heard.

Planks were put between the posts holding up the rafters to serve as additional places to lean and place bottles. Jake and Amos found room at one of these. Henri and Leroy went to the bar, got two bottles and headed toward the back to find the ladies.

"The poor bastards will go back broke," Jake said, watching his friends head toward the back. "They do it every time. I guess it is better to spend your money on rye and women rather than losing it at the card tables."

Nodding, Amos agreed. "It leaves you with better memories."

The young man pulled out his plug of tobacco. Jake raised his hand to stop him. Handing him a cigar, he said, "We are out for the night. You don't want no tobacco juice dribbling down your chin whiskers."

Amos took the rough short smoke. Raising the lantern glass, he lit it. Breathing in the smoke, he began to cough.

Smiling, Jake recommended, "Take your time and just roll the smoke around in your mouth. After a bit, you can breathe some in."

The rye had a good flavor, but lacked some of

the bite from being watered down. The two men laughed and talked about the various drunks around them. Unexpectedly, two loggers started throwing haymakers at each other. Grady and one of the bartenders came around the bar at a run with short clubs in their hands. Friends of the fighters grabbed the men apart before the clubs could be laid on their noggins.

Evidently, the owner allowed no fighting inside the building. Whoever started it, he would finish it and they would end up laying in the snow in front of the tavern. No doubt many a logger had gotten back to camp with frostbite and no memory of why he'd gotten it.

All of a sudden, the room went quiet. Five ladies were on the stage. They were dressed in corsets and some kind of lacy bloomers. Their supple breasts swelled out from under the tight corsets. The pale man began to play the concertina and the ladies sang and danced. If anybody tossed a coin onto the stage they would shake their abundant figures toward them.

With the songs done, the women bowed deep toward the loggers and away from them, displaying their best virtues while the crowd cheered with appreciation, coins clattering on the stage. Jake and Amos clapped loudly and shouted with the rest of the loggers.

The acrid smoke from the cigar burned Amos's mouth and stung his eyes, but there was no way he was going to disappoint his friend by not smoking it. He got a tin cup of beer to clear his throat. He found the brew to be excellent.

After the show was over the ladies started

working the crowd for drinks and whatever else the men could provide. A heavyset, dirty-blond woman came to visit Jake and Amos. She hadn't been in the show and had probably been working in the back.

"You boys want to buy a girl a drink?" she asked, bending just enough so they could see her ample bosoms under her loose dress. Jake handed her a coin and the damsel went to the bar and returned with a glass of amber liquid. Standing close to Jake, she laughed and talked brushing her body against him every time he said something funny.

Amos stood smiling until his cheeks hurt as he watched his friend. Several drinks later, the rye got the better of Jake's judgement as he and the dirty-blond headed for the back rooms. The young man stood still, grinning, when he felt someone close to him.

Moving a bit to give the logger room, he turned and stared into the dark eyes of an Indian girl. Her long black hair was swept back into a loose braid. Tilting her head up, she smiled and asked, "You buy a girl a drink?"

Amos stuttered, trying to find his voice. "I . . . I would, ah . . ., sure."

Awkwardly, he dug into his pocket for a coin. Handing it to the girl, she disappeared into the crowd and headed toward the bar. He muttered, "Okay, dummy. Kiss that coin goodbye."

Shane came over carrying a bottle, "I miss you on the stringers," he said, a bit of a slur in his words. "Gus is back and spends more time complaining about his foot than working."

Reaching over, he poured some of his rye into Amos' glass, spilling some on the plank. Amos picked it up and toasted the man. "Here's to warm nights and good whisky."

Nodding, Shane gulped his drink and smiled. "Damn good whisky."

Amos watched the logger walk away, when there was again a presence next to him. The dark-eyed lady was back. "Thank you for the drink," she said, leaning her head on his shoulder for a moment. She then sipped from her cup of beer.

"You don't like the rye?" the young man asked.

"Too strong for me," she confided. "Like the beer better."

The two fell silent as they drank. Amos always had trouble talking with ladies. His words felt clumsy and came with difficulty, unlike Jake, who had a quick smile and a silver tongue.

"Have you worked here long?" he asked, attempting to make conversation.

"It is my first winter," she said, playing with the cup.

"Mine too," he replied. *Stupid!* he thought.

"You work here?" she asked with surprise.

"No. Oh no, not here," he tried to explain. "I'm at the camp west of here. It is my first winter."

"Oh," she responded.

"I come from Maine," he said, struggling to think of something to talk about.

"I don't know where that is."

Unable to explain where it was, he told her, "It's far from here."

Looking at the back of the room, he wanted to

shout for Jake to finish and come rescue him.

The girl said something, and in his desperation to try and think of something to say, he missed it. "What!" he said. "The noise . . ."

"I come from Michigan," she repeated. "I am from the Ojibwa people. My name is Onaiwa. Here they call me Ona."

"Michigan! I'm headed for Michigan."

At last, something we could talk about, Amos thought.

He asked her about Michigan and about the route between here and there. There was so much he needed to know before spring.

Slowly sipping her beer, Ona answered the excited young man's questions. After a bit she set her cup down and smiled. "I must go and talk to others. Thank you for the drink."

Rubbing her hand across his shoulder she moved away to look for a logger who wanted more than conversation. Watching her go, Amos' mind raced. How much would it cost to take her into the back? He had never been with a woman and didn't know what she would expect from him. Would she be angry if he just wanted to talk?

His thoughts were interrupted as his friend returned. Jake was smiling from ear-to-ear. "The girl's name is Honey. I recommend you go back and ask for her."

"I'd have to be smarter than a hob nail," Amos muttered.

"What?"

"I said, maybe next time. I'll keep her in

mind," he promised.

It was well after midnight when the driver of the sledge started rounding up the loggers. Two of the men were passed out in the sawdust and had to be carried out. The driver from the second sledge called over, "I got mine." And he headed back for the camp.

Leroy climbed onto the sledge, next to Amos. The light from the outside lantern revealed a blackened eye. "What the hell happened to you?"

"Some drunk called my brother a cyclops, and I swung and missed. He weren't as drunk as I thought. He swung back and hit me. But that's okay, my next swing put him out cold. It were so fast that Grady didn't even see it," he said proudly.

CHAPTER EIGHT

Amos woke up the next day with a headache and a dry, sore throat. Swinging his feet to the floor, he held his head in his hands. His stomach turned for a second and he thought he was going to get sick. Slowly, it settled down.

His clothes smelled strongly of cigar smoke and some type of perfume. He hoped it was Ona's and not Honey's. He walked over to the water bucket and filled the dipper. Slowly, he took a long drink. He was about to fill the dipper again when his stomach gave him a jolt and he changed his mind.

Walking back to his bunk, Amos noticed that Henri and Leroy were still sleeping while Jake was already up and gone. Pulling his boots on, and struggling into his pea coat, he headed for the outhouse. He sat on the cold, butt-polished boards and groaned.

Once finished, he headed for the mess. The cold air was helping to revive him. The smell of wood smoke and freshly cut pine made him glad to be back at camp. As he approached the mess hall door, Jake was coming out. "Chef's shut the line down. The next feed is this afternoon."

"Damn!" Amos exclaimed. "Probably just as well. My stomach doesn't feel too good."

Jake pulled a package wrapped with string from his coat. "I talked him into letting me take something for you and the brothers."

"You are a good friend, Jacques Larue."

One day ran into another as the men harvested logs and prepared them to be floated down river in the spring. Amos liked it best when his mule was teamed with Jake's. Often Jenny was used to pull logs on to the stringers, or squared logs off. There was over two feet of snow on the ground and the temperatures had plunged. The young man found himself back in the office buying some more woolen socks from Charlie.

A man driving a dog sled arrived one morning. He ran mail from the camps to Bytown. Amos quickly put together a short letter for his father to let him know he was well. The man looked at the address and muttered, "Maine. That will cost extra."

As the man shouted mush and the dogs pulled the sled out of sight, Amos said a silent prayer, hoping that his letter found his father in good health. He wondered how long it would take to get to his father. This time of year Jacob would only go to town every other month.

The high points of Amos' existence at the logging camp were the trips to The Shanty and seeing Ona. The Ojibwa girl always smiled and visited with him for a short time. Then off she went to see others.

He knew she had to in order to make money. Saturday was the big night for the girls.

One night Amos was dreaming that he was back on the farm when the plow Jenny was pulling started to break, creating a clanging sound. Suddenly awake, he realized that it was the triangle being struck wildly. He was pulling his boots on when Shane ran by snarling, "It best not be some drunken son-of-a-bitch that brought a bottle back from The Shanty!"

Piling out of the bunkhouse door, they were greeted by flames coming out of the windows and roof of the mess. Chef was dragging supplies out as fast as he could while one of his helpers hit the triangle. The men followed him through the door, creating a chain and passed supplies out until the heat of the fire forced them to retreat.

Amos ran around to the back with Jake, pulled open the root cellar doors and started tossing hams, bacon, pemmican, squash, and as many of the potatoes as they could while the hot sparks of the fire fell down from between the boards.

When the roof collapsed and embers showered down through the floor, they had to get out. Amos climbed out, brushing hot sparks from his clothes. He could smell burning hair, felt burning on his head, then grabbed some snow and rubbed his head.

Men had grabbed shovels and were tossing snow onto the roof and into the door. The effort did little good to slow the blaze. Soon the mess was charred, smoldering logs. Charlie was there with salve to put on the several burns the men had.

Chef Pelletier sat on some sacks of flour and looked at his ruined building. "The lads left the dampers open and caused a chimney fire. It caught in the rafters and roof, then spread fast. Pine, she burns fast," he said, shaking his head.

Boss had been right in the thick of the fire and had burns on his face and hands. He climbed onto a stump and addressed the men. "I want you men to empty the bunks from number four and put them in the other bunkhouses. Four will be used as the mess until we build a new one. The cook stove should be usable, and as soon as things cool off enough we'll get it moved over."

"You men did a fine job of getting a lot of the supplies out before the roof caved. Amos and Jake saved most of the stuff out of the cellar. This food will get us by until we get some additional supplies in. Chef will cook in the wash house caldron until we get the stove going. Meals will be pemmican soup and the like. There will be no complaining. If you can't accept what needs to be done, let me know and Charlie will draw your pay. Now, let's get to moving those bunks."

Without a word of complaint, the men headed for the bunkhouse to move the bunks and men's gear. The other bunkhouses would be a little crowded, but with all their tables being moved to number four for the men to eat on, it would make additional room for the extra bunks.

Chef called to Amos, "Did you get any spuds out?"

"We did, Chef," he replied. "Most likely frozen by now."

Amos helped Chef and his two lads collect up the salvaged supplies and load them onto a sledge. There were pots and pans, utensils, tin plates and cups, and bags of food thrown all over in front of the burnt building. Jake ran to the barn and came back with the mules to pull it. Working by lantern light, the men had emptied number four and were bringing in the tables.

There was fire in the bunkhouse stove, so Chef put the coffee pots onto the flat top and sent his helpers to get water. It was just starting to get light when the morning meal was done. Many of the men dug into their packs and brought their own plates and cups. There was only room enough for half the men to eat at one time, so they ate in two sittings.

Amos sat on some sacks near Jenny's stall and dozed while waiting for them to call the men to work. The mules were still harnessed in front of him. Jake came and banged two horse shoes together. "Time to go to work. They won't have the triangle up until later today. The shoe will have to do."

The young man carefully put on his hat over his burned scalp and took his time putting the choppers on trying to avoid the blisters on the back of his hands. "I sure feel like I been rode hard."

They spent the day pulling logs off the ridge. Keeping busy helped Amos forget about the burns. It had started snowing and the men and mules were covered with the white fluff. A man came riding through the north tract shouting, "Break time, take 20!"

Jake had some jerky with him, so the two men sat on a log, chewed the meat and sipped water from their canteens. After eating their meal, both took a chew of Amos' plug. Spitting the tobacco juice into the freshly fallen snow, the men spoke little. Having stopped let the exertion from the night before catch up with them.

The sound of someone starting to chop alerted them that it was time to go back to work. The blisters on Amos' hands had broken under the gloves. Putting the choppers back on was slow and painful.

They were bringing a 30-foot log down the ridge when the sound of the triangle reached them. Amos was at the back with a cant hook, rolling it to clear a gnarled oak tree trunk. His hands were burning and his head aching. Resisting the temptation to just drop the hook and head in, the young man reefed on the cant hook and managed to roll the log enough to clear the stump.

Unhooking the log for the bucker, the two men brushed the snow off the backs of the mules and climbed on for a ride back to camp. Jake pulled out his flask, took a long draw and then handed it to Amos. The young man could hardly grip it with his gloved hand due to the rubbing of the woolen liner against his burns.

To their surprise, the charred logs of the mess hall had been dragged away and most of the smaller wood from the fire lay in a pile behind the site. The cook stove had been moved to number four and a second chimney poked up through the roof. All the damaged floor planks had been removed and a half dozen new ones had already been put in place. The fresh snow had already hidden much of the evidence of the fire the night before.

Looking in wonder, Amos exclaimed, "Damn, that was fast! Hell, they might have us eating in a new mess in a week."

Jake pointed to the pile of logs that had been

flattened on two sides. "There's our new walls."

Once in the barn, Amos took the choppers off and then his coat. Shaking the snow off the pea coat, he hung it on a peg near the mule's stall. Removing his tuque, he gingerly felt the burns on his scalp. Jake pulled the harnesses off the mules and hung them on the back wall. He then grabbed the brush and went over both mules.

"Leave Jenny," Amos told him.

"You are wounded, my friend. I was out grabbing stuff while you stood under the burning floor and handed them to me. I am pleased to do this for you," Jake replied, as he brushed down the mules.

"I got to go see Charlie and get something for the burns," Amos decided. "I'll see you at supper."

The young man found Charlie busy with his ledgers. "Got anything for burns?"

The office manager took a blue bottle out of his desk and a piece of rag. "Let me see them."

Amos held his hands out and Charlie shook his head. "They're deep, but I've treated worse. This will sting, so get a grip on something."

Spreading his hands on the desk, the young man clenched his teeth while the bald office manager swabbed the burns. "Got any more?"

Amos wanted to say no, but feared getting infection. "Just on the scalp." He tilted his head down for the man to see. Again, the young man had to fight to stop from shouting in pain.

After a few minutes the burning on his hands and scalp became tolerable. Charlie put the blue bottle back into his desk. "The scalp will heal quickly. The hands will take maybe a week. Stop by in the morning and I'll wrap them before you put your gloves on."

With time and the doctoring of the stocky old man, Amos' hands healed nicely. After the burns scabbed over, the choppers protected them and they didn't need to be wrapped. The walls and rafters were up on the new mess. In another couple of days, they would move everything back in.

The young man was walking across the camp to eat supper when he heard his name being called. It was Charlie. He was waving the young man over. As Amos walked toward the office, he called back, "The hands look fine."

"Come in, I got something I want to talk with you about," the bald office manager said.

Amos took a seat across from the man and waited. Charlie tilted his chair back a bit and looked over his spectacles. "You know we lost about half of our food in the fire." Amos nodded in agreement.

"I need someone to ride after some supplies," Charlie said.

"Where would we find supplies out here?" Amos asked.

"About 50 miles south and east of here, on the north end of Nipissing Lake, there is a trading post that has their stock in for spring. You will need to take maybe four pack horses and your mule. I'd find another man to go along with you."

"Can I take Jake with me?"

Charlie shook his head no. "Boss depends on Jake too much. It was Boss and Jake that recommended you." Then, kidding the young man, he said, "By keeping Jake here, we make sure you come back. He's going with you to California."

The mention of California caught Amos off guard. Evidently, Jake had mentioned it to Charlie, or maybe even Boss. The young man joined Charlie in a laugh at the joke.

"When do you want me to leave?"

"It will take a day to get everything ready, say the day after tomorrow. Chef is making a list for me of what needs replacing. The trip should take you about a week, maybe eight days."

Amos found Jake in the temporary mess. "So they are keeping you hostage to make sure I come back with the food?"

Jake smiled, "That what Charlie told you?"

"I wonder who will be going with me."

"Word is it will be Jamie Sharp," Jake guessed.

Glancing at the skinny kid sitting a few tables away, Amos commented, "He ain't the most ambitious in camp."

"Maybe that's why he'd be going," Jake pointed out. "All he will have to do is ride drag, making sure one of the pack horses doesn't have a problem."

"I heard he took on a man almost twice his size at The Shanty," Amos said. "He will be a good man to have along in case of trouble."

"I agree there," the broad-shouldered friend said. "Word will be out tomorrow that you will be going. You'll have a bunch of loggers wanting you to pick up things for them." Jake pressed some coins into Amos's hand. "I need cigars. If there ain't room for their stuff on the pack horses, make sure mine makes it."

That afternoon, working in the low light of the barn, Amos was with Charlie getting the pack horses outfitted. Each would have an empty pack saddle to be filled with the supplies. He also had to get his own gear ready for the trip. Several men came by, giving him money for tobacco, and one wanted peppermint sticks for a gal at The Shanty who had said she liked them.

After things were ready for the next day, Amos warmed some water in the wash house. Chef no longer needed the caldron for cooking. Boss came in while he was dressing. "Most days, Jake gets my goat, but I think he was right in sending you. I'll be needing the horses and your mule back as soon as possible."

"I will try not to disappoint you, Boss."

The young man went back into the bunkhouse, his wet hair frozen from the frigid temperature. He weaved his way through the extra bunks and knelt near his bed. Pulling his haversack out, he went through the items he would be needing. Flint and steel, candles, bullets, patches, powder horn, and caps. He had removed many of the extra convenience items. He did pack an extra pair of woolen socks and some rags. The Leman .32 lay under his bunk, cleaned and ready to go.

Sitting against the wall, he began to apply grease to seal his boots. Charlie had drawn him a crude map showing the way to the trading post. Amos had committed it to memory. He would cross the Ottawa a couple miles upstream, then travel southwest until he came to the *Petite Rivière*, or Small River. Another day's ride west should bring him to the post.

Jake placed the Colt Paterson on his bunk,

along with his shot bag. "I want you to take this with you, my friend. I doubt any trouble will be out there this time of winter, but one can't be too prepared."

"Do you know what the day is?"

"If the question is, will you be traveling on Christmas, the answer is yes," Jake told him.

It was late and time to blow out the lanterns. Amos lay on his bunk in the dark and wondered what his father was doing this Christmas. His mother had died just before the holiday, and since then he didn't hardly recognize it. One year the young man had bagged a turkey and proudly walked into their cabin and proclaimed, "We have turkey for Christmas."

His father had given him a haunted look and left the cabin for several hours. That was the last time that the young man had talked of Christmas around his pa. Once, when a schoolmate had asked Amos what he had gotten for the holiday, Amos made up something, for he had gotten nothing.

CHAPTER NINE

It seemed like he had just fallen asleep when the sound of the triangle awoke him. Groaning, he swung his feet to the cold floor boards. Someone was rattling the door of the stove, adding wood to the coals. Amos tucked his pants into his socks and pulled on his boots.

He rolled up his bedding and ground tarp. He put the Colt into his waistband and then put on the pea coat. Slinging the haversack strap over his head, he swung it under his left arm. The shot bag went to his right side. The high-cuts he had purchased from Charlie had a scabbard in which he put his hunting knife.

He put his tuque on, then picked up his choppers and the .32. He turned to leave the bunkhouse when he saw Jake. His friend had his hands on his hips. "Now don't you look like a man ready to conquer the wilds."

"Hell, Jake," Amos laughed. "I can barely

move, much less fight."

Amos went down to the barn and left his gear before going to breakfast. He had to adjust the Colt before sitting down. Chef brought a plate loaded with pancakes and crisp bacon. He placed a canvas bag next to the young man. "Something for your Christmas."

Though he wanted to say thank you, his throat tightened up and he was unable to speak. He smiled at Chef before the man hurried off to make more pancakes for the hungry loggers. As soon as he finished eating he picked up the bag and headed for the barn.

Boss was getting the pack horses ready to travel. There was a saddle and blanket sitting on the wall of the mule's stall. "You'll need it for riding the mule, Amos. You best get the animal saddled."

Charlie came in with the list while the mule was being readied. "If you can't get some of these items, switch them for something similar." Then, reaching under his coat, he pulled out a money belt.

"It should be more than you'll need in gold coins. If you get back in seven days, there will be a bonus for you," Charlie promised.

The young man put the belt on under his shirt. He knew that the trip he was taking wasn't life or death for the camp. If something bad happened and he couldn't get through, they would send another until the supplies were gotten. He was bound and determined that they wouldn't have to send another.

Jamie came in from breakfast and saddled the horse they had for him. He was looking forward to the change from doing the same work each day. "Amos, I got some money left from the last pay and am looking forward to this trip."

It was daylight and a light snow was falling. Amos led two of the pack horses out of camp with Jamie leading the other two. To reduce weight on their animals, they had put their extra gear onto one of the pack horses. He noticed the wind direction, and the sun's position. They rode past the men working on the hewing stringers and turned up the north side of the Ottawa River.

The men stopped working for a moment and waved. Amos held his arm up for a moment and then urged the mule to a trot, leaving the sounds of the logging camp behind him. The cold air and light snow hit against his bearded face.

The crossing was reached and they waded the animals across, raising their boots to keep them dry. The plan was to ride all the daylight hours and then make camp under natural shelters such as groves of cedars or evergreens. Charlie had given them an extra tarp to cover their blankets at night.

As the mule climbed the south bank of the river, Amos headed the group in a southwesterly direction. They rode through pine slashings with rotting tops and large stumps. Various smaller trees poked up, finally being able to get to the sun after the older forest had been cut.

The snow came just above the knees of the mule. The animal broke through the thin crust of the snow with ease. Amos didn't use a bit on the mule, but just the lead rope on the halter. He let Jenny pick her own trail, avoiding obstacles under the snow. If necessary, he adjusted the route as needed with knee pressure or the lead rope.

They had ridden over an hour before Amos stopped inside a tall stand of pine. These trees were too far from the river to harvest. Swinging down from the mule, he took his canteen out from under his coat. The water was cold and sweet.

Jamie rode up and got off his horse. "I was thinking you would never stop. My ass ain't use to this riding."

Amos took two biscuits from their pack and gave one to Jamie. "We have to make time. That means long stretches of riding. After another hour, we will switch our saddles to the pack horses. We can push the animals faster that way."

After finishing the biscuits, they were back on their animals and riding southwest. Amos kept an eye on the sky and wind. The weather was clearing, making keeping their direction easier. The young man was thinking that if he headed more westerly on the second day, he would hit the Small River closer to the trading post and save time.

Sunlight was rapidly fading in the tall pines when Amos called to Jamie, who was leading. "Stop near the creek and bunch of spruce trees ahead. We will camp in them and leave at first light."

While Jamie stripped the gear from the animals, Amos cleared the snow from an area under the trees, cut some of the lower branches and weaved them above their sleeping area. He then found cones and dead branches exposed under the trees and got a fire going.

After punching through the ice, he filled the pot with water from the creek. Amos set it near the fire to heat, and then went to help Jamie with the animals. A portion of grain was given to each of the stock. With the steady travel there wouldn't be enough time for them to search out grass and graze.

One at a time, the animals were watered at the creek. The two men stretched a picket rope between two larger spruce and tied the animals. The water was hot enough to make coffee when they returned to the fire. Stirring the grounds into the bubbling water, Amos then added more wood to the fire.

Chef had given them pemmican and side meat to eat on the trip. Placing the frying pan onto the red, snapping coals, Amos pulled the knife from his boot and sliced strips of the bacon into the pan. Once they had fried a bit, he added a chunk of pemmican.

Jamie had rolled out their bedrolls after spreading the ground tarps. Once the meal was cooked, the two men set the pan between them and ate directly from the frying pan. Hot cups of coffee sat next to them. The meal was quick and simple. After wiping the pan out with pine needles, Amos tossed them into the fire, looking away as they flared up.

Amos thought about taking a chew, then changed his mind and took the Leman .32 that was leaning against the tree. He laid it under the edge of his blankets. The evening had been bitter cold and the men hadn't removed their coats. Now they crawled under their blankets, taking only their boots off.

It was still dark when his cold feet awoke Amos. He curled up tighter and tried to put more of the blankets on them. Finally giving up, he pulled his boots on and went to check for coals in the ashes. The fire was cold. He had put some tinder and sticks at the base of one of the spruce. Placing it onto the ashes, he struck his flint and soon had a small blaze.

After taking a moment to warm his stiffening fingers, he put the frozen coffee pot next to the fire. Pulling on his choppers Amos added more wood. Stomping to try and get more circulation to warm his toes, he stood looking at the eastern sky. There was a hint of light.

After walking a short distance from their camp, he relieved himself and then went to check on the animals. Jenny snorted a greeting after seeing him. After making another hole in the creek ice, he led the animals one at a time for a drink. The movement was helping to warm his feet.

He heard his young companion cough and spit. "It's frozen biscuits and last night's coffee for breakfast," Amos called. As he was finishing with the animals, the eastern sky was fiery red. When he walked back to the fire, he saw Jamie looking over his .32.

"Careful with that," Amos cautioned. "Just lean it next to the tree and let's check on the coffee."

"Oh, don't worry yourself," Jamie replied. "I am quite the hand with the long gun."

"Well, I do worry and it's my rifle," Amos replied, getting a little angry.

He looked up and stopped. The damned kid was holding the rifle waist-high and had it pointing in his direction. "That's what the hell I am talking about. You don't aim a rifle in the direction of other people!"

Jamie cocked the hammer back and smiled. "That is, unless you plan to shoot them."

They stood no more than 20 feet apart. The kid had a wild look in his eyes as he squeezed the trigger. The sound of the hammer falling was loud in the still morning. Anticipating the recoil, Jamie flinched, then exclaimed, "What the hell!"

Amos took several steps back, looking for a place to run for cover. Jamie had tossed the rifle, and pulled his knife and scooped up the hatchet nearby. "I want the money, Mudd! It is more than two year's pay and I mean to have it."

"If it is just the money you want, my life is worth more than that." Shedding the choppers, he began to unbutton the coat, reaching in, his hand coming out with the Colt Paterson.

"Drop the knife and axe," Amos ordered.

"I'm not so sure the Colt will fire. Your rifle didn't," Jamie said slowly stepping toward Amos.

"You're a fool. I don't put a cap in unless I am about to shoot."

Jamie tossed the knife to the ground. Amos was watching the hatchet. As it started to come up, he fired the Colt. The kid's eyes went wide. The Colt spoke again, knocking Jamie over backwards. The young man walked toward the kid he had just shot.

The first shot had struck dead center, shattering one of the buttons on his coat. The second was in the forehead. Jamie lay draped over a snow-covered stump, his silenced mouth wide open, his sightless eyes looking at the heavens.

Amos' stomach turned and he felt panic. Clutching a tag alder, he began to throw up. The Colt hung by his side and slipped from his fingers. Spitting several times to clear his mouth, he muttered, "God help me, I am in trouble. I . . . I didn't have a choice."

"Who will believe me?" The shaken young man walked over to the fire and sat heavily. He covered his face with his hands, and after several minutes he realized that Jamie had triggered the Leman .32, fully expecting it to fire and kill him.

Amos had no memory of deciding to pull the Colt's trigger. When the arm had moved with the hatchet he remembered that the kid was good at throwing it. Then Jamie was falling, and Amos realized he had fired. He didn't even remember aiming.

It was full daylight and Amos knew that despite what had just happened, he had to get going. He tried the coffee, but his stomach wouldn't accept it. Dumping it, he stuck the cups and pot into the pack. Amos went to get their bedding.

Rolling the blankets into the ground tarps, he asked himself, "Why didn't he try and kill me while I was sleeping? Did he decide to when he saw my rifle in my bed?"

By the time he had the horses and mule ready, and the gear packed, Jamie's body had started to stiffen. They boy's blood on the snow was bright red. Amos wrapped him in one of the ground tarps and hung him over a pack horse. He had to force the body to bend before tying it on.

Amos retrieved the Leman .32 and brushed the snow off it. He tied it onto the horse with the packs. It took a bit to remember where the Colt was. After a brief search he found it, blowing and brushing the snow off the gun. It still held two shots, and he had no desire to spend more time in this camp reloading the other two. Sticking it into his waistband, he climbed onto the mule and headed out leading five horses.

Digging out his plug, he tore off a piece of tobacco and began rolling the chew in his cheek. He couldn't begin to understand what had caused the kid to try and steal the money. He had sounded excited about looking for something special at the trading post.

Riding, his mind struggling to grasp the morning's events, Amos rode unaware of his surroundings. A gust of wind sent snow from the branches above him cascading down. The startled animal jumped and pulled, attempting to get away, bringing the young man's mind back to the task at hand.

Settling the animals down, he looked around. He was heading straight west. How long he had been riding in that direction he had no idea. Jamie's saddle and bridle were on one of the other horses. He had been on the trail at least two hours. Rearranging the lead ropes, he headed out, riding the horse with his mule bringing up the end.

Suddenly, Amos' only objective was getting to the trading post. How much he may have ridden out of his way, he didn't know. The young man rode in a more southerly direction. Pulling the canteen from under his coat, he rinsed his mouth and then slowly drank. His stomach was feeling better. Reaching into his haversack, he took out some jerky and chewed on the stringy meat while riding.

The first indication that he was approaching the Small River was evidence of logging. Discarded tree tops and mounds of snow covering pine stumps became evident. The sun was getting low in the western sky. Amos had continued to switch horses so he could keep a faster pace.

While switching the saddle, he would avoid looking at his dead companion. Throughout the day he rode, muttering and debating with himself on what else he might have done. Unexpectedly, he broke out of the trees on the bank of what he guessed was the Small River. Amos had given up the thought of reaching it before dark, due to having ridden west.

Resting near the river as the sun slid behind the trees in the west, he let the horses drink their fill and then gave each some grain. Deciding that he wasn't ready to stop, Amos walked along the river, leading the horses and mule. Well after dark, the moon came up, casting an eerie light on the landscape. Amos had the mule leading the others. Tightening the cinch on Jenny, he climbed back into the saddle and continued along the river.

The twisted black shadows of the trees reached out across the snow. There was an unsettling quietness in the woods. The only sounds were the animals breaking through the snow and an occasional clink of medal on metal or creak of leather. When a cloud passed across the moon, the area would be plunged into near darkness.

Fighting to keep his eyes open, Amos kept catching a glimpse of moonlight shining off something in the distance. Once, when the moon was hidden behind the clouds, the light was still there. His foggy mind didn't comprehend what he was looking at.

All of a sudden he realized that it was the light from a cabin window, or another building. The prospect of sleeping indoors was welcome. He tried to bring the mule to a trot, but the exhausted animal refused to move any faster. As they got closer he caught the sound of laugher and music.

Amos entered the yard in front of a two-story log building. A full porch ran along the front. Next to it was a long, low building and a barn with large doors. The music and laughter were coming from the two-story building which was brightly lit on the inside.

Amos slid off the mule, almost falling due to the numbness of his feet and the stiffness of his legs. Hanging on to the saddle horn to keep himself upright, he tried stomping his feet to bring feeling back. Walking on unsteady legs, he led the mule and horses to the hitching rail. He knocked the snow off the rail and tied the mule, leaving the rest of the pack animals strung together.

Supporting himself with a post on the porch, he stepped up onto the icy boards. Standing there, he looked at the door only eight feet away and wondered if he could make the few steps without falling. Without warning it was flung wide open.

"I'll be back in a minute after using the little house!" a short, stocky man called over his shoulder. Then he saw the young man clinging to the porch post. "What the hell, who are you?"

"I . . . I come to buy supplies," the young man said and then, trying to take a step, he slipped and fell on the porch.

"Come out here and help me with this fellow!" the man hollered.

Quickly, a couple of the merrymakers inside came out and supported the young man as he entered the building. Warmth from a large fireplace and a cook stove struck his numbed face. The men sat Amos in front of the fireplace. They began to try and remove the pea coat.

Amos raised his hand. "No, you don't have to help, I can do it." His voice getting stronger, he continued. "My feet are a little numb from the cold. It was like trying to walk on stumps."

One of the men called to the ladies, "Bring him a cup of hot cider."

Amos removed his coat and hat. His face felt like it was burning from the heat of the fireplace. Accepting the cup of cider, he tasted it. It was hot and sweet with the taste of cinnamon. The young man closed his eyes, enjoying the hot liquid. He had never tasted anything as good.

Finishing the hot cider, he set the cup down and began to remove his high-cuts. The frozen laces were beginning to thaw. As he loosened them, pieces of ice fell from behind them, falling and quickly melting on the floor.

One of the men knelt in front of him. "Let me help pull your boots off." He grabbed the heel of the boot and worked it off the numbed foot. Before starting the second, he called, "Irene, bring our frozen friend here another cider."

With the second boot removed, the man took hold of Amos' feet and flexed them. He then removed the woolen socks. After a moment he smiled up at the young man. "They're just cold, no frost bite."

While enjoying the second cup of cider, Amos' feet began to warm up. The pain of the feeling coming back was severe. He pulled up one foot at a time and worked them with his hands, trying to speed up the circulation. He then pulled the warmed socks back on.

Standing and facing the people, Amos raised his cup and said, "I am Amos Mudd. I thank you for this wonderful cider."

The spell of silence was broken and the six people in the room introduced themselves to Amos. He had indeed reached the trading post. It was Christmas Eve, and the stocky owner and his wife had invited their family to a party.

When Walter, the man who had helped him with his boots, offered to put up his stock, Amos asked him to wait. "I have the body of the man that was to help me haul the supplies back."

The stocky owner, Hector, came over to Amos. "A body outside? Was there an accident on your trip?"

"No, it wasn't an accident," the young man replied. "I was forced to kill him."

Once again, the air went out of the room and everyone was quiet. Pulling their coats on, Walter and Hector joined Amos outside. Walter carried a lantern and led the way to the barn. Using a thin stick, the stocky owner lit another hanging on the barn wall.

Amos and Hector removed the partly frozen body of Jamie Sharp. The owner instructed Amos to hold the dead man's shoulder while he straightened the body. The muscles and ligaments ripped and popped with the familiar sound of disjointing stiffened game.

Standing above the body, Hector took the lamp. He then said to the round-eyed Walter, "Son, would you take the gear off Mr. Mudd's animals and tie them along the back wall? Give them plenty of hay."

He then looked at the young man with his jaw set. The way the stocky man was acting made Amos feel uncomfortable. "I had no choice . . ." he started to say, when Hector held up his hand to silence him.

Setting the lamp on a nearby barrel, the owner began, "Do you have the gun that was used to shoot this man?"

"I do, but . . ."

"Please give it to me, and also bring me any others you might have," he directed Amos.

Handing the Colt Paterson to the stocky man, Amos then retrieved the Leman .32 from his packs. Hector set the two guns onto the floor, beside the body.

"I am the closest thing to the law here on the north shore of Lake Nipissing. I have a commission from the government as magistrate. You can consider what we are doing here to be an inquest on this man, ah, you called Jamie."

He then asked Amos to tell him what happened. As best he could remember, the young man related the events of the morning. Hector listened without expression. Then, squatting next to the body, he opened the coat and shirt. Holding the lantern low, he looked at the bullet wounds.

Hector then emptied Jamie's pockets, setting the items onto the barrel head. He then asked Amos what gear was the dead man's. After pointing to the pack, Walter brought it to the stocky man. Slowly and thoughtfully, he went through everything.

"Not much to show for a lifetime," Hector said. He put a few of the items apart from the rest.

There was a small pile with bills and coins, a folded piece of paper, and a letter with the seal broken.

First he counted the money. Then the stocky owner glanced at the folded paper. The letter he opened and read. Slowly, he placed the letter next to the other items. "You're here to purchase supplies for your camp. Didn't they have enough to last the winter?"

"We had a fire in the mess hall that ruined many of our supplies," Amos explained. His thoughts wandering, he continued. "When I shot, I didn't even aim. I hardly remember squeezing the trigger."

"That may be, young man. I have heard that aiming a revolver is like pointing your finger. You fire and hit what you're pointing at," Hector said, sounding a little impatient.

"It is Christmas Eve and it is time to bring this inquest to an end. Mr. Mudd, I never doubted that you had just cause to shoot this man. Had you killed him for any other reason, you would have left the body in the wilds and he would probably never have been found. Instead, you brought him with you."

"If you would like us to take care of burying this man, he was carrying enough money to do so. I will send you back with a letter from the inquest for those at the camp."

With that, Hector's face changed from the stern magistrate and, breaking into a smile, he declared, "Now, back to the party!"

Walter and Hector grabbed the body and moved it to the unheated shed next to the barn. Amos found the bag Chef had given him and then closed the double doors. The three men went back to the bright lights and music.

After enjoying rum-laced drinks, baked ham with all the fixings, and pumpkin or custard pie, the men sat in front of the fire place smoking cigars and drinking coffee. Amos finally had time to open the bag. There was a package wrapped in paper. Cutting the string with his knife, he opened it.

Chef had made him a fruitcake. It was made with nuts and dried fruit, usually reserved for top managers or owners of the logging camp. Holding it up, he turned to Hector's wife. "I would like to share this with all of you for tomorrow's meal."

Hector's wife thanked Amos and put the cake with the other items that would be served on Christmas Day. The owner had promised Amos that he would put the list of items together the next day so he could leave early the morning after Christmas. Amos spread his blanket roll next to the fireplace, above Hector's objections.

"I been so cold today that I don't want to be any farther than necessary from the fire," Amos said.

Christmas Day was a grand affair hosted by Hector and his wife. Amos had met their son, daughter and spouses the night before. The daughter's husband had played the fiddle the night before. Gifts were exchanged. Hector gave Amos a heavy pair of woolen socks and thanked him again for the fruitcake.

It was the first time that the young man had really enjoyed Christmas since before his mother had died. When Hector told him it was time to put the supplies together, Amos regretted leaving the warmth and merriment of the two-story log home.

It had snowed during the day, and the grounds

around the trading post were clean and bright. Beyond the buildings he saw evidence of an old stockade from days gone by. It was now in disrepair, parts of it probably used in the construction of some of the present buildings.

The low long building housed the supplies. Coming in from the snow-covered outside, the dim interior made it difficult to see. While Amos waited for his eyes to adjust, he could smell leather, rope, smoked meats, and herbs. Hector hung a lantern on a post near a long plank counter.

The building was divided into two rooms by a wall with a wide opening. Steel traps, snow shoes, shovels, and axes hung on the log walls. Shelves stacked with tin plates, cups, cookware, canteens, and other items needed by fur trappers or loggers covered the wall behind the counter. Stacks of blankets, pants, shirts, long johns, woolen socks, and a row of boots lined another wall.

The second room had sacks of flour, cornmeal, coffee beans, leather bags of pemmican, grain, horse tack and supplies. Each room had a potbelly stove used to heat the building.

Hector was busy starting a fire in the front room stove. Rubbing his cold hands, he went behind the counter. "I have most of the things on this list. I'll have to give you more cornmeal and less flour."

The stocky owner hummed a Christmas tune that had been played the night before, while he pointed out the items from the list and had Amos stacked them near the door. Once the list was complete, the young man reached into his pocket for a piece of paper.

"I have some personal items some of the men

are looking for. Mostly tobacco, and one fellow wants peppermint sticks," he told the owner.

Reaching under the counter, Hector brought out the plugs of tobacco, cigars, and coarse-cut pipe tobacco. He stuck them into a canvas bag and topped it off with a dozen sticks of candy.

Amos took coins from the money belt. It took most of the gold coins to pay for the goods stacked near the door. The owner handed him a receipt, which the young man put back into the money belt. He then retrieved the money given to him by the men and settled up for the tobacco and candy. He placed the bag with the rest of the supplies, keeping the chewing tobacco he purchased for himself to be put into his haversack.

"The supplies will fit on the four horses," Hector said, "but if I were you I would pack it on all five of them."

"I will consider doing that," the young man replied. "I want to travel fast on the way back."

While the stocky owner headed back toward the two-story cabin, Amos went to take care of the animals. Hector had told him to give them some grain along with the hay. There was a creek alongside the barn. After chopping a hole through the ice, he led the animals down for water.

He was wearing the heavier woolen socks given to him for Christmas. They were much warmer than the ones Charlie sold. The mule came up and nuzzled the pea coat pocket with the chewing tobacco. "You don't want that, Jenny," he said, scratching the mule's forehead.

After putting the animals back into the barn, he

spent a few minutes going over the saddle packs and the other gear for the pack animals. His Leman .32 and the Colt lay near his saddle. Sitting next to the lantern, he checked the guns over. He loaded the two spent chambers of the revolver. Both of the guns needed a good cleaning, but he was anxious to get back to the holiday festivities.

Putting them with his saddle, Amos left the barn and strode through the calf-deep snow toward the house. The skies were overcast and the air was frosty. It was going to be a cold night. The young man paused on the porch and knocked lightly. A chorus of "come in," sounded from the inside.

It was late when Amos rolled out his blankets and settled down near the fireplace. He had eaten and drank too much throughout the day. He lay on his back, his belly swollen. In a matter of hours, he would be heading back to the logging camp. He was thankful that the memories of this Christmas would be his forever.

Someone calling his name woke the young man. It was Hector. "I knew you wanted to get an early start. I'll put some coffee on in the store. My wife put some traveling food together for you, and I got some ham and bread for our breakfast."

Pulling on his boots, Amos then rolled up his bedroll. He followed the owners out the door, pausing before going out to look back at the room where they had celebrated Christmas. When he came back from California with the gold he would find, Amos decided that he would stop back here and correctly thank them for their hospitality.

By lantern light, the young man put the pack

saddles and halters onto the horses. He made a deal with Hector on another halter and lead rope for Jamie's horse. They would tie three 50-pound bags of cornmeal onto the saddle. The rest of the supplies were distributed between the other four pack animals.

One of the animals carried Jamie's bedroll and other items. These would be given back to Charlie to determine where they should be sent. After the animals were packed and tied to the hitching rail, Amos joined Hector in the trading post and ate a thick ham sandwich and drank strong, hot coffee.

When first light showed through the small windows of the building, Amos got up and readied himself to go. Hector handed a sealed letter to him. "Give this to the logging camp and it will explain my findings. Other than the money we found on him, he had drawn a map of the rivers on the folded piece of paper. The letter was from some lady in Montreal. The gist of it was she had met another man and wouldn't be there when he returned from the camp."

"I wouldn't be surprised if he didn't start the fire to damage the supplies, knowing they would send someone after more. If he wasn't picked to go, he could follow those that were and then kill them and leave with the money. With it he hoped to win the woman back. When you get back to the camp, ask them if this Jamie took all his gear, or just some of it. My guess is he took all of it."

Amos added the sealed letter to the money belt, his mind trying to take in what the magistrate had just told him. While the information made sense, he couldn't believe someone would go to that extent to get back to a lady who didn't want him.

With the bedroll, his haversack, and the bag of food on the back of his saddle, Amos swung onto the mule. Jenny stomped, anxious to start going. Looking down at the stocky owner, the young man raised a hand. "I want to thank you and your family for the past couple days."

With that he turned the mule toward the trail, and one by one the pack horses fell in behind him as he led them out of the yard. Amos didn't look back as he passed what remained of the stockade. He wondered if he would ever have a place like this that he could call home.

All that remained of his tracks coming in were depressions in the new snow. Right now he had the Small River to guide him. Once he turned away from the river, he would have to depend on the sun, which was now hidden behind thick clouds.

After two hours of riding, Amos swung down from the mule. Walking along the line of pack animals, he made sure that everything was secure. When turning away from Jamie's horse, the animal reached out to bite him. It caught the back of his pea coat, pinching the skin beneath.

Jumping away, the young man shouted, "Keep that up and I'll put the bit back in your damn mouth!"

Amos rubbed the pinched area against an aspen tree. He mumbled as he walked back toward the mule, "Nasty rider, nasty horse. Damn, that stings."

He led the animals for a couple miles. He had no idea how far he had ridden that night going to the trading post. If it started snowing again, the trail he was following back might be covered completely. He might miss the point where he had come to the river.

Amos knew that if he missed it, he couldn't get lost because he would eventually arrive at the fork where the Ottawa and Small Rivers met. But it could add days to his trip. As he traveled the indentions in the snow would be lost for a short distance, then appear again in the heavier wooded areas.

He climbed back onto the mule. Sitting on the animal, he had a better view of the trail. Reaching into the bag given to him by Hector's wife, he brought out slices of buttered sweet bread. He ate while he rode. After finishing the bread, he drank from his canteen.

Amos was putting the canteen back under his pea coat when he saw the area where he had come to the river. The old trails indentions led into the trees. The mule turned without urging. The young man wondered if the animal was following the trail by scent. If it was, that would allow him to ride after dark if he decided to.

A light snow started falling just before sunset. Amos had let the mule have its head and it had continued to follow a trail near to, or in line with, the depressions. With the snow starting, the young man chose to make camp. The bread and meat in the bag had frozen and would require a fire to eat it.

Dismounting from the mule, he took a length of rope and strung it between two trees, aligning with the direction he wanted to follow the next morning in case the snow filled the depressions. He then tied the mule and horses to the rope.

There was a deadfall with its branches sticking out of the snow. He broke enough of them off for his fire. Using the side of his foot, he cleared the snow in front of two balsams trees. It was dark before he got the fire going and some water to heat. He then went to pull the packs and gear off the animals.

It was almost an hour before the supplies were off and stacked under a tarp to keep the snow off. Amos had to take several breaks to prevent sweating. On each pause from unpacking, he would work on his meal. He had grain for the animals, but decided to have his supper first.

Using the hatchet, he cut some lower branches from the trees and laid the boughs onto the frozen ground for his bed. The young man was exhausted by the time the animals were fed, and he had cleaned up after his meal. The remaining coffee was left near the fire for his morning meal. Amos put his haversack against the balsam trunk near his bed.

Using his saddle for a pillow, he spread his ground tarp and blankets on top of the balsam branches. He put the Colt Paterson under the saddle, and the Leman .32 under the edge of his blankets. He pulled a second ground tarp over his blankets to keep the snow off, then put his boots under it. It also covered his head to keep the snow off his face. His canteen was on the blanket next to him.

Sleep came quickly while the snow fell steadily outside his cocoon of warmth. Needing to relieve himself, Amos awoke. He pushed the tarp back, causing the new fallen snow to cascade in around him. Sitting up, he did his best to brush it off his face and out of his neck.

It was just beginning to get light. Struggling under his blankets, the young man got his boots and choppers on. Crawling out of his bed, he paused for a moment to pull the ground tarp back over the saddle to keep the snow out.

The snow-covered animals stood with their heads down. A few flakes were still falling. The sky was still overcast. Keeping low, Amos came out from under the balsams to prevent knocking the snow off the branches. A few steps from the bed, he fumbled with his coat and pants.

Finished, he looked around his camp. There had been another foot of snow overnight. The coffee pot was just a little bump on the snow. His tarp-covered packs looked enormous. The tree he had pulled the branches off for his fire had disappeared. In the gray light of the morning he knocked the snow off his campfire and coffeepot.

Breaking dead branches from the bottom of balsams in the area, he got enough wood to start a fire. To speed things up, he sprinkled some gunpowder onto the small branches and struck his flint, igniting it with a flash. Feeding a few bigger sticks into the fire, he then put the frozen coffee pot next to the flames.

There was an audible whump behind him as the snow from the balsams he'd slept under came down, burying his bed. Amos stared at it and muttered, "I guess I could have still been laying in it."

Amos went to brush the snow off the animals while he waited for the frozen coffee to thaw. There were ice crystals in their long coarse winter coats. The young man concentrated on the areas that would be covered by the saddle blankets. He made sure that he didn't turn his back to the mean horse Jamie had been riding.

With the snow off the animals, he went back to the fire to check on the coffee. He was thankful that the snow had stopped. Adding more wood to the fire, he tackled the bedroll next. The snow had packed when it had fallen from the trees and he was able to break chunks off and clear them. Setting the bedroll, haversack, saddle, and rifle near the fire, he felt the side of the pot. It was warm enough to drink.

He put some ham and bread into the frying pan on the fire, and set back to drink the coffee. Grounds had come with the dark brew as he poured it into his mug. He waited for them to settle before drinking. Using his knife, he flipped the ham and bread. It had quickly browned in the greaseless pan.

Once the ham and bread were no longer frozen, Amos fished them out of the pan and slowly chewed his breakfast. After finishing his meal, the task of packing the animals began. Again he took breaks to prevent sweating, drinking the rest of the coffee while resting.

Packing was hampered by the restless horses. The last water that the animals had had was just before leaving the river, when they'd passed an open area. They'd had to settle for eating snow until they passed a stream or pond. Amos figured that they knew they were heading for home and the warmth of the barn.

At last the horses were packed and his mule saddled. Amos went and kicked snow over the dying fire. He sighted down the rope he had tied between the trees and picked out a large, lightning-struck tree several hundred feet away. His line of sight was limited by the tall pines.

Removing and securing the rope, he then checked the packs and lead ropes one more time. Then, swinging up onto the mule, he started the pack train toward the landmark. All signs of the trail coming to the trading post were gone. Amos took note that the snow sticking to the trunks of the trees was on the northwest side. He was riding northeast, and without the sun to help guide him he would use this to keep his direction.

The snow in many areas was belly-deep on the mule. There was no crust on top to break, so that was an advantage. Still, Amos got down and broke trail for the mule, giving it some relief. At noon he noticed that the mule was headed in a more easterly direction, based on the snow on the trees. Having no idea of their true direction, he had to trust the animal.

By mid-afternoon, the snow had disappeared from the tree trunks. Overhead, the clouds had blackened, giving a gloomy appearance to the woods. Amos pulled the last of the bread from his haversack and put it under his coat. A short while later, he got down from the mule and led it, breaking trail while chewing on the dry bread.

When they hit a thick stand of pine, the snow wasn't nearly as deep. Both man and mule appreciated the break. At a small stream, he broke the ice and let the thirsty animals drink. After they were done, he filled his own canteen and put it back under his coat.

Just before dark, he broke out into a logged-out area. That could only mean that he was getting close to the Ottawa River. Then there was a flash of fear that went through his body. He could have very well ridden in a circle and be back at the Small River.

Rubbing the side of the mule's neck, he said, "You wouldn't do that to me, Old Jenny. Would you?"

It was dark when the mule stopped. Amos

urged it to continue, but Jenny stood fast. Swinging down off the animal, the young man stepped back, his feet went out from under him and he went bum over tea kettle down the bank.

He came to a stop on the ice below. He had reached the Ottawa. Slipping and falling, he climbed back up the river bank. Standing beside the mule, he brushed off the snow from his coat and pants. "You couldn't just turn downriver, hey? Had to make sure I saw the river."

While Amos wasn't certain if he was above or below the camp, he had trusted the mule this far and he was confident it had followed their original route back. Climbing back onto the animal, he urged it to move, and this time Jenny started.

Without warning, the mule turned and started down the riverbank. Grabbing the saddle horn, Amos fought to prevent going over the animal's head. They were at the river crossing! The ice along the shore broke when the mule stepped out on it and it struggled to stay on its feet. Both of Amos' pant legs were plunged into the water.

The pack horses followed them down, having an easier go with the ice broken away. Amos knew that he should have made camp once he'd reached the river, but the trip had been long and he was anxious to get back to the camp. Once he was in the river, he realized that the decision could cost him his life.

Clinging to the saddle horn, Amos prayed that the mule would remain upright. No matter what happened, now he knew that they had to make for the camp. He was wet to the knees and would have a difficult time making camp and getting dried out.

The horses behind him plunged and jumped as they crossed the Ottawa. The lead rope was pulled free from the mule and it was impossible for Amos to turn Jenny to try and find it. Once on the other bank the young man dismounted, fully ready to wade into the river and try to bring the pack horses out of the river.

In the darkness he heard the sound of steel against stone as the tethered horses fought to climb out of the river. Running blindly in the direction of the sound, Amos felt panic. He had gotten so close to being back, and to lose the animals and supplies now was unthinkable.

He was almost trampled by the frantic horses as they came out of the river. Clutching the halter of the first horse he came into contact with, he shouted, "Whoa, easy horse!" The human contact seemed to have a calming effect on the frightened animal.

Amos continued to lead the horse away from the river, hoping that the rest were still with it. On solid ground the horses stood, shaking. The young man cussed himself, knowing he should have waited until daylight to make the crossing. He realized that he had the halter of the second horse. He worked his way to the first and, finding the lead rope he tied it to an aspen.

One at a time, he checked the animals and their packs. The fourth horse had almost lost its pack and it was shifted to one side. In the dark, and with shaking hands, Amos removed the items from the pack saddle and set it back squarely onto the back of the animal.

His woolen pants had frozen and he found it difficult moving around. He managed to get the pack back onto the horse. By the time he was finished his hands were numb. Pulling the choppers from his pea coat pocket, he pulled them on with his teeth.

His eyes searched the darkness for the mule. He tried whistling for the animal. Nothing! The mule was gone! Very little water had gotten into Amos' boots, so his feet were warm in the heavy woolen socks. He had no choice, he would have to lead the horses downriver to the camp. The ride had taken two hours to the crossing. He should be able to walk it in three.

Grasping the first horse's lead rope, he pulled. For a moment it refused to move, fearful of more river in front of it. "Come on, you stubborn son-of-a-bitch!" he shouted.

Pulling again, the hesitant animal started walking. To help take his mind off his situation, Amos thought about Christmas at the trading post. His frozen pant, chafed against his legs and he was beginning to sweat. Amos did not care, because he was not stopping until he was in the logging camp yard.

Snow began to hit his face and he trudged on. All of a sudden, he found himself singing Christmas songs his mother had taught him years ago. The cold and aching in his body was forgotten. He was almost home.

His spirits high, Amos walked, leading the horse for over an hour before he saw the lantern light and heard the shouts of men coming toward him. The young man continued walking toward the light, not knowing if it was a dream or real. Either way, he knew that his ordeal was over.

Suddenly, he was surrounded by men from the camp. Jake threw his arms around Amos, shouting,

"The damn mule came in without you! We were sure you were lying out here freezing and dying."

"Hell no, Jake. I just sent it in to get you fellows ready to unload the pack horses," Amos replied.

The young man took a long draw from the flask that Jake handed him. The group had brought a horse to carry Amos if he was hurt. The men hoisted the young man onto its back and the noisy group led the pack horses and the one Amos was riding toward the camp.

The rest of the trip was a blur for Amos. After arriving back at camp, Chef and others began to unload the horses. The young man was told that his mule was in the barn, enjoying some grain and hay. Amos went into the bunkhouse and shed the wet, frozen pants. The warmth of the potbelly stove was wonderful.

Soon Amos was sitting on his bunk with dry clothes and most of the flask in his empty stomach. The men were firing questions at him, wondering what had happened. Boss came in and took one look at the sleepy logger. "You men let this man get some sleep. Amos, report to the office right after breakfast. We have some questions for you."

CHAPTER TEN

Amos met with Boss and Charlie the next day. He related what had happened on the trip and gave them the letter from the inquest. He returned the rest of the gold coins and the money belt to Charlie. A quick check of Jamie's bunk confirmed that he had taken all his gear and had had no intention of returning. The young man was told he would receive an extra £5 bonus for bringing the supplies early.

The pack horses had a few sores on their backs and one had a stone bruise from crossing the river. After a couple days' rest, they would all be ready to skid logs. Charlie took Jamie's gear and promised to take care of it. Then Amos got the best news. It was Saturday, December 28, 1850! Tonight was payday and they would be heading for The Shanty.

Amos was given light duty to recover from his ordeal. He helped the bucker mark logs as they were skidded into the staging area. Most of the men treated the young man as a hero, while those who were friends of Jamie Sharp weren't sure what to think. They found it hard to believe that the kid tried to kill for money.

When the young man had given Jake the Colt Paterson back, his friend had looked at the gun and then at Amos. "You shot the kid with this Colt? Hell, I've carried it for years and never even shot at a man."

While washing that night, Jake commented on the large bruise on Amos' shoulder. "That damn ornery horse Jamie was riding tried to take a hunk out of me," the young man explained.

Sitting on the sledge, Amos fingered the item he had in his pea coat. During the party at the trading post, Hector's wife had given the young man something to give his best girl. Amos remembered that he had blushed, not sure what to say.

He intended on giving it to Ona tonight. With the extra pay he received, Amos planned to spend a little more time with the lady. Jake sat next to him, telling him of his plans for the night. Amos hardly heard a word his friend said, deep in his own thoughts.

The heavy snowfall had left The Shanty yard clean and white. The soot-covered lanterns even seemed brighter. Amos knew that it would soon be urine and vomit-stained, but for now it was clean. The men piled off the sledge and ran for the door. The two friends hung back and let the others in first.

Jake told Amos, "If any of the kid's friends give you any trouble tonight, I got your back."

"I thank you for that, Jake," the young man said, "but they got no cause to blame me."

"Well, some are just dumb that way," his friend advised him.

Ona was talking to a logger from another camp when Amos spotted her. He got a beer and found an empty table. Stuffing his hat and choppers into the sleeve of his pea coat, he hung it over the back of the chair. Jake joined him with a bottle and the dirty blond-haired woman. "What the hell, Amos. Drinking beer tonight?" Jake questioned.

"I got to keep my head clear, Jake," the young man replied. "I got something for Ona and with a belly full of rye, I might say something stupid."

"Well, I got something for the lady here, too." Then they all had a good laugh.

The show started and Jake and his lady disappeared into the back rooms. Amos sat at the table nursing his beer. He could see the dark-eyed woman he hoped to see working the men near the bar. One of the bartenders came by the table with bottles and glasses.

Frustrated, Amos motioned him over. "I'll take one of those."

Pouring a glass of the amber liquid, he tossed it down. The rye warmed his stomach as he poured another. Accepting that Ona would be busy for a while, the young man watched the show. Shane came over and sat at the table.

"Not as busy in here tonight," he said, smoothing back his moustache. "I heard that another place opened, upriver from us. We should check it out next week, hey."

Amos sat swirling his rye in his glass and agreed with the stoop-shouldered logger. "A change is just what I need."

The show ended and Shane was up, hurrying to the stage to talk to one of the singers. Emptying the glass with one gulp, he began to refill it. "You look like a man with a problem," a soft voice near him said.

He looked up at the object of his desires. "Ona! Let me buy you a drink!"

Taken aback by the unexpected verbose greeting, Ona hesitated. Amos was normally soft-spoken. This was a side she hadn't seen before. Accepting the coin he handed her, she went to the bar to get a beer. Returning to the table, she was smiling. She had to deal with all types working in the tavern and knew how to hide what she felt inside.

Sitting with the young man at the table, she smiled and listened to his rambling story about going after supplies. Much of what he said made no sense, but Ona smiled and nodded anyway. All of a sudden, Amos stood up, almost knocking the table over. He ran for the door and added to the now vomit-covered snow.

Ona stood by the door, watching the young man as he emptied his rye-filled belly. Slowly, Amos got up from his hands and knees. He wiped his mouth with the back of his sleeve and staggered back toward the tavern door.

"Oh my God," he breathed. "It's been a long time since I done that."

The dark-haired girl took his arm, with a look of concern. "Let's go to the back room. You need to rest for a bit."

"I . . . I got money," he started to say.

"Keep it for now," she retorted as she guided

him through the tavern, stopping to pick up his pea coat on the way to the back.

The next thing Amos knew was that he was waking up on a small bed in a dim room. Around him were the sounds of goings on in other rooms. He started to get up when he saw Ona sitting on a small stool near the bed.

"What . . . where am I?" he asked her.

"You have been sleeping. I stayed to watch over you," she answered.

The young man sat up on the edge of the bed. He remembered being sick, but not much after that. Right now, he felt okay. "How long?"

"A couple hours," she replied.

"I'm sorry, Ona," he said, realizing that she had wasted a night's work because of him.

She sat on the bed next to him, and gave Amos a genuine smile. "I worried about you. You can't drink like other loggers."

Chuckling, he said, "Maybe I will get better." Then his face became serious. "I killed a man."

"You what?"

"I killed . . ."

Ona stopped him, covering his lips with her fingers. "I heard you. When?"

"It was Jamie Sharp," he began, and then told her what had happened.

The young Ojibwa woman sat in silence and listened to the young logger tell of the guilt he felt about taking a life. Then, taking him in her arms, she held him close. "You had no choice. Jamie had a meanness about him and hurt some of the girls."

For a long time they held each other. There was a shout from the tavern. "Sledge for Jasper's is about to leave!"

"That's your camp, Amos. You must go now," Ona said, reaching for his coat.

Standing near the bed, the young man put on the pea coat, shoving the tuque and gloves through the sleeve. Suddenly, he remembered and took the present for Ona out. It was a length of red ribbon. "For you, Ona."

Pleased with the unexpected gift, she smiled with delight. "I have never had a ribbon for my hair before."

She hugged the young man and kissed him. Then, pushing him toward the tavern, she insisted he go and not miss the sledge. Amos reached into his pocket and removed several coins. He pressed them into her hand. "These are for taking care of me and helping me get some of the guilt off my shoulders."

Before she could say anything, he turned and headed for the waiting sledge. Jake was leaning against one of the bunk poles. Seeing his friend hurrying toward him, he called out, "Spent your whole damn bonus in one night, didn't you?"

The next couple weeks were work as usual. Chef made Amos a special meal one evening in the new mess hall, to make up for the Christmas feast he'd missed. A series of windblown snow storms went through, shutting them down. These were considered their days off, so the men had to stay in camp Saturday nights and work Sundays. Boss showed up at the Saturday evening meal with jugs of a rum mixture. He called it grog for work well-done.

The men wanted to go and check out the new tavern when they finally got a Saturday night out. Amos waved at the departing sledge and the raucous loggers pulled away. Freshly washed, and with his beard and hair trimmed, Amos went down to the barn. He put a saddle onto the mule and rode toward The Shanty.

The mule pushed through the deep, crusted snow for the three miles to the tavern. Amos could hear the partying loggers before he caught sight of the lanterns. He tied Jenny to an aspen tree just outside the yard. He didn't want some drunken patron taking his animal by mistake.

He walked into The Shanty, pulling off his choppers and hat. Shedding his pea coat, he stuck them into the sleeve. The place was packed with celebrating men. Unable to find a table to sit at, he found a space at the bar. As the bartender went by, Amos called to him, "I'll have a beer over here!"

In the crowded, smoke-filled room, he was unable to find Ona. He leaned with his back to the bar and his coat over one arm, sipping the foamy brew. Turning to the man next to him, he commented, "Awful busy here tonight."

"Everyone is back," the tipsy logger slurred. "The new place had few women and the stuff they served had more pepper and water than whisky. A bunch of angry blokes burned the place to the ground."

"The hell you say," Amos said, and then started laughing, thinking what the men from Jasper would find when they got there.

He spotted Ona coming from the back. She was smiling at the attentive men as she went by. Amos stepped out from the bar, catching her eye. Her smile went from her lips to her eyes. It was evident that she was glad to see him.

"I wondered if you decided to start going to the new place," she said, pretending to pout.

"Better than that," the young man replied, playing along. "I chose to work the past couple of Sundays to make up for work lost during the storms."

"Work is better than me?" she kidded.

She led him to a table that had just been vacated when a couple men brought their ladies to the back room. "Have a couple beers and I will be back. I have to get a few of these men to buy me some drinks," she whispered to him, leaving before he could object.

Amos was joined by a couple of loggers from another camp. One was shuffling a deck of cards and asked the young man if he wanted to play. "It's been too many weeks since payday and all I have is enough for a few drinks," he lied.

Before they could respond, the show started and everyone turned toward the stage to watch. One of the drunk loggers tried to climb over the rail onto the stage, was grabbed by a couple of brutes and tossed out the door. His infraction required a short cooling off period, and then he would be allowed back in if he could behave.

Just as the show ended, Ona came back to the table. She looked disapprovingly at the men sitting with him. Nodding her head, she motioned Amos to come with her. Taking her hand, he followed her into the back. Once again he found himself in the small canvas room. The young woman quickly came into his arms. Dropping his coat onto the floor, he held her close.

"I had to bring you back here to protect you from those men. They would cheat you out of everything in your pockets," she confided.

"I was sort of hoping you brought me back because you wanted to be alone with me," the young man said, enjoying the warmth of her body.

Looking up at him mischievously, Ona began to unbutton his shirt. Soon she was slipping off her dress, exposing her satin skin in the dim light. She sat back on the small bed and reached up for him, comfortable in her nakedness.

Excitement surging through his body, Amos came toward her. "Take your time," she whispered.

In his state, the young man took anything but his time.

Breathing heavily next to the soft woman on the narrow bed, he panted, "Next time. Next time, I promise, I *will* take my time."

Ona giggled and held him close.

When Amos arrived back at the camp, the lights in the bunkhouse were already out. He put up the mule and gave it some hay. Pap slept in a small room toward the front of the barn. He got up when he heard noise in the barn. He saw a silhouette of a man from the light of the lantern left burning near the double doors.

"Who the hell goes there!" the bearded man challenged.

"It's me, Amos, Pap," the young man said. "I'm just getting back from The Shanty."

"Well, you best be quiet going into the bunkhouse. Got a bunch of ornery loggers in there. They spent the night looking for the new drinking place and finally found a few charred remains. Came back fit to be tied. I suppose you had a better night," the bent-nose old man said.

Grinning from ear to ear, Amos said, "I most certainly did."

As he walked out of the barn, he heard Pap lower the hammer on the revolver he was carrying. It was good to know that his mule, Jenny, had such good protection.

Amos was woken by Jake kicking the side of his bunk. "I suppose you had a better night that the rest of us," he said accusingly.

"If you mean did I see Ona, yes, I did," the sleepy young man replied. "Sorry to hear about your night."

"Sorry, my butt!" Jake snorted. "We freeze our asses off and you got a woman to keep yours warm."

The rest of the day, Amos stepped lightly around the subject of Saturday night. He took care of his normal Sunday chores. He could still smell the sweetness of Ona on his clothing. He decided he wouldn't be in any hurry to wash them.

The cold of middle winter made the work harder than usual. Chopping in the freezing temperatures slowed production. Boss put Amos to felling trees with an old-timer named Reuben. To start, the men cut narrow notches about waist-high on each side of the tree. They pounded hand-hewed planks into these notches. Climbing onto the planks they chopped the felling notch in the huge pines. Then, at ground level, they completed the cutting from the back side of the tree.

Reuben and Amos took alternate swings as the felling of a tree proceeded. Once the telltale *crack* was heard, the two men quickly moved clear of the tree. In slow motion the tree would start down, taking neighboring branches and snow, finally coming to the ground in a crash and plume of snow.

Felling trees was something that Amos enjoyed. He understood the dangers of dead branches, or the tree shifting unexpectedly, but he trusted Reuben's judgement when he looked the tree over before starting to chop.

It was March before Amos got back to working with Jake and the mules. While the young man was felling trees, Jake had skidded with one of Pap's boys. The upside was that Jenny was taken care of without costing Amos any money. The highpoint of every week was the trip to The Shanty. Ona waited eagerly for Amos and it was only matched by his eagerness to see her. As they lay in the afterglow the young man would tell her about his plans to head for California and the gold fields come spring. Sometimes she accepted money from him, often she refused it.

When the usable trees on the ridge were cut and they had moved to a valley beyond. Skidding the logs to the bucking area took more time. There were the mules, Henri and Leroy's horses, and two other teams skidding all day long. The larger logs were hoisted onto a small two runner sled that raised the larger end. Once secured, the log would ride on the runners and the tail of the tree.

When he checked his money belt Amos had nearly £30 saved up, between what he had come with and what he had earned. That was well over $100 in U.S. currency. He had never had more than a dollar or two at one time in his whole life. He was sure that the money would take him to the gold fields without a problem.

When talking about California with Jake, the young man never brought up the subject of money. He just assumed that his friend would have as much, or more, to put towards the trip. More than likely they would purchase a wagon in St. Louis and have it to use in California to haul their gold.

Some days Jake talked excitedly about California and then others he seemed doubtful. To Amos it didn't matter because he was going either way. But it would be much easier to travel with someone he could plan with and that would pick up some of the burden.

Toward the end of March some of the days were warm enough to melt some snow, but the nights kept the roads and trails frozen firm. Amos and Jake would often bring in one of the larger bucked logs at the end of the day and leave it near the stringers to be squared.

The late afternoon sun was bright and there was a cold north wind as the two men drove the mules, pulling a log to be squared. Jake was in good humor, taking a pull from his flask every once in a while. Amos sat on the log as it bumped along the road. He asked his friend what the first thing was that he was going to buy when they found gold in California.

Jake grinned, thinking for a moment. "I think I will find a nice brothel and hire all the girls for a whole night."

"After the first 20 minutes, what are you going to do with the rest of your night?" Amos asked sarcastically.

Grabbing a frozen road apple, Jake flung it at his laughing friend, causing Amos to fall off the log while ducking. Rolling clear, the young man continued to lay there, laughing. Jumping back up, he ran to catch up with Jake.

The sound of a running team coming behind them made the men pull the mule team to the side of the road. Sometimes the drivers got the sledge going too fast and required lots of room to stop. Looking back, they saw the man driving the team, frozen with fear as his panicked team ran ahead of the loaded sledge.

Tossing the mule's lead rope to Amos, Jake ran parallel to the running team and grabbed onto the collar of the closest horse, intending to get on top of the animal and stopping the runaway horses. His hand slipped from the collar and Jake hit the ground and rolled, the sledge going over the top of him.

His attempt turned the horses, causing the sledge to go sideways and flip, sending the logs and driver flying. Frozen for the seconds that all this unfolded in front of him, Amos suddenly shouted Jake's name and ran toward the sledge. As he approached, the first thing he saw was the twisted figure of his friend lying on the icy road.

Sliding to a stop next to his friend, he cradled

Jake in his arms and screamed for someone to get Charlie. Amos knew that his shouts were futile. Jake's head was crushed and the young man could feel the broken upper body of his friend. But he couldn't help himself, he just kept shouting for Charlie.

The mood at the camp was somber as the men stood, hats in hand, as the broken man was carried to the office. As it turned out, Jake's attempt to stop the horses may have saved the driver's life. When the horses turned and the load was dumped, the driver was thrown clear, suffering only a broken arm and some other bumps and bruises.

Amos refused to leave his friend's side as the stocky manager came to see what had happened. After taking one look, Charlie asked them to move the body to a shed behind the building. He then went to tend to the driver.

The young man sat with his friend's body until long after dark. The memory of the pain after his mother died was nothing compared to what he was feeling at this loss. He and Jake were going to California to get rich and live high. Women, wine, and song were the two men's future. Now there was only one.

The door of the shed opened and Boss entered, his lantern held high. "It's time for you to turn in, Mudd. Jake was a good man, good worker and to you a good friend, but he is gone. Tomorrow we have work to do. You have work, and I have work. I will put two men digging a grave tomorrow. Using picks they should be able to dig a nice, deep grave in the snow-covered area. There's a good spot just beyond the mess hall. The camp will get off an hour early for a proper funeral."

The young man sat, not moving as Boss spoke. He heard what the man was saying, but he didn't feel it was right to leave his friend lying in the cold shed alone. He felt a hand on his shoulder. He looked up at the stern face of Boss.

As he spoke, his voice was much kinder than his face, "Amos, I want you to come with me now. If you can't work tomorrow, I can fix it for you with Charlie. But you can't spend the night in here. Your friend isn't hurting. His body lays in front of us, but remember, Amos, his soul is far from here and it is warm and feels no pain."

The man put more pressure on Amos' shoulder and the young man stood up and walked out of the shed with Boss. "I have been praying that Jake would forgive me for just standing there and not trying to help him stop the sledge."

"And we would be burying two men tomorrow," Boss said. "That is the last thing Jake would have wanted. Remember, Jake turned the team and prevented a runaway sledge from entering the camp where many more men could have been hurt. You should remember him as the hero he was."

Walking into the dark bunkhouse, Amos could hear the snoring men. Everything seemed in place and normal. It just wasn't right. He felt his way to his bunk and pulled off his boots and coat. Lying under the blankets, he stared into the dark, with Boss' words running through his head and tears running down the sides of his cheeks.

The funeral was as reverent as could be expected in the wilds of Canada. The men stood with head bowed while Charlie and Boss spoke. Pap asked to say a few words and told about some of the lighter and happier times he had had with Jake. With the funeral done, the men went to the mess hall for supper. Charlie had found several bottles of cognac in Jake's gear. He had placed a bottle on each table so the men could have a farewell drink to their friend and fellow logger.

The men ate and drank, telling stories about things they had done with Jake. There was laughter at many of the tables. Amos sat wondering if when he finally died, would there be this many people remembering him? The young man couldn't explain it, but by watching he felt a part of something bigger and somehow the ache was less.

CHAPTER ELEVEN

In mid-April the ice began to break up on the Ottawa River. Large chunks rolled and crashed in the flood waters. The trails and roads the men had hauled and skidded the logs on had turned to soupy mud. Cutting trees had stopped and several of the men had left, heading back to the farms for the summer.

Amos sat in front of the mess hall, chewing on a Cornish meat pie that Chef had made. Normally it would be a meat, potatoes, and other root vegetables. This pie was pemmican, with rutabagas that Chef had found in the old root cellar.

The sun felt warm on his woolen shirt. In a few minutes he was going back to the area where the rafts were being staged for floating down the Ottawa. The mules were used to drag things into place. It was Saturday, April 19th, and he was looking forward to seeing Ona that night. With more of the loggers gone, she had extra time to spend with him.

Chef came out and struck the triangle. It was

time to go back to work. Amos walked across the muddy yard to the barn where Pap had watered and given grain to the mules. Taking hold of the lead ropes, he walked toward the river.

Boss figured that the ice would clear in the next week. There were dangers of ice jams down below, but the men would just sit tight in the makeshift quarters erected on the rafts and wait for them to clear. The ice had moved away from the camp shore and the current in the small cove was slow, so the men were launching the smaller, lashed logs to eventually be tied together and create the larger rafts.

A frame had been built over the water with a pulley at the end. Amos hitched the mules to one end of the rope feeding through the pulley, while the other would be tied to the lashed logs. They would then be pulled into the water.

The sounds of hammering and chopping were everywhere. The sun warmed the hewed logs and the smell of pine sap was strong. Some of the men were dismantling the unused bunkhouses to reclaim the usable logs. They were skidded to the hewing area and the remaining sides were flattened. They were then added to the rafts. Roof poles and some of the logs were used to erect the living quarters on the rafts.

An hour before quitting time, Boss came to see Amos. "Take the mules back to the barn and go see Charlie."

Nodding, Amos unhooked the mules from the rope and led them away from the river. He had seen this before. One or more men were sent to see Charlie, and when one got there their pay was waiting and they were on their way the next morning. That was okay.

Amos was ready to move on.

As usual, Charlie was working on his ledgers. Glancing up, he smiled. "It's been a good year, Mudd."

He then closed the book and removed his spectacles. "I been meaning to call you in for some time now. Each of you filled out a paper, or told me where you would like things sent in case something unforeseen happened to you."

Confused, Amos said, "That's good, but nothing has happened to me."

"I am not talking about you, son. It was your friend Jake."

The mention of Jake's name still caused a flash of pain through Amos. "What has this got to do with me?"

"Well, Amos, he left all his worldly belongings to you," Charlie informed the young man. "Jake had no family. He was raised an orphan in Quebec City. I guess he figured you were his family. It ain't much, mind you. Jake traveled light and lived out of a saddle bag. Now, I didn't figure you would mind me sharing the cognac with the men. But the rest is stored in a box next to the mules' stall in the barn. That is, except for this here money."

Charlie opened his desk and took out some bills and coins. It amounted to just over £11. The office manager cleared his throat and continued. "Jake liked to spend on the women and I figure most of what he made here went to them."

"I had no idea Jake would do this," Amos said, bewildered. "We just met on the way up here."

"Maybe so," Charlie said. "But it is legal and

it's what Jake wanted. Now, we would like you to stay until the rafts head down river. Pap and his boys will be taking the rest of the horses to our mills in Bytown. Henri and Leroy had to head out. They got plowing to do and a crop to get in. Can you stick around?"

Still baffled by what he had just learned, Amos nodded. "Sure Charlie, I can stay until then."

Leaving the office, Amos glanced toward the barn. He would wait until tomorrow to find out what was in the box. He looked around the camp. In all directions things were being dismantled. The smithy had the forge and his tools loaded on a freight wagon. One of the teams Pap would be bringing to Bytown would be pulling it. Only the number three bunkhouse was still standing. Talk was that the mess hall would be left and its equipment moved to next winter's camp.

Amos walked back to the wash house and checked the fire under the caldron. After supper and baths were done, the men would walk to The Shanty. With most of the snow gone, the sledge was no longer used.

The three-mile walk took about an hour. For some men the trip back could take several more hours. Shane sat with Amos at supper. The stoop-shouldered man would be riding the rafts down the river. He talked of the time when they'd floated logs down and a man took his life into his own hands trying to break up some of the jams.

With their meals done, the men took their weekly bath, put on clean clothes and were ready for a night out. Amos headed for The Shanty with 11 thirsty loggers. He could have ridden the mule, but preferred to be one of the group and walk. He suddenly realized that he owned two mules now. Jake had left him his. He shook his head. Now was not the time for thoughts of Jake.

As the first men reached the yard in front of The Shanty, they hurried for the door. Amos smiled. The behavior hadn't changed. The men ran in and often crawled out. The young man stepped in and found that like the Jasper logging camp, things were being dismantled. Many of the tables and chairs were gone. Shelves behind half the bar were empty. Beer was no longer offered.

The only ones behind the bar were Grady and one bartender. Amos walked up to the bar and bought a bottle. Grabbing a glass, he went and joined a couple men from the camp at one of the remaining tables. The young man looked around, searching for Ona.

He was on his second drink when she appeared from the back. Standing just inside the room, Ona motioned him to follow her. Amos received a good amount of kidding from his fellow loggers as he headed toward the back. Stepping into the dim back area, he saw her standing near the small room.

Pushing the curtain aside, Amos followed her in. "No drinks tonight?" he kidded her.

He saw her worried look. Pulling the curtain closed behind him, Amos turned to the dark-eyed girl. "What's wrong? I wasn't serious about the drink."

Shaking her head, Ona sat on the bed. "Grady has sent some of the girls along with the furniture and stock to Bytown. He is setting up there for the summer. He has told me that if I want to keep working for him, I would have to go when he closes this place in two weeks."

"Bytown is a nice city. You will like it much more than The Shanty," Amos tried to reassure her.

"Amos Mudd! You do not understand," she said, beginning to cry.

The young man sat and put his arm around her. "Tell me . . . what don't I understand?"

She looked up, her eyes filled with tears. "For you, meeting a woman in a place like this is a good time. For us, it isn't. Every night we give up more of our self-respect until we have nothing left. I am trapped here because a man I trusted took me from my village. When he felt I was more a burden than the pleasure I gave, he left me here."

"What can I do?" he asked. "I leave soon also."

Pounding his chest with her small fists, she cried, "You can take me with you!"

Grasping her shoulders, he held her at arm's length. "I am going to California. That will take you many more miles away from your people. If something happened to me, you would never see your village again."

The look of defeat was on Ona face. "You could take me as far as my tribe in Michigan and then go. I promise I would be no trouble."

The young man could have kicked himself. Instead of asking her what he could do, he should have suggested taking her to Michigan right off.

Trying to make up for the mistake, he held Ona and said, "Sometimes I think too slowly. I would be happy to have you travel to Michigan with me. I will be in camp, two maybe three more weeks and then we could leave."

She pushed him away. "All this crying has left me a mess. You go back to the table and I will be out in a little while."

Unsure if he was still in trouble, Amos got up and stepped out of the small room. As he walked toward the tavern, he heard her say, "Thank you, Amos Mudd."

Work was winding down quickly at the logging camp. Pap and the smithy had left. Chef would be moving his kitchen and supplies to the log rafts. Only a few beds remained in the bunkhouse. The extra barn had been taken down for the useable logs. The remaining barn would be left with the bunkhouse, mess hall, office, and the manager's log cabin. They would be used again in the fall to start up the next winter camp.

A team of horses and the mules were the only animals in the barn. The mules had been moved to the front stalls, which offered more breeze and light. The double doors were left open day and night. Amos sat on an empty barrel and looked at the box of Jake's gear. A saddle and bridle lay on top of the old rifle box. Pap had given Amos a scabbard to carry the Leman. One of the loggers had given it to Pap. It hung over the side of the stall, next to Jakes saddlebags.

Grabbing the wooden handle, Amos dragged the box near the open door. Setting the saddle and bridle aside, he flipped the metal latch up and lifted the top open, the hinges creaking. He looked at the items in the box, the collection of a man's life.

The Colt Paterson lay on top with an open top holster. There was a shot bag containing a powder horn, lead balls, patches, items for easy access while riding or hunting, and things used for cleaning the gun. The box contained a razor, a hunting knife, various items of clothing, a bedroll, a couple pictures of ladies, the silver flask, and three boxes of cigars.

Jake's gear had the smell of him on it. Amos took one of the cigars and lit it with the lantern burning near Pap's room. He closed the box and took a long drag, making the tip of the cigar glow red. Looking down, he felt a sudden chill. He opened the rifle box. Closed, it looked too much like a coffin.

During the first week of May, all of the logs were rafted up on the river. Amos walked out of the bunkhouse at the clang of the triangle. He was carrying his bedroll and haversack. He wanted to drop them off in the barn before going to breakfast. Chef was busy taking down the metal triangle to be put up on the floating galley.

"Get your buttocks back here and get your last meal before I toss it out!" he called.

"Keep it hot, Chef," Amos replied. "I got to drop this stuff off first."

The stack of biscuits, sliced ham, and cheese surprised Amos. "You got one man eating here, Chef. This is a damn lot of food."

"Oh, that. That's not your breakfast," he said, coming from the stove with a stack of pancakes. "Here is your breakfast. I figured you might want to take some of that with you when you leave."

The young man dug into the hot, maple syrup-covered cakes. Any noise the two men made echoed in the empty building. Amos had everything ready for the mules in the barn. He had offered to go and pick

Ona up, but she'd insisted on walking to the camp and meet him.

There was one more stop before Amos was done. Once breakfast was finished, he accepted the bag filled with the food that Chef Pelletier had put out. After shaking the man's hand, Amos walked across the quiet camp yard to the office. Charlie sat with a cup of coffee and an open cognac bottle on his desk. All his ledgers and items for sale had been loaded into the wagon sitting next to the building.

The stocky office manager pushed a package tied with string to Amos. "Here's your pay and a thank you from Boss and me. If California don't work out for you, you'll always have a job in the Jasper camp."

Reaching out, Amos shook the old man's hand. "You and Boss have been more than fair to me. While I doubt I will be back, I do thank you for the offer."

After a moment of awkwardness, the young man stuck the packet inside his shirt and headed for the barn. He caught sight of movement just inside the trees. It was Ona. She was wearing a doeskin dress and her black hair was braided and tied with red ribbons.

"I'm glad you're here," he said, waiting for her to catch up. "I was hoping I didn't have to wait too long."

"I have been here since before the sun came up," she told him. "I have been waiting for you to finish."

"You should have joined me for breakfast," he told her.

"No, I could not. Women are not allowed in

the camps," she informed him.

Once the mules were saddled and packed, Amos put the Colt and its holster around his hips. The Leman .32 was in the scabbard on Jenny's saddle. Pap had traded Amos an English-style saddle for the sawbuck pack saddle. It had no horn, but would work well on Jake's mule for Ona to ride.

Before leaving, Amos and Ona visited Jake's grave. A slab of board had been pounded into the ground as a marker. Jacques Larue 1851 was carved on the marker. The young man removed his round top, brimmed hat and bowed his head.

"My good friend, you were right in bringing me to this camp. I am leaving much more prepared for the trip than if we had not met. I pray you are looking down and help guide me safely on the journey we were to take together." Then, after a brief hesitation, he concluded, "Rest in peace, Jacques Larue."

Taking Ona's hand, they walked across the yard and he helped her onto the mule he now called Jake. The dark-haired woman had brought only a small pack with her. This was tied to the bedroll and other items behind the saddle.

Guiding the mules past the cove, Amos waved to all of the winter friends preparing to cut the rafts loose to start their journey down the Ottawa. He and Ona would be following the river northwest until they found a place to cross safely. The spring floods had receded some, but the currents were still dangerous.

Buds had started to come out on the trees and bushes. Crocus bloomed in the woodland, and the first signs of grass were giving the hillsides a shade of green. The mornings were filled with the sounds of robins, chickadees, and other song birds. The sharp caw of the crows could be heard from their perches in the pines.

The riders had heard the sounds of returning geese. Suddenly, Ona pointed at the recognizable V of the noisy birds. The spring had never seemed carefree like this when Amos was growing up, and he was sharing the warmth of the sun and the forest waking from its winter nap. His thoughts went to the farm in Maine.

Soon his father would start the plowing and, after a month of back breaking work, the spring planting would be done. Then the hoeing would start and the clearing of more land. There would be blueberry picking in the heat of summer to make enough money to last until potato harvest. The work was never done. Riding along the river, freedom from the unrewarding labor was giving him a new outlook of this time of year.

The first day of travel found no decent crossing. While Amos took care of gear and animals, Ona got the fire going and put on some water. The mules pulled at the aspen buds on the young trees, while the young man cut stakes to set up the fly tarp.

Coming from the trees with a load of wood hanging from a leather strap on her back, Ona stopped to look at their shelter. "What happens if the wind and rain come from the raised side?" she asked.

"Then we get wet," Amos replied, grinning at her.

Supper was a simple affair. The biscuits had to be eaten before they molded. They fried some of the ham in the blackened pan and warmed the bread over the fire using sharpened green sticks. Ona poured some of the hot water into a tin mug for tea before adding coffee to the pot.

Pouring himself a mug of coffee, Amos watched the ham heating. Taking a sip, he smiled. "You make a good cup."

"I'm not without abilities," she replied, pleased with the compliment.

The sun had gone down and mules were watered and picketed in an area with last year's grass mixed with new sprouts. Ona went down to the river to wash up. Amos spread the blanket out under the tarp. He placed the saddles at the head, placing the Colt underneath his. The Leman .32 was under the outer edge of the blanket.

He went back to the fire and pushed the coals toward the center. Shaking the coffee pot, he set it away from the coals to be reheated in the morning. Amos fidgeted. He was nervous and didn't know why. He and Ona had been together many times over the winter.

He wondered if it was because he had always had a few drinks before. Amos thought about Jake's flask in the packs. It wasn't empty, maybe just one drink first. Before he had a chance to move, Ona was back. She sat close to him and stared at the glowing coals.

"My father always told me that you should never look into a fire at night," she said. "If you are attacked from out of the dark, you can't see your enemy."

Squirming next to the sweet-smelling woman, he replied, "Let's hope we aren't . . ." He was cut off as she leaned over and kissed him.

Invariably, he pulled back. "You don't like me?" She sounded surprised.

"Ona, I feel like a knock-kneed groom on his wedding night," he blustered.

The young woman stood up and loosened the ties on her dress. It slipped to the ground and she stepped out of it, the glowing of the coals casting soft light on her naked body as she walked toward the blankets. Looking over her shoulder she said, "Then I'll have something to look forward to."

Grabbing her dress, the young man hurried toward the fly tarp, pulling at his clothes to remove them. Two raccoons walking along the river stopped and looked toward the strange noises coming from the camp.

CHAPTER TWELVE

They traveled for four days before they found a place where they could cross the river. There was a peninsula of gravel and rock that jutted out into the river just beyond a bend. It cut the time that they would be in the water. Amos stopped and checked the packs and saddle cinches on both mules. Ona had assured him that she could swim if necessary. He didn't dare tell her that while he could manage to stay above water, he hadn't had much opportunity to swim on the farm in Maine.

Jenny entered the water without hesitation. Jake wasn't as willing. Ona kicked its flanks with her heels, and finally got the mule in the water behind Amos. Thirty feet into the river the bottom went out from under them and the mules swam for all they were worth toward the far side. The riders clung to the short manes of their animals, floating above the saddles.

Several yards downstream, the mules' feet finally found the bottom and they began to lunge forward toward the steep riverbank. The torrent of water continued to push the stumbling animals downstream. A flat piece of shoreline came up in front of the mules, They climbed onto the dry ground and stood shaking from the cold and the ordeal of the river they had just come through.

Ona had been washed to the side of her mule and dropped to the ground, leaning against the animal. Amos swung down, water squishing in his low boots as he hurried back to support the girl. "I'm okay. I'm okay, Amos. Just lead the mules away from the river," she urged him.

The two soaked souls, with their dripping animals, pushed through the brush alongside the river, stopping in a small clearing. Tying the animals to the branch of a windfall, Amos started to pull the gear off the mules. There was the sound of a galloping horse coming from upstream.

The young man stepped away from the mules and checked for his Colt. The gun had been soaked during the crossing but there was the slight chance it might fire if needed. The rider burst into the clearing on a long legged sorrel. Seeing the two of them, he pulled up and practically leaped off the horse.

"Are you folks okay?" he shouted. The man had a full beard and was clothed in dirty buckskins and a rabbit fur hat. In his belt he carried a skinning knife and on his feet were calf-high moccasins. He quickly walked toward Amos and Ona.

Stepping forward to meet the man, Amos said, "We had a little scare in the river, but we come across okay."

"I caught sight of you in the water up near the

bend and it looked like you were about to go under for the last time," the breathless rider said. "The name's Jimmer. I been trapping the North Country all winter. Just bringing my catch to the Sturgeon River House. The Hudson Bay Company runs the outfit, buying furs from those of us willing to face the winters."

"The young woman there is Ona, and I am Amos Mudd," the young man said.

Smiling, his blackened teeth showing, Jimmer said approvingly, "Got yourself a young squaw. Good to keep a man warm in the snowy nights. Had me one for a while. Lost her in a poker game. Damn shame it was, damn shame."

Showing no offence, Amos invited the man to spend the night and share a fire. "You got any tobacco? I run out in February." Smacking his lips, he continued. "It has been a while."

The young man fished the wet plug out of his shirt and tossed it to the man. "It's already wet. Make for easy chewing."

Tearing off a chunk and sticking the rest into his possible bag, the man prepared to get back on his horse. "I left the pack animals back at the bend." Spitting a sluice of tobacco juice onto the ground, he continued. "Damn good chaw. I'll be right back with my goods. You got coffee?"

Amos nodded. Riding away, the man shouted, "Hot damn! Tobacco and coffee! Hot damn!"

Both of them were wet to the armpits and had planned to build a fire and dry off while keeping warm in their blankets. No such luck, they had company coming.

"I bet he was coming to see what he could get after we drowned," she sneered.

"That may be," he replied, "but we may need to go to the trading post and get a few things. Our extra powder is wet and some of our food may be soaked."

By the time the man got back with his pack horses, Ona had the fire going and a pot of water heating. She had taken her bedroll and went into a grove of balsams. It would be dark in about two hours. Taking advantage of the daylight, Amos started going through the packs, draping things that could be dried onto the low bushes. The ground cloths that wrapped their bedrolls had done a fair job of keeping the blankets dry.

The clothes in his haversack had also avoided being soaked. While their company sat on the windfall and talked up a blue streak, Amos stripped down in front of the fire and put his change of clothing on. He had set his boots upside down near the heat of the fire to take some of the water out of them. He then pulled the damp, warm boots on over his dry socks.

Feeling almost human again, Amos took the frying pan and some coffee beans. Spilling some into the pan, he set them over the fire to roast, continually stirring them with an aspen stick. The smell of the roasting beans just about drove the fur trapper berserk.

"Hot damn, them smell good. I could eat them like candy," he exclaimed. The trapper kept looking for Ona while he told Amos about the size of beaver he had trapped.

With the beans browned, Amos took them off to cool. The camp had had a grinder that had made the next step easy. He didn't so the young man went to the river's edge and found two good-sized stones with flat sides. Carrying them to the fire, he placed one down and then placed the roasted beans on it. Placing the other stone on top, he moved it back and forth, breaking down the beans.

While doing this he made sure that the trapper stayed in sight, in front of him. The young man's ears were listening for any sounds of movement in the woods beyond. More than likely, Jimmer here had been in the North Country alone too long and couldn't help himself, and just had to keep talking. Or, he could be covering the approach of a friend.

"You best get the packs off your horses while I brew us some coffee," the young man suggested.

"Damn, your right. I kinda lost my head from the smell of them beans roasting."

Brushing the coffee grounds into a small leather bag, Amos checked on the water. It was hot enough. After pouring some steaming liquid into a mug for tea, he poured part of the ground coffee into the water, saving the rest for another time.

Ona came back wrapped in a blanket tied at the waist with a length of leather. She took the mug of water and went to the packs to get tea. By the time the trapper had his packs off his animals and the saddle off the sorrel, the coffee was ready.

It was fascinating to watch the man drink the coffee. He would sip a little, tilt his head back, and after a moment swallow. Ona put a layer of pemmican into the frying pan and placed all the wet biscuits on top. There was no way to keep any after their dunking.

The trapper went to his pack and came back

with two rabbits. "I shot these earlier today. I'd like to add them to our meal." He set them down and went back to drinking his coffee.

Ona reached for the rabbits and Amos stopped her. He took them, quickly cut around the head and stripped the skin off. In short order the rabbits were ready for roasting. The young woman had cut green sticks to use for roasting the meat.

When the meal was cooked, Jimmer got his tin plate from his packs and filled his plate. Using the hunting knife to eat, he would chew and shake his head back and forth. He pulled a leg off the rabbit and ripped the meat from the bones, licking the dripping juice from his fingers.

Once the meal was done, the trapper licked his plate clean. "Saves me having to wash it," he said, smiling. Then, looking at Ona, "I must say you have a special way of making the pemmican and the biscuits. It topped off the meal."

Ona helped Amos set up the fly tarp and spread their bedding onto the ground tarp. Jimmer sat near the fire, finishing the last of the coffee. He then ran his finger along the bottom of his mug and licked the coffee grounds off.

The dark-eyed woman whispered, "At least he never has to wash his dishes or hands." Amos had to stifle the laugh that almost erupted.

After their shelter was ready, they joined the trapper near the fire. The man looked up at them, "You wouldn't have any whisky, would you?"

"Plum out of that," Amos told him. "We come from a logging camp. There was none of that for our packs."

"I reckon, hey," the man said with disappointment on his face. "No matter, in a week I'll have my furs sold and have plenty of whisky, and maybe even a squaw of my own."

The two men sat at the fire, chewing tobacco, talking of trapping, about the best routes to travel, and the past winter. Ona went through the supplies, discarding anything that was ruined and repacking that which could be saved. It was getting dark when she came back to the fire carrying two cigars.

"Hot damn, you got smoke," the excited trapper said. Taking one of the cigars, he stuck his face near the fire to light it, singeing his beard. Slapping the face hair, he puffed on the smoke. "If I didn't know better, I've figured I died and went to heaven."

The bigger-than-life visitor seemed harmless, but in the wilds one couldn't be too careful. The young man got his Leman .32 and put a cap in it. Looking at their guest, he advised him, "If your animals are skittish, you may want to hold them. I got to fire and clean this rifle."

The trapper waved his hand. "Shoot it, son. Them cayuses are used to me shooting."

Amos put the Leman to his shoulder and fired at a nearby tree. The muzzle-loader belched smoke and fire. The young man was thankful that the powder had not gotten too wet to fire. He sat back down and poured hot water down the barrel, flushing out the unspent black powder.

While the young man continued cleaning his rifle, the trapper drew on the cigar, closing his eyes and holding his breath after each drag. Ona was pulling off the items drying on the bushes before the night dew settled on them. Finished with the cleaning, Amos took the powder horn from his shot bag. The contents were protected in the watertight horn. Dumping a measure down the barrel, he then wrapped a ball with an oiled patch and pushed it home with the ramrod.

Leaning the Leman against a young aspen tree, Amos felt much better knowing that he had a gun that he could trust to fire. He was beginning to feel better about the trapper. Other than running at the mouth continually, he didn't appear to be a threat to them.

The fire had burned down and it was time to call it a night. Amos went to check on his mules, moving the animals to a new spot closer to the fly tarp. Ona had put all their supplies at the foot of the shelter. It hadn't gone without notice that she had kept herself busy away from Jimmer.

Setting the coffee pot away from the coals, he told the trapper, "We can add some water to them in the morning. I think we're going to turn in."

Raising his hand, Jimmer said, "If you don't mind, I'd like to sit here for a bit more and think on how kind you folks have been to me."

Picking up the Leman .32, Amos hefted it a bit before heading for the fly tarp where Ona waited. Behind him the trapper called out, "Thank you missus. I ain't et so good since I can't remember."

After placing the Colt under his saddle and making a show of putting the rifle under the edge of his blankets, Amos pulled his boots off and crawled under the covers. Ona reached over and touched his shoulder. "I have met his type before," she whispered. "They mean no harm, but live a rough life."

"And interrupt my love life," the young man

snickered.

The young man lay watching the trapper in the glow of the smoldering coals. He didn't want to go to sleep until the man did. He could hear Ona's even breathing next to him. The peepers called out in the night, looking for mates. Blinking his heavy eyelids, Amos fought sleep.

Suddenly, Amos' eyes opened. It was getting light. Something was wrong. The mules were gone! Throwing his blankets aside, Amos grabbed the rifle and stood in his stocking feet, not knowing which way to run. He then saw the trapper's horses tied beyond the cook fire.

The sound of branches breaking to his right made the young man turn, swinging the rifle toward the direction of the noise. It was Jimmer leading the mules from the river. "I awoke early and figured I may as well water the stock. You were damn lucky yesterday that the flat area below was there, or you'd have played hob getting out of the river."

Jimmer stopped, seeing that the young, stocking-footed man was holding a rifle on him. "Careful with that shooter," the trapper said. "You didn't think I took your mules now, did you?"

"No, no, Jimmer, I was just going to put it against the tree near the fire." Quickly pointing the Leman toward the ground, Amos walked over and set the rifle down.

Feeling rather foolish, Amos walked back to the fly tarp and sat down to pull his boots on over the socks, now damp from the dew.

By the time that the young man was finished, the trapper had the fire going and the coffee pot filled with water against the flames. Amos went into the brush to relieve himself. Coming back, he looked for any evidence of where the trapper had slept. No sign could be seen.

Breakfast was kept simple. It consisted of coffee made from last night's grounds and the last of the ham. By the time the mules were set for travel, Jimmer had his horses packed. Amos noticed that the trapper had two single-shot pistols and a Hawken .50 caliber rifle. The young man had heard of them, but had never seen one.

"That a good-looking rifle you got there," Amos commented.

"Got that for griz," the trapper replied. "If one of them big brown buggers get on your trail, you best have something to stop them."

Meeting up with the trapper turned out to be a good thing. Several miles were cut off the route to the Sturgeon River House. Amos would have followed the rivers going out of his way. Jimmer had made the trip many times and had a more direct route.

The man never ran out of things to say. Most of the time the young man just smiled and nodded, half-listening to what was being said. While they were riding by the falls on the river, Jimmer said, "The post is less than a mile ahead."

They passed several longhouses made of bark and wooden poles. Each one held several N'Biissing families and their dogs. Ona told Amos that these were their winter homes. Soon they would leave them and travel north to hunt and fish. Each family would live in a wigwam of poles and hides that could be taken down and moved. She told him N'Biissing, or

Nipissing, meant *little water.*

The young man was anxious to continue west. After purchasing what they needed, they only spent one night in the Sturgeon River House area, sleeping under the fly tarp on the river below the trading post. They saw Jimmer once during the day after leaving him. He was busy dickering with the fur buyer from the Hudson Bay Company.

When Amos and Ona awoke the next morning, they were surprised to find a package near the foot of the fly tarp. It contained a bottle of whisky and a deerskin dress decorated with beads and quills. A short note said, "ta kep ya werm goin ouest Jimmer".

Packing the gift along with the rest of their stuff, Amos thought of all the people he had met on this trip. He was only a day's ride west of Hector's trading post, where he had spent Christmas. Right now, too many days would be lost going there. Once again he promised himself that he would do so when he returned with gold from California.

Jimmer had trapped both north and west of the Sturgeon River House. Ona had told him her village was near the falls of brown water they called Tahquamenaw, or Tahquamenon Falls. He had been there and estimated that they would make it in less than three weeks of steady travel. He told them to keep west until they hit a large lake, then follow the north shore maybe five days until it narrowed. Then if they found a man with a proper boat, he could take them across. If they didn't find a boat, they would continue another day or so to the St Mary's River between the two big lakes and cross there.

The young man found the land west of

Nipissing untamed and exciting. They rode through river valleys, densely forested areas, and treeless expanses of rock ledge covered with small bushes he recognized as blue berries. Even the black flies couldn't dampen his enthusiasm.

The young woman's excitement grew when she spotted landmarks she had seen on her trip east. Occasionally they would pass some traveling tribes, and in most cases Ona was able to speak with them. They would trade items for food, or leather goods such as moccasins.

When they reached the big water, Ona told Amos that it was called Huron, named after the Huron tribes. The first night they camped on the lake, Amos had caught several fish and had them roasting over their fire. The dark-eyed woman came from the fly tarp wearing the dress that Jimmer had left. The young man caught his breath. In the setting sun she looked like a princess.

That night he held her close and told Ona that he never wanted them to part. The bond between the two had become strong during the days traveling alone. They were just over a week from her village. The young man figured that they could travel to a mission and get married. Amos envisioned them traveling together across the country, all the way to California.

Amos intended to share his plan with the young woman after meeting her parents. He noticed that the mules were getting a little gaunt from the continuous travel. They would have to spend some time in the village to get some weight back on them.

It was the third week of June when they arrived at the village. The young woman slid off the mule and was immediately surrounded by excited friends and relatives shouting "Onaiwa!" Amos climbed off Jenny and tied the mules to post near a bark-covered longhouse. He hadn't heard Ona called Onaiwa, and for a moment he didn't understand what they were saying.

The Ojibwa village was neatly laid out with several longhouses and a few wigwams. In the center was a fire pit where communal cooking was done. Ona's parents were away catching whitefish, but were expected back in a couple days.

Speaking breathlessly in Ojibwa, Ona introduced him to everyone. She said he had found her and taken her home. Several of the women surrounded Amos, touching him, some hugging him. They were about to eat and invited them to sit. Bowls of a fish soup with wild greens was placed in front of the young man.

Using the wooden spoon offered, he tasted the soup. Smiling, he swallowed. The soup was bland and had a seasoning he did not recognize. While it wasn't unpleasant, it was unusual. The fish was sweet, but had bones to tend with. He guessed that the greens were dandelions. Once the bowl was empty, he was offered a second but declined, motioning that his belly was full.

The next week, Amos was busy taking care of the mules, moving them to the best grass. Ona took him to see the falls. The amber water flowed like a ribbon over the edge. Several children played in the river. He asked her about the tree bark structure near the falls. She told him it was a sweat lodge used to cleanse the body and spirit.

The two of them were given a wigwam to stay in. The villagers just accepted that they were husband and wife. When Ona's parents returned they were older than he had expected. Her father had white, shoulder-length hair and wore a beaded headband to keep it off his face. His face was creased from the many years in the wind and sun. He was slightly bent, but well-muscled.

Her mother wore her salt and pepper hair in a single braid in the back. Like her husband, the sun and wind had taken its toll on her skin. Like Ona, her mother smiled with her eyes. She spoke no English.

The father took Amos around the area, showing him the second falls and taking him by canoe to the bay they fished in. He had the young man use the net to catch some fish. The young man roasted them over a fire they built on the shore. It was the best meal he had eaten in a week.

He got back one evening and Ona told him they would be going to the sweat lodge to purify their spirits. They both put on a loose cotton garment. They walked together to the falls. Amos didn't care for the feeling of having nothing on underneath. He pulled back the hide and ducked under the low doorway, followed by Ona, who put it back to cover the opening. Hot rocks sat in the middle of the room. The only light came from an opening in the ceiling. Amos shed his cover and laid it next to the one Ona had taken off.

A bucket of water sat near the heated rocks and two reed mats lay on the floor for them to sit on. Ona poured water onto the rocks, creating clouds of steam. She sat on one of the mats, folding her legs with her feet on the opposite knee. She placed her hands on her legs and sat straight back with her eyes closed.

Amos tried to duplicate her position, but his muscular frame didn't have the same flexibility. He pulled his knees up and hugged his legs. "Are we allowed to talk?" he asked.

"Yes, but you must speak from within. From your heart," Ona replied.

He glanced over at her in the dim light. Perspiration was running down her cheeks, dripping off her chin, dropping onto her stomach and flowing down in tiny streams of water. Her breasts and sides glistened from beads of water. The stay in the village had been good for her. She had gotten far too thin and was now filling out. He felt a warming in his loins and looked away, remembering that they were in the spirit house.

It was time to tell her what he had been thinking about. "In a week, maybe two, we need to continue west. We passed a mission not far from here and we can go there and have a Christian wedding. We can also have a ceremony with your people."

Amos caught a slight movement of the young woman beside him. She spoke softly. "I was hoping we could stay in Michigan and raise a family. You enjoy hunting and fishing. You can raise our sons to be great hunters. We don't have to live in a wigwam. I can help you build a cabin. I know the ways of the white man and can make you a good wife."

Her response was not what he'd expected. Shifting to face her, Amos spoke, keeping his voice low. "We can come back after we go to California. There is gold for the taking. We can work together and be back in a year, no more. I can't see going without you."

Her head dropped, her chin on her chest. "And I can't see me going. I left here with the trapper a year ago because life in my village wasn't enough. I have seen what life has done to too many woman in that place. I was trapped with no way to escape, never to see my parents, my people again."

"We'll come back, I promise," he urged her.

"Amos Mudd, if I followed you across this country to the place you call California, I will never see my people again. I will die in a strange place, my spirit wandering alone for all time."

"I will be with you, Ona."

"For now and maybe for a while, you'll want to be with me," she agreed. "But I have seen your eyes as you look at the horizon, wondering what is over the next hill. It is not the gold, Amos. It's the adventure of the search. Once we are tied down with children you will find yourself right back on the potato farm in your mind. Again, you will dream of leaving the farm."

The room had cooled and now it was tears running down her cheeks. The young man felt desperate. "I love you, Ona. It will break my heart if you don't come with me," he pleaded.

"It will break your spirit if I were to go."

The young man took her in his arms. She laid her cheek against his chest and whispered, "I will always love you, but if this isn't enough, you must go."

For a long time, the two sat in the sweat lodge holding each other, knowing that when they moved what they had would be over. There was a rapping on the bark near the door. "You must come out and wash the bad spirits off in the river."

CHAPTER THIRTEEN

Amos led the mule off the steamboat and onto the pier in St. Louis. The afternoon sun was hot in early August. It had been a month since he'd left the Indian village. He had given Ona Jake's mule and much of what he had gotten from his dead friend, except for the Colt and saddle.

While both Amos and Ona had been devastated by their decision, her parents had been pleased. The Ojibwa had ranged as far west as the Minnesota territories, and her father had sketched out a route he could take to Fort Snelling to go down the Mississippi to St. Louis.

After he had arrived at the fort, he had booked a Mississippi steamboat at Pig's Eye landing. He had sat at a tavern by the same name, drinking rye while he'd waited for the boat. Amos had found himself quickly riled after the breakup. The 400-mile route had been full of fights. One man who had made disparaging remarks about his mule had pulled a knife when Amos had come at him. The two of them had slashed and circled each other, both drawing blood until a local constable had fired a shot in the air and had threatened to put a bullet into the next man who tried to use his knife.

While on the steamboat a gambler had tried to cheat the young man, and Amos had pulled the Colt, fully intending to kill the man. Grabbed from behind, he'd had the gun wrestled from him and had received a knock on his head that had left him senseless until the next morning.

The crooked gambler had been put off at the next landing, and Amos had found his money back in his pocket when he'd finally awoke. The young man had realized how close he'd come to killing a man over his loss, and had vowed to control is temper in the future.

Amos sat on some bales of rags as he watched the travelers coming and going along the pier. A wagon driven by a man dressed in a dark suit, western-style boots, and a black, flat-brimmed hat with a silver band was coming his way.

The man's face was lined, showing his age. He was cleanly shaved and sported a thin moustache. Amos saw the .31 caliber Colt in a holster on his hip, and a Hawken rifle leaning on the seat beside him. Everything about the man said he didn't lack for money.

"You looking for a day's work?" the man driving the wagon hollered.

Acknowledging the man on the wagon, he replied, "Not really looking. What I need is to get to Independence and join a wagon train."

"You got money?" the man asked.

"Not enough, I'm a feared," Amos said,

shaking his head.

"Climb up, maybe I can help. That your mule? I can get you a good amount for it."

Tying Jenny to the back of the wagon, Amos climb up next to the man. "The mule's not for sale. My name's Amos Mudd."

"I'm Jon Tupperman, folks call me Jon T," the man said, flipping the reins to get his team going.

Adjusting his Colt Paterson and holster, Amos asked the man, "What kind of work you got?"

"I got a pile of supplies up the pier and need to get them loaded." Jon T replied.

As the wagon bumped along the pier, the young man sat impressed with all the goods piled along the side. Freight wagons were coming and going. He looked back at the steamboat he had arrived on as it spewed clouds of black smoke out its stacks as the paddle wheel churned the water, backing it into the river.

The wagon stopped in front of a stack of wooden boxes guarded by a red-faced security man. Jon T flipped him a gold piece and sent him on his way. "This here is whiskey out of Kentucky. There's a powerful thirst for it out near the mountains and I plan to bring it to them."

Laughing, he continued. "I can cut it by half with water and it is still better that the man-killing brews they sell out there. There are buffalo hunters, mountain men, and soldiers that will put up their hard-earned money for a good drunk."

Amos climbed down and moved his mule a short distance away. Hanging his holster and Colt over the saddle horn, he then began to load the crates of bottles onto the wagon. Removing his shirt, he continued to load the wagon, his long john top wet with sweat. It felt good to do the lifting. He had been sitting or riding too much.

Jon T was looking toward the mule when Amos finished. "Can you hit anything with those guns?"

"I can hold my own," the young man replied.

"You ever killed anyone?"

Taken aback by the question, Amos snapped, "Ain't none of your damn business. I loaded the wagon, now pay me."

Reaching into his pocket, Jon T apologized. "I didn't mean to pry, but I need a man to help drive and guard this wagon going out west. I'm looking for a man that isn't afraid to shoot if it comes to a firefight."

He held out a $5 gold piece. Amos looked at the man and said, "That's a hell of a lot of money for just loading your wagon."

"Consider it a down payment if you agree to go with me."

Taking the coin, Amos shoved it into his pocket. He then pulled the tobacco plug out of the shirt lying next to him and took a chew. He offered one to Jon T, who declined.

"I am headed for California. I had hoped to be in Independence a month ago, but things slowed me down. Does guarding your goods here include my meals?" the young man asked.

"It does, but that squirrel gun is a little light for the job. You wouldn't have means to get a Hawken or something like it?"

"Tell me where we meet and I'll be there with a .50 caliber," Amos replied. Then he added, "That is, if the pay is $40 a month."

"That, and a bonus if we don't have any breakage or theft." Jon T said, smiling. "I'll be a mile west of town. We leave in the morning to join up with Alberts' train in Independence. Suppers at five."

The young man arrived at the camp with a Hawken .50 in the scabbard. He had traded in the Leman and the lead balls in his shot bag. The Hawken had two triggers. The back one set the hair trigger on the front. He had a 33-inch barrel, making it easier to carry on the saddle scabbard.

Jon T had a pot of beans bubbling over his fire. Amos noticed that while he had two horses hitched to the wagon in town, he had three additional horses in camp. The freight wagon weighed down with the cases of whiskey would require a four-horse team for the trip across the plains. The extra horse would be used for riding.

While the two men started eating, Amos saw a covered wagon heading toward them. The man pulled the four-horse team up near the camp. "I got the supplies you wanted, Mr. Tupperman."

"Come and get something to eat, Albin. You can put the team up after supper," Jon T replied. "Albin, this here is Amos Mudd. He'll be going with us."

Thrusting his work-hardened hand out, he said, "Albin Doolittle is my full moniker. Folks other than Mr. Tupperman call me Doo."

Albin was dressed in buckskins that had seen better days. His wore low-heeled, calf-high boots. His jowls were covered with a week's growth of whiskers, and under the sagging, brimmed leather hat he had thinning white-hair.

Squatting next to the fire, the man filled his

plate with steaming beans. A Dutch oven near the fire had slightly dark biscuits. Reaching in, Doo fished out a couple and sat next to Jon T and began eating. Talking around a mouthful of biscuits and beans, he said, "Prices was up. This hot weather has caused some items to be scarce."

Jon T set his plate down and reached for the coffee pot, refilling his and Amos' cups. "As long as we got enough to get to Fort Kearny. We don't want to have to buy anything in Independence."

Noticing that Doo didn't have any coffee, Amos offered, "Can I get you a cup for coffee?"

Shaking his head vigorously, "Nah. Don't like the stuff. Makes me jumpy. Now this here Kentucky whiskey, that settles me down just fine," the old-timer said, laughing at his own joke.

After the meal was finished, Amos helped the old-timer unhitch the team. Doo reached into the wagon and pulled out a Hawken .56 caliber. It had been converted to percussion caps and was well scarred showing its age.

In the wagon Amos saw bags of rice, beans, coffee beans, and corn to be ground into meal. Keg barrels held flour, sugar, salt, dried meat, and hard bread. There were also several other items needed for living on the trail for the months to come. There were several bags of grain to supplement the horses' feed. While oxen and mules could live on the prairie grass, it wasn't enough for horses. Each wagon carried a water barrel on one side and a spare wheel on the other.

The young man's gear would also be stowed in the covered wagon to take the burden off the mule. Jon T had put a tightly fastened tarp over the wagon carrying the whiskey. Amos had noticed the different spelling of whiskey labeled on the cases. He had asked Jon T about that. He was told that the Scots and Canadians spelt it whisky, while the Irish and Americans spelt it whiskey. Why? He didn't know.

The sun was just coming up when they pulled out of camp. The leftover beans, coffee, and water had made a quick breakfast. It would take about two weeks to reach Independence. Doo and Jon T rode on the whiskey wagon, while Amos drove the covered wagon. The mule and extra horse were tied to the lead wagon with the two men. The young man was surprised at the amount of supplies that would be needed to make the trip.

During a brief meeting before leaving, Jon T had told them that they would be traveling fast and everyone was to keep their rifles loaded and ready at all times. They were not traveling with the safety of a train for the next two weeks, and the supplies and whiskey they carried would be a valuable target for thieves.

One other thing carried next to the riders in each wagon were English-made, 12-gauge double barrel shotguns loaded with buckshot. Amos was surprised by the arsenal Jon T felt he needed, but it did make the young man aware that they could be in for trouble along the way.

The well-traveled road was dusty, forcing Amos to put a cloth across his face. Throughout the day they passed several wagons heading west. There was one train consisting of 10 wagons. The leader asked Jon T if he wanted to join, but the boss man declined.

On the sixth day of travel, there were three horsemen under an oak tree, waiting near the road for them. Amos was riding the mule, while the other two were driving the wagons. The three men moved their horses into the road to prevent the wagons from continuing. Rocks and logs had been placed out from the side of the road to prevent a wagon from going around.

A crude sign said, "$5 each wagon." Doo pulled his wagon over on the right and stopped abreast the boss. Amos rode his mule wide on the left side. The men sat with rifles across their saddles. Their spokesman touched his hat and smiled. "You are about to go through the town of Kroft. The wagons tear up the road and the animals eat our grass. It will cost you $10 for the two wagons and another dollar for the man on the mule."

Amos noticed that both Jon T and Doo had moved their shotguns forward when they'd seen the riders. The young man had removed the loop off the Colt Paterson. Jon T tilted his hat back just a bit. "I don't recall a town out this way. Now move your horses and let us pass."

The young man's stomach began to churn. There was no doubt that the boss wasn't planning to pay any toll. "The town is legally registered in the territory and we are within our rights . . ."

In a quick movement, Jon T brought the shotgun up and pointed it at the bold toll takers. Without thinking, Amos drew his Colt. He noticed that Doo also had his shotgun out. The riders froze. They had been overconfident with their show of force and had let their guard down.

"Now, don't make me shed any of your polecat blood in this here town of yours," Jon T threatened. "You boys are wasting my time." With that he fired, shredding the sign and startling the men's horses.

One of the men tried to bring his rifle around and Amos fired, the ball striking the man's shoulder and knocking him off his horse. The other two men dropped their rifles and held their hands up.

"Albin, pick up their rifles," Jon T said, and then to the men, "We will leave your guns a way up the road. After you fix up your friend here you can come looking for them. We will also let the sheriff in the next *town* know about what you boys are doing here and I am sure he will be paying you a visit."

Doo climbed back into his wagon with the rifles and a revolver taken off the wounded man. Then the two wagons continued west while Amos kept his Colt on the toll takers. After the wagons were clear he followed them, keeping his Colt out until he had put some distance from the three riders.

"That was a hell of a shot, Amos," Jon T complimented him. "You saved the man's life. I was about to put a load of buckshot into him."

"You and me both," the old-timer said.

The young man rode tall in the saddle, enjoying the moment. Truth was, he had shot dead center on the man, but the movement of the robber's horse had made the bullet hit the shoulder. The men continued well after dark, to put distance between themselves and the toll takers. Amos noticed that they never dropped the rifles for the men.

It was late afternoon when the two wagons came within sight of Independence. Everywhere surrounding the town were wagons and cook fires going. People they passed waved and called out, asking what train they would be taking.

Jon T would holler back, "Jack Alberts'!" hoping they would point out where the train was.

The city was the starting point for the Oregon, California, and Santa Fe trails. Several buildings had signs offering goods for the wagon trains. Amos saw no less than three church steeples. Jon T stopped at a blacksmith shop. A man with scarred arms and a heavy leather apron was working on a glowing piece of steel. The smithy looked up, wiping his forehead with the back of his gloved hand.

"Can you tell me where Jack Alberts' train is?" the boss asked.

The apron-clad man struck the steel a couple more times and then stuck it back into the glowing coals of his forge. "Alberts is set up two miles south and west. When you see him, let him know I got the oxen shoes ready for him."

Amos followed his boss, driving the covered wagon. Jack Alberts was a tall, square-shouldered man with a matter-of-fact manner and white hair. Jon T had told the young man that the man had been guiding wagon trains since they first started crossing the South Pass going to Oregon.

Jon T wasn't going to Oregon or California. He was heading for the South Pass area, where he had set up a tavern not far from an area where many of the wagon trains stopped to rest and make repairs before the 300-mile trip to Fort Hall where the various trails would start to split.

Doo had been a trapper, but when the beaver pelt prices had dropped with the change from felt top hats to silk, he had hunted buffalo, bear, and even done some prospecting. The old-timer had thought about going to the gold fields of California.

Unlike Amos, Albin Doolittle knew what to expect when he got to California. This wasn't the first gold rush he had chased. The results were always the same. After backbreaking work, he would get enough gold to stay drunk and chase whores for a few months. Then he was back to looking for work to buy his next meal.

Jack Alberts ran the wagon train like a general. If one didn't like his rules, they were invited to leave or follow them. He was also smart. None of his trains had experienced cholera like so many others had. It was unknown what caused it, but 50% of those who got it died of dysentery.

Jack knew that where large groups shared the same watering spot the illness often thrived. He knew of less populated ones and adjusted his route. He understood how to set up a defense against Indian attacks and how to keep the train grouped in dangerous areas. And, most importantly, he could bring the trains safely through the passes.

The day after arriving at Independence, Jon T had Doo and Amos move the wagons to an area about a mile from Alberts and quickly set up a store selling extra goods from the covered wagon, and whiskey. For three days he sold or traded items from the wagon. He had Amos and Doo run the tavern area. Nobody complained about cutting the whiskey with water. One evening a couple of fiddle players showed up and played for their drinks. Some men brought tables and chairs and played poker.

The rifles that were taken from the toll takers were sold to needy emigrants. By the time they were ready to join Alberts' train and depart, Amos had a better understanding of why Jon T had so much money. Everything he touched made him a profit.

With lighter wagons and a heavier wallet, they

took their position in the wagon train and continued west. The boss had them rotate from driving to riding the mule or horse, and sometimes just walking. A canvas was tied under the covered wagon to hold buffalo chips or any bits of wood they found for the cook fire.

The grass-covered plains stretched out as far as the eye could see. The Platte wound like a ribbon through the plain, with occasional clusters of trees on its bank. Wild plums and choke cherries could be found in the brush lining the river. Travel was easy, but slow. The train could only travel as fast as the slowest wagon. Those pulled by oxen could only make about a mile and a half an hour.

At first they would see a few bison at a time in the distance. One morning they awoke to a sea of buffalo passing the train. Jack sent Amos and another man named Alan Woods to shoot and butcher one for fresh meat.

Amos took the Hawken .50 and rode toward the wall of woolly beasts. Alan led three pack horses to carry the meat back. Stopping 100 yards from the buffalo, Amos swung down from the mule. He offered to let Alan take the shot if he wanted to.

Woods shook his head. "I'm much better at cutting them up than killing them."

The young man saw one that was moving away from the others. It was curious of the movement that the men were making. It came within 50 yards and began to turn away. Amos's heart was pounding in his chest as he raised the Hawken. The buffalo in front of him was the largest animal he had ever seen. Pulling the set trigger, he settled down and aimed just behind the front shoulder. Letting his breath out slowly, he touched off the hair trigger.

The Hawken bucked against his shoulder. The buffalo turned, trying to run. After a couple steps it rolled to its side, and after a kick or two lay still. Amos wanted to run over and check his kill, but the rest of the buffalo were too close. He and Alan watched them for over a half-hour before there was enough distance between the herd and the felled buffalo to go in.

The young man knew that they should have cut the throat and bled the animal as soon as it was shot, but there was no way they dared to move in, even if the monster animal was alone, until they were sure it was dead. It took two hours to skin and cut the animal into small enough pieces to lift. They folded the hide and put it onto one horse. They loaded the best cuts on the other two horses.

Amos looked at the large amount of meat they couldn't take, that would be left to rot. It would feed the hungry wolves that followed the herd. The wagon train was out of sight by the time they were finished. Riding along the rutted trail, they caught up to the train near a fast-running stream an hour later.

The fresh meat was a welcome change after days of beans, rice, and dried meat. Amos brought the tongue back for Doo. The old timer promised that they were in for a treat. He skinned and sliced the meat and fried it with wild onions. As the young man chewed on the tough tongue, he couldn't quite say that it was a treat, but it was the best and first buffalo tongue he had ever eaten.

The hot sun burned down on the wagon train relentlessly as they slowly rolled across the expanse of grass-covered hills. Early one afternoon, Alberts stopped the train. A lone wagon was stopped a half-mile in front of them. Amos was riding his mule that day. He rode to the front to see what was going on.

Jack was swinging onto his horse. He turned the bay and rode toward the young man. "I want you to join me to find out what's wrong with the wagon ahead. If they're broke down we'll help them get going again. The two men rode abreast as they approached the wagon. A hatless man leaned against the wheel.

A hundred feet away, Jack held up his hand for Amos to stop. "What's your problem?" Alberts asked.

The man started walking toward them. "Stay put right where you are," Jack snapped.

The man halted. "Me and my family are low on water and food. We hoped we could join up with you. I got some money."

"Where's your train?" Jack demanded.

"We left them two days ago," the man replied. "They come down with a sickness and we left them right off."

"You are welcome to follow us, but keep your distance and camp alone. In a week, if you're all well, you can join us." Jack told the man.

"My boy, he might be sick. He can't keep nothing down. All we need is water and I'm sure he'll be okay," the man pleaded.

"It's probably cholera, mister," the wagon master warned. "You can't come with us. We will leave you some water and food, but if you try to follow us, my man here will shoot your animals."

To Amos he said, "I'll have two water barrels and a week's food left for these folks. More than likely they'll be dead before it's used up. You keep your distance, but don't let them follow us. Once we put a few miles between them, you come on and catch up."

Amos sat on the mule, stunned at the task before him. He watched Jack ride toward the train and wave them to come on. The young man pulled the Hawken out of its scabbard and held it across the saddle. The man returned to his wagon and stood there, his head hanging.

Jack had the food and water dropped off next to Amos and then he took the wagon train wide of the man's wagon. After the train had passed, the young man rode around to the west side of the wagon.

"You can't just leave us," the man begged.

Sitting on the mule, Amos wished he knew the words that could help lessen the fear he saw in the man's eyes. "Mister, you got food and clean water. If you got a bible, I would recommend you read it and pray real hard. Maybe by the grace of God, your son will get better."

Suddenly, the man ran around his wagon and pulled down his pants, relieving himself. Then, falling forward on his knees and elbows, he held his head and began to weep. In his heart Amos knew that Jack was right. This family wouldn't live to eat the food or drink the water.

Feeling helpless, the young man started the mule, following the wagon train. He prayed for the family as he rode. Frustrated, Amos kicked his heels into the mule's flanks, galloping toward the train, wanting to put what he had just seen behind him.

When Amos came alongside, Doo stopped the wagon so he could tie the mule to the tailgate and take over the driving. The two men sat quietly for a while. The old-timer took out his tobacco, cut a piece off and stuffed it into his cheek.

"It ain't right leaving them folks," Amos

complained. "They're alone out there sick and probably dying."

Sitting for a few minutes without comment, Doo spit before speaking. "It ain't being alone that will kill those folks. If that was so, President Polk would still be with the living. He had the cholera and was surrounded by folks but died just the same. There just ain't no cure for the sickness. Jack Alberts couldn't bring the sickness with us, and us sitting around them, possibly catching it our own selves, wouldn't keep them alive."

"Polk died from cholera?" the surprised young man asked.

"Sure did," Doo replied. "They say it was brung in by English or Irish emigrants. Now we got it on the trail with us. We'll bring it to Oregon and California."

What the old timer said made sense, but Amos still didn't feel right about it. It brought his thoughts back to his mother. One day he was helping her with the wash. The next day something went wrong inside her. Before his father got back with the doctor, she was gone. He had been sitting by her bed and she was rubbing his hair, telling him not to worry. Then she had stopped. Amos blinked back tears. He didn't want to think about that day anymore.

That night Jack held a meeting at the fire. He told everyone that they would arrive at Fort Kearny in another week and each wagon should check their supplies. It was the last chance to purchase any until Fort Laramie. Finishing with that business, he said, "Today we left those folks with the cholera behind. Riding away from the sick is one of the most difficult decisions I have to make. I'd like to ask all of you to remember them in your prayers tonight. 'That is all.''

Without waiting for any questions, he left, heading for his wagon. Amos slowly walked back to Jon T's wagons. The boss and Doo were busy lubricating the wagon wheel spindles. The young man picked up the tallow bucket and swabbed some on the dry spindle, so the two men could lift the wheel in place.

"Did Jack have anything interesting to say?" Jon T asked.

"Just to check our supplies before Fort Kearny and to pray for the folks we met."

Once the wheels were done, the three men sat near a small fire, keeping the coffee hot. Jon T was smoking a cigar, Doo a pipe, and Amos had a short, blunt cigar called a cheroot. Their meal that night had been boiled rice mixed with wild plums and honey.

"We need meat tomorrow," Jon T said. "Amos, you take my horse in the morning and get us some prairie chickens. We been flushing them regularly. You have been practicing with your Colt. See if you can hit anything."

Early that morning, the young man rode out ahead of the wagon train. He liked Jon T's horse. The tall chestnut had a smooth gait and stood 13 hands high. By mid-morning he had three birds in the game bag. The horse never flinched when Amos fired. He had stopped and was taking a drink from his canteen when he caught sight of movement near the tall switchgrass. A prairie chicken had ducked into the tall growth.

Turning the chestnut into the saddle-high grass, he hoped to flush one or more birds into the open, getting a shot. Carrying his Colt, barrel up, he anticipated the sound of their wings as they flew. All of a sudden, the horse sidestepped, and he felt something grab at him. He turned just in time to see an Indian swing up behind him and shove him violently off the chestnut.

The young man grabbed at the thief, but missed and fell to the ground on his back, hitting his head. Dazed from the impact, Amos couldn't have been down for more than a second or two because he could hear the hoof beats of the chestnut as it galloped away.

Struggling to sit up in the tall, tangled grass, he realized that he had dropped his Colt Paterson. With his head throbbing, he crawled around looking for the gun. Finding it, he stood up. The top of the grass was at his eye level. Jumping up for a better view, he was unable to see the thief.

"Damn! Come back here you son-of-a-horse thief!" the angry young man shouted. Rubbing the back of his head, he scooped up his hat and slammed it onto his head. Pushing his way through the switch grass, he made his way to the trail. Amos sat next to it, stewing over the theft, while he waited for the train to catch up to him.

Slowly, the wagons went by. Amos stood as he saw Jon T's. Running up to it, he tossed the game bag on top of the canvas-covered whiskey and then, grabbing hold, he climbed up into the seat. "Aren't you missing something, Amos?" the boss asked.

"I had the horse stolen. I was cutting through the tall grass, flushing birds and they were on me before I had a chance," the young man explained.

"The chestnut was a good horse," Jon T pointed out. "When someone uses something of mine, they are responsible for it. The horse was worth more than I'm paying you for working the trip. I like you Amos, so I am willing to figure we're even, or you can sign the mule over to me."

Trying to absorb what he had just been told, Amos asked, "In other words, if the mule was lost, you would owe me for it?"

"If I took your mule and it was lost, I would pay you it's value. If the wagons were attacked and stock was stolen or killed, each man would bear his own loss," Jon T explained.

"We need to go after the chestnut," Amos suggested. "They took it from us, we can take it back."

"At what risk?" the boss asked. "The Arapahoe or Cheyanne aren't going to give the animal up without a fight. We are a business, Amos. Most of the time we hope to make money. Some of the time we face losses. We need to accept the losses and learn from them."

Amos sat next to his boss, steaming. Jon T could afford to lose because he raked in the profits. Had he realized that he was responsible for the horse, he would have taken Jenny. After riding in silence for a while, Amos came to the conclusion that it was better to have lost the horse rather than the mule. He would give up the pay. He would still be well west at the end of the trip, and he was eating well.

He and Doo were sitting near the buffalo chip fire, drinking coffee and tea after supper. The old-timer took a long draw on his pipe and blew several smoke rings. "Have you thought about going after the horse?" he asked.

"Boss said we couldn't. There was too much risk," Amos said, disappointment in his voice.

"Depends who is taking the risk," Doo pointed out. "Jon T has little reason to go after the animal and end up losing more. You again, have little more to lose if you go after it and much to gain if you come back with it."

"And if I get killed?" the young man mumbled.

"Why hell, you still win. You no longer owe boss for the horse, and you wouldn't be working the rest of the trip." the old timer said, chuckling.

"You are just funning me, right?"

"I guess so," Doo replied. "I think I know where the horse is, though."

"You think you know?" Amos questioned.

"About a mile up there is a stream coming out of some sand stone cliffs. Maybe three or four miles up the stream the Arapahoe like to camp. They hunt and make jerky or pemmican. They trade it at Fort Kearny for things they need," the old timer said.

"You think I could just ride in there and take the horse with the whole damn tribe sitting and watching?" Amos snorted, spitting tobacco juice at a passing beetle.

"I figure it was a couple of young bucks watching the train for something to grab and run with. You stumbled into the waiting place and they thought, hell, why not take the horse," Doo said. "There ain't no reason you couldn't go into their camp and take the horse back. They probably wouldn't even kill you if you got caught, if you brought something to trade your life for."

The young man stood up. "I'm going to do it. Damned if I'm not."

The old-timer pulled a Colt from his belt and handed it to Amos. "In case I'm wrong and it turns into a fire fight, you'll need this."

Amos found a piece of paper and a stub of a pencil from his haversack. He wrote quickly and handed the note to Doo. The old man read it out loud. "I trade my good mule for the Colt, unless I bring the Colt back."

Sticking the paper into his shirt pocket, the old timer said, "Fair enough. If you come back, we trade back."

Amos stuck the Colt behind his belt and smiled. "Yep, that way if I don't come back, Jon T don't end up with the mule."

"You best come back though," Doo called after the departing Amos. "If you don't I will catch hell from Jon T."

The young man took Jake's knife and things to trade from the haversack and then walked toward the setting sun. He should be at the camp in less than two hours. If the Arapahoe weren't there, or another tribe had stolen the horse, he would only be out a little shoe leather and some sleep. If he got the horse, he had his pay back. Amos didn't want to think about the third option of him getting killed.

Just as the sun set, he reached the creek. A wagon train was camping near it. He walked wide around them. Jack had made him wary of any other trains. In the glow of their fire he could see a circle of people singing. The songs were hymns Amos was familiar with.

He climbed onto the sand stone cliffs and walked out onto the plain. The quarter-moon had just risen, offering enough light for Amos to avoid hazards next to the stream. An hour later, he caught sight of a fire. Taking his time, he moved toward the flickering light. He hoped it was the Arapahoe camp.

The stream near the camp had a grove of wind-stunted trees, undoubtedly why the spot had been chosen. Amos had always stalked when hunting. Now this ability could get him the horse or, if spotted, get him killed. The young man realized that the horse might not even be in the camp.

Hiding in the grass less than 30 paces from the fire, Amos looked for the Arapahoe horses. They had to be tied in the trees. He began to work his way around the camp toward the trees. From out of nowhere, two braves stood up from the grass, blocking the young man's way.

Both held spears ready to run him through. Amos was trapped, his right hand only inches from his Colt. Before he could pull it, one of the spears would stick him to the prairie dirt like butterflies to the board like he had seen at school in his youth.

The young man raised his hands to let them know he was giving up and then he pushed himself off the ground and stood looking at the fierce faces in front of him. With nothing to lose, Amos said, "I need to talk to your chief."

One of the braves moved around behind him and took both of the Colts and his knife. Amos still had his shot bag with the extra knife. Little good it would do against the two spears. The sharp point of the spear against his back started the young man toward the fire burning in the center of the camp.

Several men sat eating from earthen bowls. Two women were roasting meat over the fire. The two braves grabbed his arms and stood him in front of a brave who Amos guessed with their leader. The Colts and his knife were placed in front of the leader. They said something to him in Arapahoe.

Setting his bowl beside him and licking his fingers, the brave looked up. "You have come into our camp and interrupted our meal. Is it because you are hungry?" the leader asked, his voice heavy with sarcasm.

The young man had no idea what would happen in the next few minutes, but at least the leader spoke English and Amos could possibly reason with him. The best he could hope for was leaving with his life. His guns and knife now belong to the Arapahoe.

Amos decided that honesty might be best. "It was not right for me to come here the way I did. I should have just walked in. I would like to compliment your braves. They came upon me like a ghost. The reason I have come to see you is a horse was taken earlier and I think some of your young braves may have done this. My leader wanted to make a complaint to the commandant at Fort Kearny. It may cause trouble for you trading jerky and pemmican at the fort."

The leader spoke quickly to one of the braves who had brought Amos in. The man moved away into the darkness. He then spoke to the women and one of them brought a bowl with meat to Amos. The leader motioned him to sit.

Having no appetite due to the circumstances, Amos fished out a small piece of the meat and put it into his mouth. It was tender and juicy. Setting the bowl into his lap, the leader motioned him to continue eating. By the time that the young man had eaten the meat, he heard the brave coming back leading a horse.

Fighting the temptation to look back, Amos continued to look straight at the leader. The young man no longer knew if he was a guest or prisoner.

Maybe he had just been fed his last meal.

"Is this the horse you speak of?" the leader asked.

Amos looked at the chestnut. "This is the very one. It also had a saddle when taken."

"My son said you had fallen off the horse and they caught it in the tall grass and brought it here."

"They are correct, I did fall from the horse," Amos said, picking his words carefully. "I am responsible for the horse. If I do not bring it back, it will mean trouble for me."

"You come with many guns," the leader said. "Did you mean to harm us to get the horse?"

"I must admit, I was unsure of what to expect. I wintered with the Ojibwa in Michigan and learned much of your ways, but still have much to learn," Amos admitted.

"The Ojibwa are our friends. We trade with them. If I give you the horse back, what do I tell my son who caught and brought it here?" the leader wanted to know.

Amos now feared that he was about to lose the Colts and his knife. He asked, "May I take something I have brought for you from my bag?"

The leader nodded and Amos reached for Jake's knife. "I have brought this for the brave that found the horse." He then reached in again and took out four cheroots. "These I bring for you to thank you."

The leader stared at the young man, eyes unblinking. Amos breathed deep and once again reached into the bag and brought out Jake's silver flask. Holding it out in front of him, he said, "This gift came to me from a friend that died in my arms. He said it would watch over me and give me strong medicine. He would want a great man like you to have it."

The leader's eyes lit up. He took the flask and held it up in the firelight. He then removed the cork and smelled the contents. "It is filled with very powerful medicine called cognac that comes all the way from across the great sea beyond the sun," Amos said, pointing to the east.

The leader put the cork back into the flask and placed it next to the knife and cheroots. Again he spoke in Arapahoe to the braves. Shortly the man returned with the horse's saddle and bridle. The leader stood and told Amos to saddle the animal. Amos noticed that the blanket was missing.

Once the horse was saddled, the leader walked toward the stream and asked Amos to come with him. "My son was mistaken for not taking the animal back to you. I will tell him of your bravery and of the gifts you brought us. Who do I tell him you are?"

"Tell him I am a friend. My name is Amos Mudd."

"You can call me Okomi."

One of the braves that had caught Amos brought him the Colts and his knife. The young man climbed onto the chestnut and held his hand up, palm out. He then rode away from the camp, unsure of all that had happened. He regretted having to give up the flask, but he thanked God that he'd had it with him.

CHAPTER FOURTEEN

The look on Jon T's face when he saw the horse the next morning made the risk worth it. There was a look of respect on his face like Amos had never seen before. Many of the other men on the train looked at him differently.

After Jack had the wagons in order and underway, he rode back, next to the wagon with Amos and Doo. He rode without speaking for some time, like he was deciding what needed to be said. "That was a stupid stunt you pulled last night, Mudd. I have thrown men off my train for less. If I didn't need your gun and good men on this train, I would never overlook this."

Alberts rode away, heading toward the front of the wagon train. Doo rolled his chaw in his cheek. "I ain't sure what he said, but I think you just got a chewing with a compliment."

Fort Kearny was impressive, with a large parade ground and cottonwoods around the border. There were wagon trains camping for miles. Supplies were priced much lower than Independence. Amos was told that the fort was authorized to sell supplies to emigrants at their cost. No wagon was to leave the fort without enough supplies due to money.

Jon T took advantage of the low prices and purchased as much as the teams could pull. Amos expected him to set up his makeshift tavern, but Doo told him with the number of wagons, his stock would be gone before they left. Much of it might be stolen if everyone knew he had it.

The next morning the Alberts wagon train left an hour after sunrise. In the distance they caught a glimpse of another train that had left before them. Amos was driving the covered wagon while Jon T and Doo followed with the liquor wagon. It would take a month to reach Fort Laramie from Fort Kearney. Then it would take another month to make the South Pass. It was now the beginning of September. They would reach the South Pass in November. Amos had to accept the fact that he wouldn't be seeing California this year.

Once they arrived at Fort Laramie, they would only be halfway on their journey. Many of those in the wagon train would winter between the fort and South Pass. Jon T was only going as far as the South Pass area. Amos planned to stay with him and then start off alone for California as soon as the snow cleared in the passes. The wagon trains had to wait until the grass was plentiful enough for feeding the stock. His mule could feed on tree buds as well as what little grass they would find. It would put him a month ahead of the first trains.

A week out of Fort Kearny they arrived at the split of the Platte River. The North Platte River was the one they would be following. They would have to cross the South Platte. Jack decided to spend the night before crossing.

Amos and Alan accompanied Jack to check the crossings. Lack of rainfall had left the river low and would make it easier. The young man rode the mule across the river to check for any deep holes. The water wasn't over belly-high on Jenny. The bottom was muck, which would make pulling the wagons across more difficult.

Heading back to the wagon train, Amos spotted the ruins of several cabins. He rode the mule through the old compound and wondered who might have built them. The layout indicated it may have been a military encampment. There were only poles for the roofs. He guessed that they had had tarps stretched over them.

He caught sight of two apple trees in the brush near the river. Amos was pleased to find they had some fruit. Although fruit was scabby and had worms, not an apple was left to rot. That night the Dutch ovens emitted the wonderful aromas of apple pie and cobblers.

The first wagon across the next morning was Alberts'. His was more lightly loaded than many of the others. His mules struggled but pulled it across. The canvas top swayed back and forth due to uneven deposits on the river bottom.

A man named Tully and his wife had one of the heavier wagons. A mile downriver from the crossing was a ferry. There was a short debate over whether they should ride down and use the ferry or cross with the rest of the wagons. They decided to cross. Two additional oxen were added to the four pulling his wagon.

Amos rode ahead of the team with lead ropes to the first oxen. With his wife sitting next to him in the driver's seat, Tully shouted at the oxen and slapped them with a long switch. Amos had a harness on the mule, with the lead ropes tied to the tracings. He kicked the flanks of the mule to put tension on the lead ropes. His purpose was not to help pull the wagons, but rather to guide the oxen.

The six team oxen floundered and slipped on the muddy bottom. The front of the wagon dipped on the right side, and cloudy river water splashed on the man and his wife. As quickly as it had gone down, the wagon lurched back up. The back wheel following the same track hit the same hole. Tully was shouting and striking the oxen. His wife clutched her arms around her husband's stout middle, hanging on for dear life.

One of the middle oxen went down. The wagon stopped as the animal struggled to get back onto its feet. Finally it got up, and with Amos pulling the lead team and Tully shouting at the top of his lungs, the wagon moved across the South Platte River.

One by one the wagons moved across the river. Knowing where the dangerous spots were, they were avoided by the rest of the wagons. The wagon train camped another night on the west side of the river. Items in the wagons needed to be dried and the exhausted teams rested.

Amos spent time brushing the mule. It had made several crossings during the day. Jon T gave him some grain for Jenny. The young man also had a couple of the smaller apples in his pocket. Before heading back to the fire, he fed them to the mule.

"You worked hard today, girl. I won't ride you

for the next few days and let you have it easy," he promised the animal.

For the next several days the fall sun burned down on them. The relentless wind blew in their faces, giving the emigrants wind burn during the day and chilling them at night. The monotony of the slow travel across the plains was wearing on the members of the wagon train.

More than one fight broke out between drivers blaming each other for bumping, crowding, or taking more fuel for their fire than was needed. Any small personal difference could flare into something big. One evening Amos and Alan Woods were walking, checking on the stock. The sound of an angry voice caught their attention.

"Damn you, Chester," the man threatened. "You look at my wife like that and I'll skin you alive!"

The man, Chester, was a large, muscular man and not intimidated by the stocky husband, "You best take care of that woman or I will do it for you, Tully."

Tully, being the shorter of the two, had his dander up and was not thinking straight. Stepping toward the large bruiser, he snarled, "You take that back, you son-of-a-polecat! You take that back or I'll kill you!"

Alan and Amos were standing behind Tully, looking on with disbelief. Not far away was the man's wife, smiling. Many on the train considered the woman to be flirtatious. It was clear that she liked being fought over.

Chester spat and turned away when the stocky man pulled a gun from his waist band. Without hesitating, Mudd and Woods grabbed Tully, with the young man struggling to keep the revolver pointed at the sky while Alan tried to bring the stocky man to the ground.

The sound of the revolver firing was loud in the circle of wagons. Amos twisted the gun from the man's hand before he could fire again. The white-faced Chester stood looking on in shock. "Tully, you bastard! You were going to shoot me!"

He came at them as the two men got the disarmed Tully to the ground. "Stop right there Chester, or I will shoot you myself!"

It was Jack, coming on the run, bristling with anger. Jack told both wagons that they would be leaving the train at Fort Laramie. If anything else happened in the meantime, they would be left behind to fight it out that very day. Alberts then walked by the wife, glaring at her. She was no longer smiling.

The two men got up, leaving Tully lying on the ground. Brushing themselves off, they continued to check on the stock. "She is a damn pretty one, ain't she," Alan said.

Glancing back at the wife, Amos agreed. "Pretty, but trouble. You take on a woman and she will give you comfort. But with it comes a whole new set of problems. You end up right back on the potato farm."

Confused, Alan looked at his friend. "Potato farm?"

Two days later the camp awoke to find Chester's wagon was gone. The man had stopped a few miles early to fix something on his wagon. He'd told Jack he'd be along shortly after dark. Nobody remembered him coming in. Everyone noticed that along with the wagon being gone, so was Tully's wife. The stocky man stood looking at the back trail while the rest of the camp had breakfast and started to get the wagon hooked up.

Jack came back to find out if Tully was going after her. "I should have killed him, Jack. It would have been less trouble for him than she will be. I'm going with you."

A week from Fort Laramie someone pointed out a low cloud on the horizon. Jack galloped his horse to a rise to have a look. Wheeling the horse around, he hurried back shouting, "It's a fire! Get off your wagons and grab your powder!"

The trail was around 120 paces from the river. The men were ordered to spread gunpowder in the grass along the trail and ignite it, setting the grass ablaze. While the men lit the grass, most using their firearms, the women and children were wetting blankets in the water barrels. The wind rapidly pushed the fire through the grass, burning toward the river.

The wildfire tearing across the grasslands was quickly gaining on their position. The wagon train could see flames taller than their wagons marching across the plains. Thick black smoke billowed high into the air in front of the fire. Once the fire they'd set reached the river, the nervous animals pulled the wagons onto the burned-off area close to the river.

"Grab anything that carries water and get it from the river and wet down your canvas and wagons!" Alberts shouted.

Jon T yelled at Amos and Doo, "Wet the liquor wagon first!"

Chains were set up, people passing buckets to the wagons and wetting them down. The horses and oxen were staked down between the wagons and the river with short lead ropes. Amos tied the mule to the back wheel of their covered wagon.

Doo pointed to a group of wagons racing towards them just ahead of the smoke and fire. The emigrants with Alberts' train watched in horror as the smoke enveloped the trailing wagons, which turned toward the river, going right over the bank and piling up below. The smoke covered the devastation and the roar of the fire masked the screams of the animals and the people.

"Get down close to the ground and cover yourselves with the wet blankets!" Jack shouted.

Amos lay with his soggy blanket over his body and closed his eyes as the thunderous sound of the fire reached them. It was as though the air around him had been sucked away and replaced by smoke. Burying his face into the crook of his arm, he struggled to breathe, coughing as his lungs seemed to fill with smoke.

His wet blanket was being torn at by the winds created by the fire. Amos grasped at it to pull it back over himself. It took only moments for the raging fire to sweep by the wagon train, but to the young man it seemed an eternity.

He was sure that he was going to die when the blanket covering him was pulled away. A soot-covered face was shouting at him to stand up. It was Jack. He was running from person to person, checking to see if they were okay. The air was still filled with smoke, but Amos was able to breathe. His throat and lungs were raw from the ordeal.

The grass fire had claimed the lives of two children and one man on Alberts train. Several people were suffering from the effects of the smoke and might take days to recover. Jack's quick actions had saved the wagon train from sure destruction.

The golden grass of the plains was blackened as far west as he could see. Everything around the wagons was blackened by the ash. One of the oxen had to be put down due to burns. It was butchered to save the meat.

As the wind blew the smoke clear from the smoldering grass, the tangled mess of the group of wagons that had gone over the bank became evident. Amos and several of the men led their animals toward the carnage. They passed two wagons that had turned away from the river and had been overtaken by the flames.

The blackened animals lay dead, still harnessed to the charred wagons. The canvases had burnt off, and the bodies of the occupants lay in and around the wagons. When Amos turned one of the bodies over to check for life, the area underneath was unburned and the unseeing eyes of a young woman looked up at him.

Shaken, Amos moved to another, looking for survivors. Had there been any alive, they would have died from the burns in a matter of days. After the men checked the wagons, they continued to the river. The cries of trapped people could be heard. Several dazed occupants of the wagons sat on the bank, many burned severely.

Climbing among the wreckage, the men helped desperate people, freeing them by lifting the wagons or using the animals to pull them over. A dazed woman mumbled, "There were 62 of us this morning."

"Where is the leader?" the young man asked.

"Mr. Waxman. Fire caught his wagon first," she replied without expression.

Amos looked around. He counted only 12 huddled on the bank and he doubted that they would find many more alive in the river. In the distance he saw a couple of wagons that had tipped before the fire caught them. The rest of the afternoon was spent pulling what they could from the river. Some of the bodies had been pushed into the silt-covered bottom of the North Platte River, never to be seen again.

Two of the wagons that had been pulled out of the wreckage could be used. Some of the men had hitched their oxen to them and went west to collect the bodies of those who had not reached the river.

The dead recovered from the unfortunate Waxman wagon train totaled 37. Those found alive totaled 16, although burns that some had received could still be fatal. If the dazed woman was correct, there were still nine missing. There was the chance that the panicked teams had pulled them further out onto the plain. More than likely they would never be found.

Many of the animals had broken free, running in front of the fire or swimming out into the river to get away. One team of oxen stood on a small island in the middle of the river, still in their harnesses. Those injured in the wreckage of the wagons had to be shot. One oxen was dragged out to feed the survivors. The rest were left to be scavenged by the plains animals.

Salvaged blankets were used to wrap the bodies. Jack had taken charge of the occupants of both wagon trains. Shallow graves were dug alongside the trail. More than one body went into each grave. Some of the survivors searched for their departed before they were buried. None of the graves were marked. Jack Alberts said brief words over the dead.

In the next few days five additional graves were dug for those who died from their burns. The sounds of weeping and cries of pain could be heard day and night. Amos fought the feeling of guilt from having seen their train sustain little damage. The canvas covers had some holes where larger embers had landed on them.

Future rains would wash the soot from the wagons and plains. Time would wash the memories of the tragedy from all but those who had endured it. Grass fires moved rapidly across the ground, using the oxygen to fuel their fury. Immediate death by smoke inhalation or suffocation took most of the victims. Burns from the heat of the flames killed more slowly. Jack had been aware of this and knew what to do to save his wagon train.

It was over a week before the wagons rolled toward Fort Laramie. Two days of rain helped cleanse the blackened plain, offering a hint of green. It would be next spring before the blackened switchgrass and big blue stem would regrow.

While Alberts' train recovered and helped the other wagon train, several passed them moving slowly by, some asking if they needed anything, but none stopped when the answer was no. Once underway it took just a day before they drove out of the blackened prairie and were again surrounded by the golden fall grass.

It was another day to Chimney Rock. As they passed the 300 feet-high wonder, hope was renewed. The train had traveled one-third of the emigrant trail to Oregon or California. Jack camped the night on the trail, which passed on the north side of the rock. It also meant that they were only five days from Fort John, also known as Fort Laramie.

The fort was built on the west side of the Laramie River where it met the Platte. The white walls of the fort finally came into sight across the river. Several buildings offering supplies sat next to the main fort. Like the South Platte, the Laramie River was also low. Jack planned to stay on the east side of the river to winter, which has better grazing and areas to camp. Prior to the spring floods, he would move the train to the west side in preparation to continue west.

Jack asked for volunteers to take the worst burnt people across and find a doctor. Jon T offered Amos and Doo. Turning to the men, he smiled. "We will only be here a couple days. I thought you might want to spend the night near the fort and shake out a few kinks."

"If you insist, boss," Amos replied.

One of the wagons from the burned-out train had been used to carry the four burned emigrants. Three of them were lone survivors, and another was accompanied by her husband. Looking forward to a night out, the two men drove the wagon pulled by a team of mules.

Many of the wagons from the burned train had money boxes in them. In most cases there were no survivors. This money was being kept by Jack Alberts to purchase supplies for the survivors. He gave Amos some money to pay the doctor and for the livery to put the mule team up for the night.

Doo and Amos checked at the fort about a doctor. They were directed to a small clapboard building a short distance from the fort. A sign hanging in front said, "*Doctor Herbert Ward.*" Pounding on the door, a voice beyond told them to come in. Pushing the door open, Amos saw the ruddy-faced doctor with gray hair sitting at a small desk. A sturdy wooden chair used for pulling teeth stood in the middle of the room.

When to the doctor learned what had happened, he hurried outside to see the patients. Looking into the wagon, he ordered, "Help me get these people into my office."

He had a couple of beds at the back of the room, behind a curtain. The worst were placed on the beds, while the others sat on chairs in the office. Snapping instructions, the old doc had Amos, Doo, and the husband of the woman busy assisting him as he began to work on the injured.

Two hours later he had another bed behind the curtain, and the three people, two men and one woman who had nobody left, lay in them. The wife had burns on her arms and some broken ribs. Doc Ward sent them to stay at a boarding house.

Sitting in the office with Doo and Amos, the old doctor ran his fingers through his tangled gray hair. "I can't do much for the middle fellow. I gave him laudanum for pain. His burns are infected. I would be surprised if he lasts until morning."

The bad news had little effect on the two men. While they wished that the doctor could do something, they didn't know the patient and had a night out waiting for them. Amos and Doo sat in Doc Wards office, wondering how long they were supposed to stay.

The doctor had continued to work at his desk. Looking back up at the two men, he said, "You may as well go. Nothing more can be done. Come by in the morning and I'll give you an update."

The two man almost stumbled over each other trying to get out of the office. Amos stopped just before closing the door. "Let us know what we owe you and we can settle up tomorrow." Slamming the door, he hurried after Doo.

After bringing the mules to a livery, they headed for a saloon on the Laramie River below the fort. The place was a two-story building called the Elk's Head. Doo led the way in and went straight to the bar. A man in a stiff white shirt and a half-apron tied under his belly was running a rag over the well-polished bar.

Turning to the men, he slung the rag over his shoulder and asked, "What'll it be boys?"

"Hell," Doo said, "I ain't been called a boy in a long time. We'll take a bottle and we are looking for some ladies."

Setting a bottle of rye down in front of them, the bartender slicked his greased hair back with his hands before speaking. "They'll be down in about an hour. I can go hurry a couple if you want."

"No hurry," the old-timer said. "Just point the madam out to me when she comes in."

Amos lit a cheroot with the low burning lamp on a pole near the bar. Doo poured the rye at their table. Holding the glass high, he said, "Let's drink to a night we won't remember."

The rye had a bite to it. The young man looked around the room. Four men were playing cards near the window. Another was slumped over a back table, sleeping.

The Elk's Head had some cheese and bread at the end of the bar. After a couple drinks, Amos's stomach was growling. He went and made himself a thick sandwich. He ordered a beer to wash it down. He talked to Doo about California.

It had been over a year since Amos had left the farm in Maine. He knew that he should already be panning gold along the banks of the American River. He had traveled over 2000 miles and still had another 1000 to go. He planned to travel alone when he left the south pass in the spring. That would put him in the gold fields by the end of July.

He was asking Doo how long it would take to pan a good amount of gold when the door opened on the second floor. Six ladies slowly came down the stairs, looking over the room. Nine more men had come in since Amos and Doo. Three had started a card game and the others leaned against the bar.

The old-timer slapped his knee. "By jingles, here they are."

The bartender called one of the ladies over. Speaking low to her, he pointed to Doo and Amos. Smiling, the buxom, brown-haired woman motioned to one of her girls and walked over. "Abe at the bar says you are looking for the best in the house."

The middle-aged blond woman sat next to Amos and cooed, "Buy me a drink and I will take you to places you've never been before."

The night got wild with drinking and even dancing. Before the two men were too drunk to walk, the ladies took them upstairs. When Amos awoke he was sleeping in the hayloft of the livery. His head was pounding and he was fighting the urge to vomit. A few feet away he could hear the snoring of Doo.

The young man crawled to the edge of the loft and hung his legs over. He held the back of his aching head with both hands. Flashes of the merriment the night before went through his mind. How he'd got to the loft, he couldn't remember.

Coughing and a groan alerted him that Doo had awaken. "Mighty oh James," the old-timer croaked. "That was one hell of a night, me boy."

Doo sat next to Amos, rubbing his face vigorously. He looked at the young man. "Looks like that there woman rode you hard, son."

Amos just groaned and leaned forward. Suddenly, the young man exclaimed, "Where the heck are my boots?"

Looking over the edge at Amos' stocking feet, Doo shook his head. "I can't remember if you had 'em or not when I helped drag you over here."

"Dragged me over?"

"Yep. You were fast asleep in the blond one's bed and she needed you out for another customer," the old-timer explained.

Amos felt himself blushing. Evidently he had lost control last night. Then he thought about his money. The belt was still around his waist. He was thankful that it wasn't empty. Slowly he counted, then snorted, "Damn night cost me half month's pay."

Doo swung onto the ladder and said as he climbed down, "I could go for a big breakfast. Let's go to the café near doc's."

"What about my boots?" Amos complained.

"You been barefoot before," the old timer said. "We'll check at the saloon after we eat."

Amos looked around before climbing down. "Damn hat's missing too!"

The young man had coffee and sweet bread while the old-timer drank buttermilk and wolfed down a steak served with eggs. The thought of tackling a breakfast like that turned Amos's stomach. He could smell the sickening sweet smell of the woman's perfume on his clothes and beard. He vowed that he would have a bath before leaving the fort.

Sitting on the end of the bar were Amos' boots and hat. The tired-looking bartender sat drinking coffee and pointed to them. "Leanna said they were yours."

Embarrassed again, Amos sat on a chair, brushed the dirt from his woolen socks and pulled the boots on. He noticed that the seam on one side had split, no doubt when he was kicking his heels up on the dance floor. Planting his hat onto his head, he asked the bartender to thank the lady.

They went to Doc Ward's to check on the patients and settle up. The old sawbones was adding wood to his small stove. "Kinda cool this morning."

The young man leaned against the rugged wooden chair. "How are the folk we brought in?"

A broad grin spread across the doctor's face. "A little better than you by the looks of it," he snickered.

"I didn't have much hope for the one fellow when you brought him to me, but he looks better today and there is less fever," the doc said, sharing the good news with them.

"We got to head back across to the wagon train," Doo told the doc. "We are supposed to settle up with you."

The old doc hemmed and hawed for a moment before answering. "Right now the charge would be $10, but these are hurt folks and the amount owed will go up."

"Fair enough," Doo replied. "I'll give you $20 now and you can settle up with Alberts' wagon train if there are any more charges."

The young man was glad to be out of the doc's office. The antiseptic smell mixed with the smells of infected flesh were unpleasant to his sensitive stomach.

"I need to find a bath, Doo," Amos told the old-timer. "I got to get this stink off me."

It was late afternoon when the two men arrived back at the wagon train. Jon T has cooking something in a pot over the fire. "Bring the wagon and mules back, and by the time you finish this pemmican and bean soup will be ready."

The young man's stomach had finally settled and the soup sounded just fine. Doo jumped off to talk with Jon T while Amos turned the mules toward the Waxman group. He told them what the doctor had said and about the husband and wife staying at the boarding house.

Upon his return, Amos found Jack talking with Jon T. The wagon master was trying to convince him to stay at the fort for the winter. By the time he reached his tavern near the South Pass the trappers would be in the mountains and there wouldn't be much reason to be there.

Jon T shook his head. "I got people waiting for me and these supplies."

"You got another month to South Pass. November often brings snow. You shouldn't take the chance of getting stranded on the high plain in a blizzard," Jack warned.

Giving up, Jack left to check on the rest of the wagon train. The boss told Amos that they would only be staying one more day, to pick up a few supplies and give the animals a little more rest and good feed. Doo had already told the boss about their night in town.

Jon T smiled when Amos sat near the wagon wheel. "You up to a meal tonight?"

"You damn right I am. I could eat the bark off

a tree."

That night Amos lay next to the wagon in his blankets, the cold north wind doing its best to get to him as he looked at the stars. The schoolmaster back in Maine had told him he would see the same stars as he traveled west. He knew that he'd been right, because the North Star and the dippers were still above him. He wondered if his father was looking at the stars tonight.

While he never wanted to go back to potato farming, he did miss his father. After he found the gold in California, he would travel back and visit. All of a sudden, he made a decision. Tomorrow he would write a letter to his father and mail it from the fort before they left.

The next day Jon T had them drive the wagons across the river to purchase supplies, Amos walked to the fort and mailed the letter. It was a dollar for sending it. The letter was much shorter than he had planned. He did say he would be wintering at the South Pass.

As the man dropped the letter into a bag behind the counter, Amos felt good. It was almost like he had talked to his father. He had closed with the promise that he would be back. The young man left the fort and headed back toward the wagons. He was anxious to get back to the supply house, because he had to get another pair of boots before they went. Water had soaked his sock this morning, reminding him of the ripped sole when he had stepped into a puddle before crossing the river.

As he passed the Elk's Head, he heard the sweet voice of Leanna calling to him from an upstairs window. Pulling his hat down, he blushed again as he hurried by. Jon T had considered traveling on the north side of the Platte River for a while. Unsure of a good place to cross, he'd decided to stay on the south side.

The next morning after saying their goodbyes, the two wagons left Jack Alberts wagon train and continued west. The men of the wagon train had already started to set up shelters for the coming winter. The sounds of chopping and hammering filled the air.

Amos was wearing his pea coat to fend off the cold north wind. It was the first week of October and snow wasn't far away. The wagon train only traveled 15 miles each day. Without having to travel at the speed of the oxen, they could make as much as 25 miles a day.

From Fort Laramie to the South Pass the elevation continued to rise. The trail was also filled with more hills and valleys, plus small rivers and streams to cross. The Sweet River alone would be crossed six times. The first day out, they traveled through a rock cut that had depressions worn by the iron rims of the wagon wheels. The stone would preserve the marks as a testament to the many wagons that had traveled west.

Being more vulnerable traveling alone, Jon T instructed the men to keep the shotguns and their rifles loaded at all times. They also had their revolvers at the ready. As they traveled the taller grass started to disappear as they began traveling the high desert area with sparser grass and sage brush.

Jon T's horses need some grain every day. Amos' mule did just fine foraging on the variety of high plains plants available. It wasn't long before Amos wore the tuque at night to keep the cold off his head.

The high desert lost its heat quickly during the night.

Six days into the trip they camped at the sight of the ferry operated by the Mormons each summer. There were vacant buildings on the south side of the river that were used for living quarters. It was three more days before they camped at Independence Rock.

Doo and Amos walked up to the 130 feet-high humped rock. It was over a quarter of a mile long. The old-timer pointed to the names chiseled into the stone. "Emigrants have put their names into this rock for years. Wagon trains are supposed to reach here by July 4th to make it over the mountains before winter." Chuckling, he continued, "Damn glad we don't have to go over the mountains this year."

Amos looked at all the names and wondered how many of them were in the California gold fields. He stood there wishing that he had been here in July. While waiting for supper, the young man brushed the mule. "I sometimes worry that we won't ever see California," he told the mule. "Everything has taken longer than I planned."

Rubbing the mule between its ears, he said, "I know you don't understand what I am saying but I just needed to tell this to someone."

CHAPTER FIFTEEN

For several days they'd had a band of Cheyenne shadowing them. Jon T figured that they were looking over the horses. "Hell," he said, "if they knew how much liquor we had in the wagon, we wouldn't ever be able to stop them."

"Yep, we would be quite the haul with whiskey, horses, and our guns," the old-timer agreed.

The men started to take turns standing watch at night. The animals were kept close, to make them easier to protect. Everyone slept with their rifles and revolvers at the ready. Doo had just relieved Amos for the last watch and the young man had barely gotten into his blankets for a couple more winks when there was an ear splitting sound from the plain.

The Cheyenne swept down on the camp just before sunrise, trying to scatter the horses and mule. The animals were tied to a picket line strung between the two wagons. Doo fired the shotgun, knocking one of the braves from his horse. Amos ran stocking-footed with his Hawken in one hand and the Colt in the other. The sound of arrows striking the low brush and wagons were everywhere.

Amos emptied the Colt Paterson at the charging braves as they rode by again. One dropped his bow as a bullet creased his arm. The young man tried to sight in on the departing braves with the Hawken. He fired, doubting he'd hit anything.

The sound of the panicked horses drew their attention. Jon T ran to calm them, and came back swearing. "They got two of the damn horses."

The attack turned out to be a diversion. While they were defending from the attacking braves, others had come in and cut two horses from the picket line. Doo sat looking out into the darkness, his shotgun at the ready, "Well-played you son-of-a-bitches, well-played."

The mule was added to the liquor wagon team. Its reward would be getting grain each day with the horses. The Cheyenne seemed satisfied with the two horses and weren't seen again.

The wagons arrived at the tavern the last week of October. A light snow was falling from the overcast sky. Amos was wearing his high-cut boots. The tavern was a long log building with a cedar shingle roof. It had a long, wide porch in front, facing west to watch the sunset. The main room was the tavern and trading post.

The south wall had several small rooms with blankets covering the doors. A large fireplace was on the north wall. A small, open kitchen had a nine-plate stove for heat and cooking. Shelves were filled with items needed by emigrants or trappers. Amos noticed that the prices were higher than Fort Laramie. A plank bar ran out from the wall near the fireplace.

Jon T's trading post survived because Fort Hall had refused to sell to those going to Oregon in the past and Fort Bridger was another two weeks for a wagon train. The boss knew of sheltered valleys if a train had to winter. Timber was available for fuel and the trading post had supplies. This trip was Jon T's last before winter. It would be June before he needed to send wagons to replenish.

Behind the tavern was another log building that stabled the animals. Stacks of hay were piled next to the building to feed them. Amos and Doo put the horses and mule into box stalls. Against one wall were five milking cows.

Next to the barn was a three-sided building with a forge, and boxes filled with horse and oxen shoes. The two-piece oxen shoes were needed due to the cloven hooves. An anvil sat next to the forge and metal working tools hung on the wall. A tarp could be pulled down in the winter to keep snow out.

Amos walked back into the tavern and saw four women sitting at a large community table with Jon T. He had just given them gifts purchased in Independence. A man was stocking the bottles of Kentucky whiskey under the bar.

The boss called to the young man, "Amos come here and I'll introduce everyone. The ladies are Hazel, Uma, Tilly, and Shelly. The fellow putting away the whiskey is Stan."

Shelly had light brown hair and breasts pushing out of her dress. She leaned forward and told the young man, "If you want anything, let me know and I will tell the girls."

Amos felt trapped. He was at the table and had no good excuse to leave. "I appreciate that, Shelly."

Finally, Doo came in and shouted his hello to the girls and Stan. "I'm in the mood for some buttermilk, Tilly. The cows are looking healthy. Hope they're milking well."

"Their milking just fine Albin," she said, her whole face smiling.

Jon T sent the woman away, wanting to talk with Doo and Amos. "You men did a great job on the trip. Albin, I imagine you want your wages in supplies, like usual."

"I'll be needing them for trapping," the old-timer agreed.

"With bonus, you will have $50 credit in the trading post. Now, don't waste it all on Tilly," Jon T suggested.

Amos had thought that Doo worked full-time for Jon T. It turned out that he needed work and meals for the summer and had taken the trip.

He looked at Amos. "I promised you $40 and a bonus if things went well. You did your job well, so there is a $10 bonus. I do have to deduct the horse blanket you lost when the chestnut was taken. $2 should cover it. Then there was the advance I gave you in Missouri."

"Wait a minute," Amos objected. "Part of that was for loading the wagon and I would have still had all $5 if I didn't come to work for you."

"Okay then. Do you want it in supplies?" the boss asked.

The young man was taken aback. He hadn't thought about winter or needing food. He had just assumed that he would be here doing some kind of work for food and a bed. "Supplies . . . supplies I guess."

The old-timer slapped him on the back. "Hell yes, he'll need supplies. We're going trapping for the winter. Come spring we will sell you our furs if the price is right."

Confused for a moment, he agreed with Doo, "Yes, I'll need supplies . . . for trapping."

"Well fine," Jon T said. "Albin will show you were to store your gear until you leave."

Carrying his bedroll, haversack, and his saddle bags, the young man followed Doo back to the barn. There was a small tack room off the barn. The three-sided building leaned against the sidewall with a sloping roof. There were two bunks built against the back wall.

"I leave the door open and the heat from the animals keeps it comfortable in here," the old timer informed him.

"When do we go trapping?" Amos asked.

"I figure we spend about a week resting and spending a little time with the ladies, then we leave. I want to head for the Yellowstone area," Doo informed the young man. "I got a cabin in the area."

Brushing the dust off a shelf, Amos placed his haversack and saddle bags there. He rolled his bedding along the upper bunk. At least he wasn't sleeping in the weather, the young man figured.

The week of getting ready was more enjoyable than Amos had expected. The days were busy selecting items that they would need and putting them into packs. Amos couldn't help but notice that Jon T charged them his regular prices. The nights were filled with storytelling, rye, and getting to know the ladies.

Amos was concerned about the dent it was putting into his money belt. Doo told him not to worry. They would make $5 for each wolf skin, $1 for most small furs, $3 for mink and fishers, and for the claws, head, and hide of a grizzly they would make $20, maybe more.

A Crow woman came to the trading post to sell items she had made. Doo suggested the young man buy buckskins. Amos also ended up with calf-high moccasins and a possible bag. He still had to get a pack saddle for the mule.

Jon T had a sawbuck pack saddle hanging on the wall. The young man asked about trading his riding saddle for the pack saddle. "You know this is a well-built sawbuck," the boss informed him. "Your saddle has had some tough days. Most I figure I can repair, but it will cost me."

Feeling like his back was against a wall, Amos asked out of frustration, "Damn it, Jon T. What will it take for me to get the sawbuck?"

The boss scribbled on a piece of packaging paper with a stub of a pencil for a moment. "I will lose on this deal, you should know. And I already lost when you bought the buckskins from the Crow. If you throw in the scabbard, $10 and your saddle for the sawbuck pack saddle."

"I need the scabbard, Jon T," the young man said, feeling a little hot under the collar.

A wounded look crossed the boss' face, "I'm giving you a fair deal here, Amos. It hurts me to think you don't believe me."

Both men sat in a locked stare for a long moment. All of a sudden, Jon T's face broke into a broad smile. "I like you Amos. It goes against me, but I'm going to let you keep the scabbard. Maybe you'd be willing to throw in the haversack. A mountain man doesn't carry one. They're for town folk."

"Jon T, we got a deal and I will shake on it," Amos conceded, "but I want you to know I will be counting my fingers after we shake."

The young man took the sawbuck and headed for the barn. Doo followed close behind. "I wouldn't let Jon T bother you, Amos," the old-timer said. "With the boss it is the dickering, not the deal, that he enjoys. When he came back with you he told me he offered you a job guarding and driving back here. I told him we don't need another man. He said he knew that, but the man needed a ride."

"Don't get me wrong, Amos. You more than carried your weight on the trip from Missouri, but I just wanted you to know what kind of man your dealing with."

Suddenly, the frustration left the young man. "Did you hear him call me a mountain man? Damn, that sounded good."

There was a small log building a short walk from the trading post, near a clear running spring. The outer room was a dressing room. The inner room had a small fire place with stone sides. A small reservoir held hot water. Benches built at three levels were on the wall across from the door and fireplace.

Jon T had said it was a sauna. He had met another trader named Franklin, south of the pass, who had built one. By throwing water onto the heated stones, steam was created. After a good sweat, they would use cold spring water mixed with the heated water to wash.

It was the third week of November when the two men led their mules away from the trading post. They had enjoyed a good, hot steam bath the night before. Doo and Amos were pleasantly surprised when Tilly and Shelly joined them.

Jon T, the ladies, even Stan, stood outside in the early morning chill and shouted goodbyes. The mountains in the distance were white. The four inches of snow in the pass crunched under their moccasins. Promises had been made that they would come back in the spring and trade their furs with Jon T, not with Fort Bridger or Fort Hall.

The old-timer set the pace as they walked north. He had told Amos that it was slow enough to prevent them from sweating and fast enough to cover some miles. Amos asked Doo if they would be trapping any beaver.

"Was a time when we got $4 for a good pelt. Then the silk hats made our pelts worth only $1. We won't be going after beaver," the old-timer assured the young man. "Was a time, though when beaver was king. A man could spend a winter trapping and need two, three mules to bring out his catch. We would come out of the mountains and go to the green river, Popo Agie, Wind River, or where ever the rendezvous was being put together. Many tribes would be there with their firs. There was drinking, dancing, foot races, knife throwing, and all kinds of good fun."

"You could find a woman for the night or if you wanted, to marry. There was every kind of thing a trapper would need for the next season. You'd come in and set your furs down and walk away with a pocket full of money. Too often you would leave with supplies and empty pockets. But we always left looking forward to next year."

As the two men walked, Doo kept up a constant stream of stories of the old days that the young man enjoyed hearing. They made simple camps at night, keeping their fires small. Most of the time, Doo would drink tea in the evenings while Amos drank coffee.

The young man had seen mountains in Maine and New Hampshire, but never the likes of what he was traveling through in Wyoming. The majestic peaks rose far into the heavens above the trappers. Amos took in every wonder, hoping to never forget them.

They reached the Wind River on the third day. The old-timer told Amos that they were in Crow, Shoshone, and Flathead territory. Most tribes would be in their winter camps by November and shouldn't cause any problems. They followed the river northwest, with plans to cut over to the Snake River.

The young man had heard that this range was a destination for trappers after beaver. He felt chills knowing that he was following the same trails walked by the many early mountain men he had read about in a magazine published out of Portland, Maine. His father would scold him because he would read and reread the articles over and over, shirking some of his chores.

Jedidiah Smith, Jim Baker, Liver-Eating Johnson, Jim Bridger and so many others had called the Wind River Range their home during the winter. Doo frowned and remembered, "When we learned that the summer of '40 was the last rendezvous, it was like they took Christmas from us."

The two men continued to climb. Amos spotted something white on a ledge ahead of them. "Doo, would you like some fresh meat?"

Smiling, the old-timer shook his head. "I figure you could hit the sheep, but look down into the valley. We would spend a day or more getting to the other side to fetch it. And then it might get caught on one of them crags and be impossible to get to."

When they reached an area where the land fell away, Doo pointed to the long valley. "We call it the 'hole'. It got elk, buffalo, deer, and all kinds of good hunting. Them mountains on the west side is called the Tetons. It was named by the French, and meant 'three breasts'. Some figure it was from one of the tribes. Now, when we get down to the valley, you can shoot us some fresh meat."

Descending into the hole was slow and dangerous. There were snow-covered gaps that could swallow a man and his animal. Amos was thankful when they finally reached the bottom. Pushing his tuque to the back of his head, he looked up at the mountain peaks in front of him.

There were no foothills in front of the mountains. The towering 7,000 feet granite mountains capped with snow were breathtaking.

"Ain't they something?" Doo asked. Amos just looked at them, unable to put the view into words.

As promised, the young man saw movement in some cedars along the river. A whitetail deer was tearing at the tender ends of the boughs. Amos removed his choppers and took out a primer cap. Placing it onto the nipple of his Hawken, he brought the rifle to his shoulder. The shot echoed in the valley.

The deer bounded away, disappearing over the bank of the Snake River. Amos reloaded the Hawken before following the animal. "I am sure I hit it, Doo."

Hurrying through the knee-deep snow, Amos caught sight of the blood trail of the deer. The animal had made it just over the bank before it had collapsed. The young man slid down to the river and poked the deer with the barrel of his rifle. The spike horn was dead.

The men camped in the cedar grove and, spearing venison steaks with green sticks, they roasted the meat over their fire. They ate their fill of the young buck and then wrapped the rest of the meat inside the hide. Doo had pulled together some of the lower branches of the cedar, making a snug shelter for the night.

In the morning there was snow masking their view of the Tetons. They carved frozen slabs from the deer and again roasted them. The old-timer poured himself coffee, with the surprised young man looking on. "I didn't think you drank coffee."

"I don't like coffee. Sometimes I drink a cup or two to save on my tea," Doo replied.

Amos looked at the empty pot. No second cup this morning. It was still snowing when the two men led their mules across the valley. "We got another two days and we'll be at the cabin," the old-timer informed Amos. "Now don't expect too much. It's small and easy to keep warm once we put some moss between the logs."

"Where do we keep the furs and hides we get?" the young man asked.

"In the cabin with us. We stretch and dry them on one side of the cabin and sleep on them on the other." Doo explained.

They were climbing out of the valley when the snow stopped. Amos stopped and looked back at the mountains. He promised himself that he would come back sometime and hunt and fish the summer away under the towering Tetons.

Toward evening, they spotted a fire in the

distance. The size indicated that it was white men and not Indians. Sparks were carried into the night sky as wood was added. Stopping a distance from the camp, Doo called, "Hello, the camp, we're coming in."

Three men dressed much like Doo and Amos sat around the fire, drinking coffee. One of the men stood and watched them approach. He cradled a rifle in the crook of his arm. "You're welcome to come in and set. Coffee is hot and we were about to start our supper."

"Only if we can add some venison we got yesterday to the meal," the old man replied. "They call me Doo and this is my partner, Amos."

"We're the Bradly brothers. They call me Pete, and these are True and Tony," Pete Bradly said introducing themselves.

"I heard of you," Doo replied. "You boys usually work the Green River area."

The man seemed pleased that the old-timer had recognized the names. "We'll take you up on the meat. We was about to boil up some pemmican."

The Bradly's put on another pot of coffee while Amos got the deer meat ready to roast. Doo stripped the packs off the mules and put them onto a long picket rope to allow some searching for grass. He then made up a shelter in some balsam trees.

Their hosts had a large cast iron pan and put that on to fry the venison. The young man noticed that there was a Dutch oven on the fire that smelled like it was baking biscuits.

While the supper was being eaten the conversation was about hunting and trapping conditions. They all talked about areas they had hunted, being careful not to give too much information out. Amos noticed that the Bradly's travelled heavy. They had seven horses and several large packs nearby.

"Planning on settling in this area?" Amos asked.

"Come spring we plan on going to the Montana territory. We'll build us a cabin and maybe go up to Canada and drive down some horses and start ranching," True said.

Doo and Pete talked about the good old days of trapping beaver. Tony told Amos about buffalo hunting this past summer. In great detail he talked about the rotting carcasses and the smell of green hides in the wagon. He vowed that he would never spend another summer doing that.

With the meal finished, the men checked on their stock, bringing them closer to camp. Then they went to their beds. Amos kept his Colt handy, in case there was a need during the night. The snow had started to fall again.

Shortly after daylight, the two parties wished each other good hunting and moved out. Doo had a worried look on his face. "Something bothering you about the Bradly's?" the young man asked.

"No, the Bradly's are good men," the old-timer replied. "The snow has me concerned. If we get wind with it, the passes we need to go through will be blown full and we'll have a tough time of it getting through to the cabin."

"I got no problem walking until we get there," Amos told his partner.

"We got one high pass to get through. The walls along the snake are too steep to stay near the river. I wouldn't want to get caught up there in a storm at night. We'll camp this side and if the weather holds, we'll go over first thing tomorrow. The cabin is a half-day's walk down the river from there."

It snowed on and off as the men pushed through drifts waist-deep. They took turns leading and breaking trail. Exhausted from the travel, they camped near the river. The series of foothills that led to the pass were in front of them.

They turned in right after having weak coffee and hard bread. Amos had let Doo make the coffee while he took care of the mules. He would make sure that that didn't happen again. The young man had trouble sleeping. The weather was on his mind. He lay listening for the wind to pick up.

Morning came with a clear blue sky. Tree branches were heavy with snow. Looking back, the falling snow had wiped out any evidence of their passing. The ground was covered with a foot and a half of newly fallen snow. It was light and fluffy so it wouldn't hamper their travel. Should the wind start, there would be a white-out.

While Amos heated water for coffee, the old-timer brushed off the mules and packs. Then the two of them lifted the pack onto the animals and secured it with leather ties. The two men stood drinking their coffee and soaking hard bread to soften it.

Doo pointed to the mountain tops. "The wind has started over the mountains. Soon it will sweep down the valley and we will be in for a full-blown blizzard with all the loose snow."

The young man could see the snow swirling over the ragged peaks. Gulping the last of his coffee, he stuck the rest of his hard bread into his mouth and grabbed the coffee pot. Kicking snow over the fire, he shook what grounds he could out of the pot and tied it to the packs.

The snow was almost waist-deep as they approached the first rise. Slipping on the icy footing and pulling on the lead ropes, the men worked their way over each of the series of ridges. The passage kept them close to the steep drop to the river below. Amos prayed that they wouldn't hit a slippery slope that would send them plunging to their deaths.

Looking back, the snow coming off the mountain looked like a wide waterfall with a white, boiling mass below. The wind was coming, and coming fast. The mountains were eight to ten miles behind them. There was no doubt that the storm would engulf them before they reached the other side.

The men crossed the deepest part of the pass and began to climb the final ridge. The wind was beginning to tear at the new snow. In desperation, Amos got behind the mule and began to swat its rump, shouting, "Go Jenny! Get up! For God's sake, get up!"

The mule charged forward through the chest-deep snow, leaping and plunging ahead, breaking trail. The young man was trusting the judgement of the sure footed animal to recognize the safest route ahead of them. Slipping and falling behind the animal, Amos regained his feet and kept encouraging Jenny on.

By the time that the men and mules went over the final ridge and started down, they were in blowing snow. Amos and Doo both knew that if they were caught in white-out conditions on the ridge they would be lucky to get out of the ordeal with just frostbite.

Before starting down the other side, Doo tossed the lead rope to Amos. They added a length to it and tied the end to Jenny's packs. As they started down, the two men let the mule take its lead and they hung on to the rope, knowing that soon the blowing snow would be blinding.

The young man glanced back, and snow was shooting over the ridge propelled by the wind. The leeward side of the ridge was offering some protections for the moment, keeping the storm above them. It was as though the mule understood the danger of the situation as it pushed forward through the snow.

The men and animals were surrounded by blowing snow as the raging storm caught them, on the downward side of the ridge. Jenny kept going and the men continued to cling to the rope. Amos knew that the mule was now just moving with the storm and seeking shelter.

He had seen a stand of pine trees at the base of the ridge. He had no idea if the mule was headed toward them or toward the drop-off to the river. Amos knew the animal was as blinded as the men it led. Suddenly, the rope jerked down, almost pulling it from the young man's choppers. Doo had fallen.

There was no way that Amos could stop Jenny during the steep descent. If his partner lost his grip on the rope, the young man was helpless to go back and get him. The rope slacked and came back up. The old-timer had lost his grip.

"Doo! Get up! Grab something!" the panicked young man shouted, the words being lost in the wind. Stumbling along behind his mule, Amos prayed, "Lord, don't let Doo die. Give me strength to go back for him when the mule stops."

The young man fell to his knees when the downward slope disappeared and the bottom was reached. After being dragged several yards, he was able to get back on his feet. The blowing snow began to swirl, its velocity becoming less as the mule led them into the pines.

Amos pulled himself toward the head of the mule. The snow was no longer waist-deep under the trees, but visibility was still near zero. Getting to the front of the mule, the young man tied its lead rope to a pine. He then headed back, feeling his way along the animals. Something hit his legs and down Amos went, face first into the snow.

"Son-of-a . . ." the young man said, spitting snow.

"Don't blame me, it seemed like I been dragging behind this mule forever."

It was Doo! He wasn't left on the slope. "You sure as hell had me worried!" Amos shouted above the wind, moving closer to his friend.

"You were worried!" the old-timer exclaimed. "I thought I was a goner when my glove slipped from the rope. I grabbed up as my mule passed me and caught the breeching and held on. I was hoping the hell it didn't kick out at me. I just bumped the rest of the way down the hill behind all of you."

The two men stood leaning on the mule for several minutes, catching their breath. Then Doo went to the front, led the mules deeper into the pines and stopped behind a large root base of a windfall. Protected from the force of the wind, they loosened and dumped the packs off the animals. Amos cleaned the crusted snow from around the animal's eyes.

Amos led Jenny behind the root base and reached into his possible bag. Withdrawing two pieces of hard bread, he fed it to the mule, "This is the second time you saved me in a snowstorm. All I got for you right now is this bread. When I get to California and find gold, you'll get the best feed possible for the rest of your life."

The men and their animals sheltered behind the windfall for two days until the storm blew itself out. The first day they chewed jerky and drank water from their canteens kept under their coats. After daylight the second day, they felt their way along the windfall, breaking dead branches to build a fire.

The mules moved a short distance away when they had the fire going. Amos couldn't describe how good the heat of the flames felt. They put on a pot of beans to boil, and coffee. The rest of the day they spent searching nearby for wood to feed the fire.

After the animals got over their initial fear of the fire, they moved back into the close quarters behind the root base. Amos dug some corn meal out from the pack and put a couple cupful's each in their nose bags. He knew it would do little to fill their bellies, but he hoped it would do some good. The men then settled down, chewing tobacco and waiting for the storm to blow out.

Once the wind died down, the men got the packs back onto their mules. "The cabin ain't but a couple miles along the Snake from here."

CHAPTER SIXTEEN

The two miles took the men most of the morning to travel, as they had to break through the stiff crust of the drifts. Suddenly, Doo shouted, "There she is!"

All Amos could see was another drift. Getting closer, he saw part of the cabin exposed from under the snow. The old-timer told Amos that there was a lean-to on the end of the cabin for the mules. They pulled the packs off the animals and led them around the end of the cabin. The three-sided structure for the animals was made of balsam poles lashed together. It sagged a bit but appeared sound.

They tied the mules on long picket ropes to allow them to forage for food on the trees and under the snow. Amos followed his friend back to the cabin door. Doo grasped the latch and hit the door with his shoulder. It gave way and he stepped in.

Following the old-timer into the cabin, Amos was greeted with the foul smell of rotted meat. The snow-covered dirt floor was littered with rusting tin cans, animal bones, and rotting bags. Daylight came through many of the ill-fitting logs.

"Welcome to my humble home," Doo said.

The small cabin was even smaller than the old-timer had indicated. If half was used for drying and the other for storage, he couldn't use the fireplace built into the north wall. Doo began tossing trash into a corner of the cabin. "I was in a hurry to leave and didn't do any straightening up."

Whatever the conditions of the cabin were, Amos accepted that it would be their winter home. The first thing he did was to check the bags lying around. Ripping them into strips, he went outside and used them to caulk the logs. While they were rotting, they still did the job.

Amos then went into a stand of balsam and began to cut and limb several trees. Doo checked the fireplace over. For the next two days the men worked on the cabin. Amos built a set of bunks using balsam boughs for the mattresses. The evergreen scent helped to freshen the cabin.

He also built pole racks to dry hides, a rough table and two wooden benches. Amos added an enclosure in front of the cabin for scraping hides, to keep the fat and meat out. Doo spent time cutting up windfalls for firewood and stacked it against the wall cabin wall.

The last thing that the young man worked on was a small structure made up of poles leaning against each other, somewhat like a teepee. It had a catch trough in it and a split bench to sit on. When finished is was a functional outhouse.

With the improvements done and the supplies put away, the men were ready to start trapping and hunting. They had heard big cats and wolves almost every night. It was late November and most grizzlies would be in hibernation. The men would watch for their dens, found mostly on northern slopes. The bears would often take advantage of natural caves and deep openings on the rock walls.

While Amos worked to enlarge the shelter for the animals, Doo went hunting for meat to add to their supplies and to bait the traps. Late in the morning, the young man heard a shot north of the cabin. He was lashing some of the last poles when the old-timer's mule came back without him.

Speaking softly to the mule, Amos was able to get a hand on the lead rope. The sawbuck pack saddle was on the animal and it appeared to be unhurt. There was a chance Doo was tracking game and the mule had slipped the knot on the lead rope and had just wandered back. Then again, maybe the old-timer was in trouble and the mule had been frightened away.

Amos got his Hawken, possibles bag, and Jenny. He climbed onto her back, riding without a saddle. Leading Doo's mule, he began to backtrack to find his friend. There were three hours of daylight left. The young man strained his ears for any sound. All he heard were the mules breaking through the crusted snow.

Jenny suddenly stopped and raised her head, ears forward. What she heard or smelled, Amos didn't know. Sliding off the mule, checked the Hawken to make sure it was ready. Under his pea coat he had the Colt Paterson. He began to tie a secure knot into the lead rope but changed his mind, tying them with a slip knot. If he ran into trouble, they might need to run.

He was moving slowly when he heard a

horrible roar. Then there was shouting. It was Doo! The young man's heart was in his throat as he moved forward as quietly as possible. The sounds in front of him were growing louder.

There was a loud growl and then the tearing of branches and bark. "Take the damn meat and get the hell out of here you bastard!" Doo shouted.

Amos stepped from behind a drift and not 150 feet in front of him was a silver tipped grizzly beside a dead elk. It was trying to get at Doo high in the branches of a red pine. The bear roared and pushed at the trunk of the tree, attempting to uproot it or shake the trapper down.

Before Amos had a chance to react to the sight, the bear turned, standing on its back legs and looked directly at him. He was upwind of the bear and it had caught his scent. The huge animal was protecting the elk that Doo had killed and considered the trapper a danger to its meal. Now it had its attention on Amos.

Tearing his chopper off, the young man cocked the Hawken. He brought it up to his shoulder and pulled the back set trigger. Then, sighting on the large bear's chest, he touched off the front trigger. Smoke burst from the hexagon barrel.

At the same moment the large bear lunged forward, coming at Amos. Dropping the Hawken, the young man ran for his life, seeing a pine with branches he could reach. He grabbed at them and started to pull himself into the tree.

There was a severe blow on his moccasin-covered foot, almost knocking him out of the tree. The bear, in its rush, swept by the tree and turned, giving Amos enough time to recover and climb out of reach. The grizzly shattered the lower branches and reached for the young man. Its paw swiped only a few feet below the treed trapper.

Amos looked up. He couldn't gain much more height in the tree he had climbed. How he could have missed the animal he did not know. It had moved about the same time he'd fired, but the shot should still have struck high on the chest at worst.

Looking down, he could see blood spatter on the snow near the base. For all he knew it could have come from his throbbing foot. The bear might have torn it wide open. Amos reached under his pea coat for the Colt. The bear was pushing on the tree. The young trapper could hear the breaking of the wood fibers in the pines trunk.

Clinging to the tree, Amos aimed and fired into the gaping mouth of the grizzly. The bear turned and took a few steps away from the tree. It looked up at the treed man. Rising on its back legs, the bear put down its head. It roared, blood and saliva spraying from its mouth, and it charged the tree. The impact had Amos clinging with both arms, his eyes closed tight, unable to look at the horror raging below.

He heard something hit the snow and then there was silence. The young man looked down. The giant of a bear lay on its back, unmoving. Unable to stop shaking, Amos slowly climbed down from the tree. As he lowered himself to the ground the foot gave way and he collapsed onto the snow. He was sitting looking at the 3 inch claws extending out from the bear's back paws.

"You okay, Amos!" It was Doo with his Hawken at the ready.

"I'm . . . I'm not sure, my foot . . ." the young man said.

Doo poked the bear with the barrel of his Hawken. It was dead. "By God, Amos. You got it. You killed the beast."

"I got the mules a way back." Amos told his friend.

The old-timer headed after the mules, leaving Amos with the dead bear. The young man sat clutching the Colt, ready if even a hair moved on the beast. His foot was buried in the snow and Amos didn't dare look at it. If it was broken or severely torn, there was no doctor to come and fix him.

Doo came back leading the mules. The animals wanted nothing to do with the bear and began to pull and bray as they got closer. Tying them to some small trees, the old-timer came to check on Amos. The foot was badly bruised but the claws hadn't penetrated the moccasin.

Limping on the injured foot, Amos went with his friend and the mules to get the elk. "We best get this one to the cabin and in a tree before wolves get scent of it," Doo advised. "They won't be as anxious to go at the bear."

Once the elk was at the cabin, they came back for the bear. It was all the men could do to get the mules tied to the grizzly. Amos held their heads while Doo ducked the kicking feet and secured the ropes.

It was after dark before they had the elk hanging out of reach of any wolves and the bear lying in front of the cabin. Amos found that walking was helping work the pain out of his foot. Freezing temperatures would work against them, so they had to keep processing the day's kills.

The old-timer skinned the bear and removed the paws and head. "Hey, Amos. You had a good shot in this beast. You missed the heart by an inch. There was enough damage that the bear bled out."

"Another minute for the bear to bleed out and it would have had me out of the tree," the young man replied.

Amos quartered the elk and cut out the tenderloins. Once the work was done, he would cut steaks from it for their supper. After hoisting the elk meat high into a pine, the young man went into the cabin to start a fire.

"After you get the fire going, come out and help me get this bear carcass in the trees," Doo called.

Soon the two men had the bear meat out of reach of the wolves, Amos stood looking at it. "Damn, that looks a lot like a large headless man hanging there."

The next morning, they headed out to set up three trap lines. Blazing the trees as they went, the men set foot traps for wolves, fox, or cats. Others were set for mink or fishers. The plan was to check one trap line each day. They used both bear and elk meat for the bait.

It was clear that the wolves had come close to the cabin grabbing whatever scraps they could, so Amos decided to build a platform in a tree to keep him safe, then put some of the meat to lure them in. Choosing a moonlit night, he sat with the Hawken loaded and waited. After several cold hours, he climbed down and headed for the warmth of the cabin.

The second night in the stand, he thought he saw a shadow move. Sitting, hardly breathing, he watched. There it was again! Two wolves were coming to the bait. Dismayed, Amos realized that when he cocked the Hawken it would spook the wolves.

Holding the set trigger down, he pulled the hammer back, then released the trigger. Amos had not tried this before and hoped that all he would have to do was touch off the front trigger and the rifle would fire. There was a moonlit space between two growths of balsam trees. When one of the wolves crossed the opening he would shoot.

The wolves lay in the shadows, unwilling to move across the opening. Amos sat with the rifle inches away from his shoulder, waiting. There was the sound of a growl that let him know that the wolves were still there. There was an impatient whine and then another sharper growl.

Let the little bugger come out, Amos thought.

The next move caught him completely by surprise. A flash of a shadow crossed the opening as a wolf went to the meat, grabbed it and continued on. The other wolf ran away from the platform, offering only a glimpse of its tail waving.

The next morning, Doo was making corn mush for breakfast. Amos told him about the wolves. The old-timer chuckled, "They knew you was there. Only thing was they wanted the meat more than they feared you, so they took their time."

"I was downwind from them and sitting in the shadows of the tree branches," Amos objected.

"You go back and follow them tracks and you'll find they circled you and the bait before coming in. Hell, the wolves may have passed right below you. Once they knew where the danger was, then they found a way to get to the meat." Doo was still laughing as he filled the wooden bowls with steaming mush.

The trapping proved to be more successful

than the hunting. By the end of the month they had four wolves and three fox. They had spotted the tracks of a large cat, but it wouldn't come into the bait. They did catch bobcat, mink and fisher.

One afternoon Amos came back with two raccoons. His excited partner said, "I will make us some fine caps out these rascals."

The two men were playing cards by candle light and smoking when Amos asked, "Did we miss Christmas?"

Doo sat studying his cards. "I don't rightly know. It must be passed by now."

"Well, I heard some turkey this morning," Amos informed his friend. "I'll shoot us one tomorrow and we'll roast it and call the day Christmas."

The short days of winter left the men with little to do during the long evenings. While they worked on making some snowshoes, Doo would talk about the old days when he'd gone after the beaver. Amos would talk about growing up on the farm in Maine. The lack of adventure growing potatoes became very apparent to the young man when he listened to the old-timer talk of growing up on the frontier.

When Doo was a youngster, he had traveled with his folks up and down the Mississippi and Missouri Rivers, hunting and fishing. After he was old enough, he had struck out on his own, panning gold in Georgia and Alabama. After that he'd come west in the '30s to trap beaver. He had met and trapped with many of the men Amos had read about.

It was during these months in the Rockies that Amos came to grips with the fact that he would never return to live on the farm. Riddled with guilt from knowing that he wouldn't be keeping his word to his father, the young man spent hours trying to come up with the right way to explain it to his father.

It was February before Amos had another moonlit night to try for the wolves. Every night they could hear the packs hunting. The young man tied a bobcat carcass to a young aspen tree. The winter night was frigid and he sat with his toes aching from the cold.

The Hawken lay cocked with the set trigger pulled. Amos took care not to bump the front trigger and accidently fire the rifle. His eye caught movement in the trees. The game had begun. For an hour the hunter sat, fearful of moving and alerting the wolves.

If his eyes weren't playing tricks on him, then the young man was sure that there were at least three stalking the bait. The shadows of the trees reached out over the snow. As the night dragged on, Amos watched and waited. He began to believe that the wolves had abandoned the bait.

All of a sudden he realized that one of the shadows wasn't right. Rather than falling away from the moon, it was falling from right to left. He finally saw an almost undetectable movement. Right in the open a wolf was crawling on its belly toward the bobcat.

Confident that the shadow was a wolf, he decided to shoot. Bringing the Hawken to his shoulder, Amos sighted down the barrel and touched the front trigger.

The Hawken bucked, the gunshot loud in the stillness of the night. The shadow rose from the snow, leaping and crying before falling and laying still. Amos climbed down from the tree, stiff from the cold. He cradled the Hawken in his left arm and reached under his pea coat for the Colt. If the wolf wasn't dead, he would finish it with the revolver.

Walking slowly up to the dark hulk, he held the Colt ready. There was movement to his right. Amos turned just in time to see the outstretched form of another wolf leaping onto him. The impact caused the revolver to fire and he was knocked to the snow.

Swinging out with the Colt Paterson to try and strike the wolf, Amos found nothing but air. The wolves had disappeared into the trees, frightened by the Colt going off next to them. The shaken hunter collected the Hawken, which had fallen, and grabbed the tail of the downed wolf. Hurrying toward the cabin, he expected another attack at any time.

Amos burst into the cabin, dragging the wolf behind him. His startled partner sat up. "What the hell happened?"

"Got me a wolf and almost was got by one," the breathless young man said.

The young man gave up his night hunting. With game being scarcer, the wolves were becoming more brazen. When checking the traps, they would often find the animal still alive. After dispatching it, they would skin it on the spot and carry the fur rather than the whole animal.

More than once Amos had caught sight of movement in the woods while skinning. Wolves had taken to following the trappers. When the carcass was discarded and the men had barely gotten out of sight, the sounds of the wolves fighting over the kill could be heard.

If the wolves got to the trapped animal first, the trappers would only find hair and blood left. One evening the men were eating beans and roasted rabbit.

The usual conversation about California and the gold fields had been exhausted when Doo suggested. "We only got another month before heading back to the pass. I ain't showed you the Yellowstone. Tomorrow, after checking the north trap line, we'll head up that way. We'll be back here in maybe a week."

Amos awoke the next morning, excited about the new adventure. He had heard talk of hot water shooting right out the earth, and colored springs. The young man found that he was always anxious to see what was around the next bend in a river or over the next hill.

They had had a week of snow squalls, but this morning the sky was clear and the sun bright. The nights had become shorter, giving the men more hours to work outdoors. Much of the trappers' time was consumed finding feed for the mules. The animals looked shaggy with their heavy winter coats. It helped to hide the fact that they had lost weight over the winter.

The two mountain men finished checking the trap line and walked briskly, leading their mules towards the Yellowstone. Both men had a chew in their cheeks. Their beards had grown long over the winter months and their hair covered their ears. Both were wearing buckskins, and Doo had a rabbit skin hat while Amos wore his tuque. Their new snow shoes were tied on the packs of the animals.

The men walked abreast in areas where the wind had blown most of the snow clear. They went single file in the deeper snow. The Snake River was frozen over except for areas with rapids, so they could cross from one side to the other, choosing the best routes for travel.

Leaving the river, they stopped next to a lake for the night. The hills surrounding the men were covered with trees, many over a hundred years old. There were the sounds of wolves or coyotes chasing prey. Amos could imagine the deer struggling through the snow while the hunters ran after them, held up by the crust.

While Doo was putting their meal together, the young man worked in the balsam, making a shelter for them. After the sun went down the temperatures dropped rapidly in the high elevations. Amos pulled his pea coat over his buckskin top.

The nerve-shattering scream of a mountain lion set the mules to braying. Amos went and got the animals and brought them closer to camp. Doo called him to supper. He had mixed a little flour and water in some pemmican and warmed it in the frying pan. It was sort of a stew without potatoes, carrots, and other things a stew normally had. They had run out of coffee beans, so they were drinking tea. Soon, that too would be gone. Amos pulled off his choppers and kept his hands warm, holding the tin plate with his supper.

Deer and elk had been forced to leave the area for better grazing at lower elevations. Doo had hoped that they would get some fresh meat in the Yellowstone. He said there were springs that attracted the animals.

Late the next day, the men were crossing a valley when a spout of steaming water shot above the trees. Amos froze not believing what he was seeing. "What the . . . what is that?"

"Hell of a sight, ain't it?" Doo said.

"Can we camp near it?" Amos asked.

"I wouldn't recommend it, but if you want we

can."

The men walked closer to the mound that the water had appeared from. The nearby trees were covered with frost from the water settling and freezing. With an open view of the mound the two men set up their camp.

"Do you think it will shoot up again?" the young man asked.

"You can depend on it, Amos."

That night a rumbling could be heard, then the rush of steam, then the water would come. It came every hour to hour and a half. While Amos found it fascinating at first, by morning, with his sleep interrupted throughout the night, he was ready to move on.

At a high point, the men could see steam rising from several geysers. Doo took the young man to another hot spring and they stripped down for a good soak. A light snow was coming down and the world around them was white. In the distance there were buffalo wandering. Amos doubted that he would ever see such a sight again in his life.

While the old-timer put an afternoon meal together, Amos tied on the snow shoes and walked a large circle. He watched the buffalo plowing the snow off the grass by moving their wooly heads back and forth. He saw an emerald pool of water with yellow deposits around the edges.

The next day the two men headed back south, each in their own thoughts about the wonders they had just seen. Amos told his friend, "When I get the gold in California, I'm going to build a cabin near here."

They were crossing over a ridge when Doo reached out and stopped the young man. Amos looked to where the old-timer was pointing. A bighorn sheep was standing 300 feet above them, staring down.

"You could hit it from here," Doo whispered. "We could use the meat."

Amos fumbled in his possibles bag for a cap, and put it on the Hawken. The sheep had turned, looking like it was about to run. The young man pulled the set trigger. Putting the sight just behind the shoulder, he touched the front trigger. The shot echoed off the hills. The bighorn turned its head and jumped sideways, going off the narrow ledge it was standing on. It lay sprawled in the snow just below the upper ridge.

The old-timer slapped Amos on the back. "Good shot. Now we got to get up there and drag it over here."

The young man's heart was pounding with excitement. He looked at the sheet of snow that continued below that ridge they were on. "You stay here, Doo. I'll climb up and start it sliding down the snow and we can pick it up at the bottom. It will save us dragging it here."

Handing Jenny's lead rope to his friend, Amos reloaded the Hawken and then began climbing to the higher ridge. He had fashioned a sling on the rifle to make it easier to carry when checking the trap lines. He slung it over his shoulder then, gripping the ragged rock outcroppings, he made his way up to the narrow ledge.

Hugging the wall behind him, he worked his way to just above the downed sheep. The snow started about three feet below him. When the bighorn had jumped its front legs had broken through the crust, preventing the sheep from sliding down.

Squatting down on the ledge, Amos supported himself with his right hand. The ledge was too narrow to sit on. While struggling for a way to step onto the snow, he wondered how the bighorn was able to travel the ledge so easily.

Straining to reach the snow, Amos' feet slipped. He shot off the ledge, landing on the animal. Suddenly, the bottom went out from under him and the whole side of the mountain was moving. The young man fell backwards trying to grab onto anything. He was on top of a snow avalanche!

Desperately, he fought to stay on top of the snow as he plummeted down. The snow hit another ledge and shot off it like a waterfall sending him into space. With his arms flailing uselessly, Amos was at the mercy of the sliding snow.

As quickly as it had started, it stopped, the impact knocking the air out of the young man. He was buried in the snow! Gasping for breath, he felt panic rising. He was unable to move his legs, and one arm was pinned underneath him while the other was twisted behind his back.

He got his breath back and shouted Doo's name. For all he knew, he was several feet below the snow. There was no way that his friend would hear him. He began to scream for help, stopping only to catch his breath. The snow was crunching around him. It was settling tighter!

A pain shot through the arm twisted behind his back. The snow was beginning to move. It was going to start sliding again! "Amos! Amos, are you alright!" He felt someone pulling at his clothes and the aching arm.

Finally, his head was clear of snow and he

looked up at the apprehensive face of his friend. "My arm hurts, don't pull on it," Amos pleaded.

A short time later, Doo had Amos dug out and lying on the snow on his back. Doo was kneeling over him, continuing to brush the snow off. "It was your rifle, Amos. When the snow stopped sliding the barrel was sticking out. I dug around it and you was at the other end. The sling was tangled around your arm."

"Did you see my sheep?" the young man asked.

"Your sheep! Oh, I was going to dig it out first, but figured I might need your help to load it on the mules." Frowning Doo grunted, "Your sheep."

The arm was only sprained, and with time it would be fine. His tuque was gone, not to be seen again. One of the back legs of the bighorn was sticking out of the snow just above the men. Doo went back up the ridge to get the mules while Amos rested.

With the sheepskin, head and meat packed onto the mules, the men headed away from the snow slide. Memories of the Yellowstone quickly boosted Amos' spirits back up. The meals of the bighorn's meat were enjoyed. It reminded Amos of lamb. The screech of the large cat was heard each night. Doo told the young man that it was crying for the meat they carried. They arrived at the cabin two days later.

The passes would open up in a little over a month. Amos was looking forward to getting back to the South Pass and make ready to head for California. Doo had told him that he was too old to chase gold in California. He planned to prospect in the Rocky Mountains, maybe even as far as the area that the Lakota had called Badlands.

In early April two mountain men stopped by the cabin and joined them for supper. They had a large mountain cat tied across the back of one of their horses. The other horse showed evidence of deep claw marks on its withers. The cat had attacked the animal the night before while they'd camped just south on the Snake River.

The taller of the two men whose name was Ed, had just finished cleaning and reloading his rifle when the cat had jumped onto the animal's back. A quick shot had knocked the cat off the horse. Wounded, the lion had headed up the rocks above their camp.

They'd spent most of the day tracking the injured cat and had finally cornered it in the afternoon. The animal had been game. It had come right at the men and had made it within a few feet before they'd killed it.

The shorter of the two men, named Soot, skinned the cat and offered to roast some meat up for their meal. Amos was doubtful about eating cat, but to his surprise it was great. The four of them enjoyed it for supper. It was good to have company. Having been in the mountains all winter, none of them had any current news, but having someone new to talk with and share a smoke lifted the spirits of the two trappers.

The next morning the two mountain men left with their trophy and its remaining meat. Amos walked with them a way as he headed to check the south trap line. Doo went to run the north line. When the men broke off toward the west, the young man stood watching them go. After Ed and Soot disappeared into the trees, the mountains felt empty. That night Amos lay in his blankets and missed hearing the cry of the mountain lion.

Spring came late to the high country, and many of the passes remained filled until mid-summer. Doo told the young man that it was time to pull in the traps and ready their winter's catch to travel. "I awoke this morning and the air smelled like it was time to go," he told Amos. "In a week or so the ice will be out of the Snake and we'd be stuck here a month waiting for it to go down enough to cross."

It took three days to cache the traps for next year and ready the packs for the mules. Doo and Amos carried their personal items and bed rolls on their backs. The winter's hunt and trapping had been good, and the mules would be heavily loaded.

Memories of walking into the filthy building last November motivated Amos to clean the cabin and leave a stack of wood near the fireplace for Doo's next visit. The young man could also smell the difference in the air. While they weren't the warm breezes that forecast the end of winter in Maine, they had something that told them a change was coming.

CHAPTER SEVENTEEN

Doo led the way across the Snake River to a cut in the mountains that ran toward the east. Amos worried a little about the condition of their animals. The winter had been tough on the mules. He hoped that carrying the heavy loads wouldn't be too much for them.

They reached one pass that was still blocked, and had to go back and take a higher route. They spent a night above the tree line and awoke the next morning to clear skies. Amos sat looking over the mountain range and felt like he was sitting on top of the world.

Finally reaching the eastern slopes, the men and their mules started down. By midday the sun warmed them and they walked in long john tops. Only the deepest drifts were left in the wooded mountain sides. They would break trail through the packed drifts and soon be in the clear again.

The change in the season as they came out of the mountains and onto the plains was unbelievable to Amos. Just the day before they'd been walking in a spring snow storm and now they walked out onto an area with new grass poking out of last year's dead, brown cover. Splashes of color could be seen from the spring flowers.

In a valley below, the men could see a low log structure with a few scattered out buildings. Nearby, they set up camp near some hot springs to rest the animals. There was ample grass for them to eat, and a local resident had a small trading post offering a few supplies for grocery-poor trappers coming out of the mountains. The two men sat soaking in one of the springs with a bottle of questionable rye, washing away the memories of the cold winter.

The buckskins they had gotten before leaving the South Pass had been light in color. They were now dark and stained from their winter's work. That night the merchant's portly wife had a hardy stew, fresh bread, and strong coffee. It cost each man 50 cents, but truth be known, they would have spent more for the hot meal.

The trading post owner was Dom Levesque. He slicked his thinning hair back with grease and had a thin moustache that he liked to twist with his fingers. His heavyset wife's name was Corrine. The owner tried to convince the two men to trade some of the furs at his place. He promised good prices and would save them from having to pack the furs all the way to South Pass.

Levesque didn't have a large supply of goods and his price for them was high. The owner pointed out that the men had used his spring and the mules were eating his grass. What finally broke the trappers down was the smell of the apple pie Corrine was baking.

They spent another day near the trading post and used most of it dickering with Dom while trading some fox and fisher pelts. Amos let Doo bargain with the stubborn owner while he went fishing in a stream that ran by the post.

He caught several trout and was heading back to the trading post to clean them when he saw the wife coming from the woods. She had a bag of greens and fiddle heads. Amos grinned widely. He hadn't had fiddle heads since his mother had passed.

That night they ate fried fish, the fiddle heads and greens, with apple pie and coffee to finish the meal. Once again there was a 50 cents charge for each man. The men should have objected, but the meal was good and come tomorrow they would be eating beans and the little pemmican they had left.

The old-timer had traded for coffee, some tea, a couple bottles of rye, chewing tobacco, and jerky. He also got some corn for the mules. They left the trading post before daylight the next morning, not wanting to talk anymore trade with Dom. They had already taken a beating on the furs they'd exchanged for the supplies they had gotten.

They had another week of travel before they reached Jon T's trading post. Three days from Dom's trading post Amos spotted a fire. As they approached the camp, Doo recognized the men as the ones who had shot the mountain cat.

"Hello the camp, can we share some of our coffee with you?" the old-timer called.

"Is that you, Doo?" Ed replied.

"Sure is. Me and Amos got us some coffee from the place north of here and would be happy to make a pot over your fire."

"If you bought it already ground by old Dom, it is probably half sawdust," Soot kidded him.

Amos stripped the pack off the mules and picketed them near the horses. Heading back toward the fire he said, "I see you got six horses. Must help for fast travel."

"Four of them was the Bradly's" Ed informed them. "We was heading for their cabin, and found it burned to the ground. Soot here spotted what was left of two of them in the ashes. Didn't see hide or hair of the third one. Course, he could have been in and mostly burned up. We're bringing the horses into Fort Laramie."

"They had seven horses when we come across them back in November," Doo said.

"We followed the trail of some that had left the cabin, but they seemed to be wandering more than being ridden. We decided to round up these four and head back for our camp," Ed replied.

While the men ate the meal and drank their coffee, they talked about the winter's trapping. The fate of the Bradly's was forgotten. Ed asked them what their plans for the summer were.

"I'm going to the gold fields in California and Doo here plans to hunt for gold here in the Rockies." Amos replied.

Shaking his head, Ed said, "Chasing the yellow metal ain't for me. Most folks come back from places like California poorer than when they left."

Amos just sat there, smiling. He was tired of being told that there wasn't any gold to be had in California. If folks just read like he had, they would know. Doo pulled out one of the bottles and the men sat sipping the rye from their coffee cups. The next morning before leaving, the old-timer promised to let the folks at South Pass know about the Bradly's.

The water was high with spring runoff when they reached the Wind River. They led their mules downstream until they came to a long series of rapids. The current would be strong, but the deepest part should only be to their waist.

Doo tied enough lengths of their rope together to reach across the river. Amos stripped to his long johns, putting his gear and buckskins onto the mule. They then tied the rope around his middle. If the current knocked him off his feet, then Doo could pull him back to safety.

Lacing his high-cut boots tightly to prevent them from being washed off, he led the hesitant Jenny into the rolling water. Fighting to keep his footing, Amos decided to let the mule lead. Holding on to the upstream side of the pack, he shouted, "Get up, Jenny!"

The mule's inclination was to walk down stream, but Amos held the lead rope taught and kept it walking into the current as they crossed. Boulders on the bottom were the biggest hazard. More than once he stumbled and was saved by the sure-footed mule.

The icy water was numbing the young man's legs and the splashing water was soaking him from head to foot. His teeth were chattering as he urged the mule on. Suddenly, the water went chest-deep and the mule was swimming. The current swept Amos behind the animal. Reaching out, he grabbed the tail and hung on.

The mule regained its footing and continued across the river. Unable to get his feet back under him, Amos clung to Jenny's tail, praying that they would reach the other side before the rope around his waist reached its end.

The mule climbed up the bank and Amos' cold hand was no longer able to grip the tail. He lay half out of the river, the current tearing at his legs, trying to pull him back in. The mule stood above him on the river bank, waiting for his master to follow.

He looked back and Doo was knee-deep in the river, holding the rope. The current had washed Amos several feet downstream. Knowing that he had to get moving, Amos scrambled along the water's edge, heading back upstream to give some slack to the rope.

Finally, there was enough so he could climb the bank. Doo had tied the rope to the halter of his mule, standing in the frigid water, and waited for Amos to tie the other end to Jenny's pack saddle. Amos called the mule over and grabbed the lead rope. He pulled himself up the bank.

The rope around his waist was being tugged at by the river current, and he feared it would be jerked from his cold hands when he untied it from his waist. Amos tied the rope to his packs, leaving it around his waist.

He looked back and Doo had started across with his mule. Amos headed Jenny away from the river, keeping tension on the rope. Once the old-timer's mule hit the hole, the young man gave the rope some slack to prevent pulling the swimming mule's head under water and turning it belly up and losing everything.

Wide-eyed, Doo clung to the upstream side of the pack, keeping his legs up alongside the mule to prevent the swimming animal from kicking him. It seemed an eternity before the mule touched bottom and lunged to the river bank.

His friend climbed up the bank behind his mule and the men sat, blue from the cold, and in a tangle of rope, trying to muster the strength to get up. The bright sunshine was helping to warm them as they dressed in dry clothes. It was early afternoon, but they had no intention of continuing travel until tomorrow. Amos put a fire together while Doo pulled the furs off the mules.

With the animals taken care of and a quick camp set up, the two men sat next to the fire and warmed their insides with Dom's rye. They had set things that needed drying onto the tall winter grass, or on low bushes. They were about three days from the trading post. The side of Amos' high-cut boot had split open while tripping over the rocks in the river.

He cut the top of a moccasin and pulled it over the boot to keep dirt out of the opening. He then tied leather straps around the boot to keep the moccasin from slipping off. The men then checked and cleaned their guns. In the open country a man couldn't be too careful. There were those who would rather steal a man's winter work and leave him dying on the plain rather than earn it themselves in the mountains.

The next three days to the South Pass seemed to take forever. Memories of the paydays at the logging camp came to mind as Amos anticipated selling the furs. He would keep a nice mink to give to Shelly. It was late afternoon when the trading post came into sight.

Both men were weary from the pace they had kept as they got closer. One of the girls was coming from the barn after milking and screamed when she saw the men. Soon, everyone was streaming out of the trading post to welcome them.

A happier time Amos couldn't remember. It was like coming home from a long trip. Jon T stood near the door. waiting for them. "Have a good winter?"

"Only one grizzly and one big horn, but we got a good number of other furs," Doo replied.

"Dump them inside the back shed and we'll tally them up in the morning," Jon T told them. "Supper will be another hour and I'll have the sauna warmed for you."

Amos knew that the last offer was because of the smell. A winter of skinning your catch and living in the mountains left a man and his gear smelling plenty ripe. While the sauna was heating up, the men leaned on the bar and kept Stan busy pouring shots. The bartender kept marking them down on a ledger. Tilly and Shelly claimed their men and kept the other girls clear.

The two mountain men kept their extra clothing in the tack room and stopped to get some on the way to the sauna. Sitting on the top bench, the men threw plenty of steam. They scrubbed from top to bottom with the brown soap that the trading post made.

Doo dried off, and dressed quickly and headed back to the bar at the trading post. There was a mirror in the outer room, and after drying off and pulling on clean long johns, Amos took his scissors to trim his beard and hair. "I'll help you with that."

It was Shelly. She took the scissors and ran her fingers through his hair. Amos watched in the mirror, hardly recognizing himself, as she trimmed his unruly beard and hair. The face and eyes of the young man who had left Maine were gone. He was only 20 and had developed the hardness of the frontier man.

The woman leaned close to him as she worked on his hair. If Amos was to take a bet, it would be that he wasn't going to make supper. As the two of them lay on the upper bench of the sauna, Shelly traced her fingers along the many scars that Amos had gained since leaving Maine.

The next morning, Amos climbed out of his bunk in the tack room. Doo and Jon T were already counting the winter's take. Though his stomach ached with hunger, he went to the shed and helped with the tally.

"We missed you at supper last night," Jon T said.

With a twinkle in his eye, Doo added, "And at breakfast."

Jon T stepped away from his counting. "There are a couple of men having breakfast inside. I think you should talk to them."

Amos was damned hungry and it took little encouragement. "I'll grab something to eat and be right back," he promised.

Two men dressed in faded woolen shirts and patched woolen pants sat eating at the big table. There were stacks of pancakes with a bowl of butter and a jug of maple syrup. A pot of coffee sat on the stove. Amos grabbed a plate and cup. Sitting at the table, he loaded his plate with pancakes and smeared them with butter before pouring a generous amount of syrup.

He began to stuff forkfuls in his mouth before he remembered the two men. "Jon T says I should talk to you."

The older of the two men looked at the hungry

trapper. "I understand you are heading for California."

Swallowing the mouthful of pancake, Amos replied, "Yes sir! I hope to be on the American River by the beginning of July."

"Going to work for the mines?" he asked.

Smiling, Amos replied, "Heck no. I plan to find me a spot and pan some gold."

"You're going to do this on the American?" the man said. "Bring plenty of money. You might be able to buy a worthless claim."

"You're wrong," Amos said, correcting the man. "I plan to stake a claim and work it up. I know grub and stuff will cost a lot, but I got a mess of furs in the back room. I'll have money."

"Let me tell you what will happen," the man said, his eyes looking tired. "You'll risk your life getting there over the next 900 miles. If you make it, there will be men willing to sell you a claim. They'll poke a little gold in a shotgun and shoot it into the gravel along the river. They will let you pan a little and you will find gold. Then, if you have enough money, they will sign over the claim to you."

"More than likely the piece of paper they give you will be no good anyway. But if it is, you will spend the next month or so busting your back looking for more of the gold. There won't be any more because all the placer gold has been found. By this time, you will have spent everything you came with, or it will have been robbed from you."

"Like me and my brother here, you'll go to work for the mining companies, which will pay you in scrip that can only be spent in their stores for overpriced goods. You will hoard whatever food you can until you have enough to run, and you will run because after working for them you end up owing more than you make. They got goons that keep you in line. We ran in the night and walked over mountains and across deserts to get back."

"Jon T put us up for the winter and let us work enough to eat. We will be driving some of his wagons back to St. Louis once the grass is high enough. Don't get me wrong. There was a time that a man could stake a claim and pan some gold. If he didn't get killed for his gold and claim, he got out with a few dollars. I never met one, but I hear there has been those that did."

Amos sat at the table, his appetite gone. Futilely he said, "If not the American, there are other streams and rivers."

"When you get there, if you find one of the places that still has gold, and I doubt you will, keep it quiet. If word gets out, you won't last the week." The man wiped his mouth, then he and his brother went outside.

"They're not the first ones that have come back with the same story." Shelly had come out of her room and sat next to Amos.

"You don't understand," he said. "I gave up everything for this dream. My father sits in Maine, not knowing where I am. I have lost blood, friends, and someone I loved for this dream. How can I not go?"

"You talk of seeing over the next hill, or around the for next bend in the river. Its new places and experiences that drive you, Amos Mudd. They won't make you rich with money, but you will be rich with memories. Who knows, maybe you will find that gold mine. Will you stay and work it like your father worked his farm?"

Amos felt trapped. Right now he wished that he was back in the Yellowstone, watching the water shoot out of the ground. He wanted to be on the top of a mountain and see for miles so his head could clear and he could think.

"I got to go and help Doo count the furs." Leaving his half-finished plate, he walked out, his head spinning.

The old-timer came walking around the building, his eyes shining. "We done good, Amos. Each of us will get over $300 after Jon T takes out our expenses. We got $75 for the grizzly alone."

His dream shattered, Amos leaned against the wall and watched his friend head inside to find Stan. He heard footsteps and turned to see Jon T. "I been meaning to give this to you. A fellow from our wagon train brought it from Fort Laramie." The boss handed him a letter. The seal was broken. Jon T's face was sober. "I'm sorry."

Confused about what Jon T had said, he watched the boss disappear around the corner. Amos looked at the address. It was addressed to Amos Mudd, South Pass or Fort Laramie, Wyoming.

January 18, 1852
Amos Mudd,

I regret to inform you that your father, Jacob Mudd has died. He was found by a neighbor lying in the potato field on June 20, 1851. Not knowing of your whereabouts the farm was sold and the money put in his account at our bank in Ashland, Maine.

Your letter was brought to me January

12, 1852. It was sent from Fort Laramie. I am sending this hoping it will find you. The amount in the bank is a considerable sum. I will wait to hear from you.

My condolences,

Jonathon Daggett

President, Ashland Bank

Shocked, Amos read and reread the letter. His father had been dead almost a year and he was only learning about it now. He had been traveling with Ona when his father had died. Guilt flooded over him. Amos wondered if his leaving had killed his father. Maybe his father had just been hurt, and if he had stayed he may have been able to help him.

Amos squatted against the wall, his eyes filled with tears. He had sent a letter from the logging camp. He hoped that his father had received it. Suddenly, he realized that he had nothing to go back to Maine for. He would send the bank a letter and ask them to keep it in an account in his name until he sent for it.

A considerable sum, the banker had said, a considerable sum. Amos knew that the farm had been sold, but it would have been worth much less than a considerable sum. Had his father been putting money in the bank while they'd barely gotten by? Did he sacrifice so his son would have money?

Doo came around the corner of the building with a bottle. "Let's go celebrate our winter earnings. Shelly and Tilly are waiting for us."

Looking at his friend, he said, "Why not?"

Amos was thankful that he was surrounded by people whom he considered family. Slowly, the dark mood that had absorbed him began to lift. He and his good friend Doo spent the rest of the day buying drinks and telling stories of their winter adventures.

Those sitting around them were wide-eyed, listening to their adventures. Amos began to understand that he and Doo had had an exciting winter that those who had stayed back envied. While a person could visualize the places they talked of seeing, no words could describe the smell and feel of where they had been, the roar of the water spouts, the quiet of the mountain tops, or the grandeur of the majestic Teton peaks.

Jon T joined them at the bar and asked Doo, "What are your plans for the summer?"

The old-timer leaned back and smiled at Amos. "Me and my partner here will be prospecting."

The boss looked at Amos. "Prospecting, where? In California?"

Looking around at those who sat around him, Amos realized that something had changed. He had not felt like this since before his mother had died. Amos replied, "No sir. We're going prospecting in the Rockies, or maybe the Badlands. But, definitely not California."